SALT RIVER ROAD

Cover art: 'Quandongs' by Glenda Williams

'Every season when quandongs are starting to reproduce on the trees, a lot of our mob look out for them when driving. The quandongs grow along the sides of the road. Our mob travel for miles to pick them. They know all the places one can go. Quandongs are used to make jams and chutneys. Quandong jam, when made, is also used as a topping for ice-cream. My painting, "Quandongs", came to me as I was sitting in front of the blank canvas. It shows quandongs in season and is painted in acrylic on canvas.'

– Glenda Williams, Noongar Elder and artist based in Albany, Western Australia.

SALT RIVER ROAD

MOLLY SCHMIDT

In honour of the Traditional Custodians of Noongar Boodjar.
For the Goreng and Menang Noongar people, with deep respect and gratitude.

~

This book is dedicated to my magnificent mother, Jenny Schmidt.
And to my father, Gavin Jürgen Schmidt, the heart of this story.
It is also for Little Molly. We did it. We can tell a different story now.

Author's note

This book was written on Menang, Goreng and Whadjuk Noongar Boodjar. I pay my respects to the Traditional Custodians of this land, past, present and emerging.

As a Western Australian author, my goal with this book was to write a story that honoured the Traditional Custodians of the country it is set upon. I believe it is my responsibility as a writer to not only purchase, read and celebrate work by Indigenous authors, but also to ensure my own work is respectful and inclusive of the world's oldest culture of storytelling (while never writing from their perspective or telling these stories as my own).

Salt River Road was informed by an Honours thesis that explored the question: 'How can non-Aboriginal writers include Noongar characters in their fiction in a manner that avoids misrepresentation, cultural appropriation, stereotyping and tokenism?'

But the very first question I asked the Goreng and Menang Noongar Elders of my hometown in the Great Southern region of Western Australia, was if, as a non-Indigenous writer, I should be referring to their people and culture in my work at all. And in this case, the Elders said yes. They preferred a work of local fiction be inclusive of and refer to the Noongar people who have long called this region home.

The completion of my thesis and the writing of this book would not have been possible without the guidance of five remarkable Noongar Elders: Aunty Averil Dean, Uncle Lester Coyne, Aunty Carol Pettersen, Uncle Ezzard Flowers and Uncle Glen Colbung. These Elders sat with me, shared copious cups of tea, told stories, read this one, gave feedback and inspired much of what you are about to read. They have all given their blessing for this book to be in your hands, and it was with their careful guidance that I have included references to Noongar people and culture in my writing.

My thesis found that when time is taken to consult with, listen to and learn from Aboriginal Elders, the inclusion of their people and culture in local fiction can form an active part of reconciliation. My Honours thesis, 'Bridging the literary gap in Western Australia: Wadjela authors writing Noongar characters well', was supervised by Professor Kim Scott and Dr Brett D'Arcy.

Ngank

There are six cars and a caravan in the front yard of the Tetleys' house. The humble Tetleys, who don't get too many visitors. If they had neighbours, they'd be craning their necks over fences. But they haven't had neighbours in years, nor very good fences, for that matter.

From above there's no order to the picture. People pile out of cars. Some clutching flowers, others holding plates stacked with almond biscuits and cream-filled cannoli. The sound of wailing drifts over the tin roof. Your sister gets her hands stuck in her pearls as she waves them about. Pearls ping down the garden path, roll in the gutter, fall down the drain. Your niece slips on them, your dad tries to grab her elbow. Down they go, into the orange gravel-dust.

Some of the visitors are inside now. Flapping those hands and filling the kitchen with noise. Your children climb out of corners, peer around doorframes, and one climbs right out of the living room window.

Your sister, Lisa, is holding shortbread biscuits to their lips, but they blink at her with tight shut mouths. You watch your father hug your daughter close. He never seemed that tender, back when you were young. The only language he spoke was botany, and so you learned. Fast. A small child, reciting scientific names.

Rose is thinking about how you didn't stick around for this bit, nicked off before your own family arrived from Perth.

This is the part no one considers. When the life has ended, but the chaos continues.

You drift up above the karris and turn, look back down.

Your husband, Eddie, is making a noise that makes everyone else close their eyes. You remember when you first saw him, crouched over a bucket at Emu Point. A boy in a blue flannelette shirt. He was calling out to his friend over on the rocks. You heard his mate shout something back, and the boy in blue stuck his head in the bucket.

'Got about a dozen whiting and a coupla herring.' His voice echoed round the red plastic.

'Hi,' you said.

He looked up then, smiled shyly. His eyes were the same colour as his shirt. You reckon you knew, even then. Just as you held your hand out, the other fisherman plonked his bucket down on the jetty. He was wearing a red flanno in the same chequered print.

'Hey, lady, I'm Bert,' he said, and he took your hand and shook it. You'd never been touched by a Noongar before.

'Elena,' you said, and he winked.

Blue shirt bit his lip. Chuckled softly and elbowed his mate out of the way. 'Eddie.'

You remember his hand was calloused, tacky with salt and fish bits.

Those calloused hands were heavy and warm, made of the earth. Hands that grounded you, held you. Tickled your children, lifted their chins to the stars, traced your lips. Shook the soft, cold hands of doctors. Trembled as they held your test results, did their best to keep you here. Were laid gently on your heart as it beat its final dance.

Now, those hands are clenched.

Open.

Shut.

Open.

Shut.

Open shut open shut open *shut*.

Chest heaving and knees wobbling.

There are Christmas carols playing faintly on the radio. Your eldest, Steve, is smacking Eddie's back as if the grief-sound is a cough that can be beaten away. He's brown and square as the paddocks and his hair carries licks of sunshine. Steve filled your belly when you were young and times were different. When you, Eddie and Bert rented a room in a fishing shack by the sea from an old lady who told you, 'God speaks louder on the waves than from the altar.' You studied for your teaching certificate at an old wooden desk, with second-hand books and scratchy pens, while Eddie and Bert stood knee-deep in water casting line after line. They came home with buckets of fish, and salt in their hair. Your belly grew, and your family shook their heads, looked down their noses at you, a long highway and five hours drive away. When times were hard, you heeded the old woman. You sat beside Eddie in his little boat and you found God on the waves.

Is that where you will find him now?

Joe is dunking teabags in scalding water. A different cut, this one. The peace and calm inside a storm of Tetley kids. He came not long after you moved to the farm, to the cottage still smelling of fresh paint, unpacked boxes. The bees told you he was coming. You were out at the hive with Aunty, collecting honey. They'd never been as flighty as they were that day, buzzing at your wrists, getting in your ears. *Today, today, today*, they seemed to hum. The bees chased you back to the house, bumping into your back and tapping at your ankles. Aunty washed honey from her hands, held them to your forehead, rubbed your temples. An ache, a pulse, a funny feeling in your belly that he'd be joining you soon. And then there he was, without a fuss, you on your back in the bath and his head landing neatly in Eddie's hands. The three of you in the warm water, steam and blood and love.

Then Frank, your lovable little villain. He came on the eve of a hot summer storm. Late, grizzly after a seven-hour labour. Aunty sang songs while the lightning lit the sky. The worst pregnancy, and yet the most beautiful baby. Unpredictable, from tantrum to tender love, his hand gripping your finger or locks of his own dark curls. Always jumping off things, breaking things, loud and temperamental like the storm that brought him in. But the giver of laughs, and the bravest of the lot. That kid won every race he ever ran, could do anything he put his mind to. But losing you has stopped him believing.

Rose is standing with your father. They're leaning on each other, wordlessly taking in all the noise around them. She came exactly one year after Frank, another summer storm. The tin roof cracked with the heat, and rain beat the windows. Eddie had the record player in the bathroom. Hours and hours he flipped the vinyl, dropped the needle. Aunty sang sweetly while you clenched and relaxed, clenched and relaxed. Just as Billie Holiday's 'Moonglow' began to spin, Rose started to crown. Right from the beginning, she talked. Softly, to herself, as if she was figuring everything out. Humming and da-da-dumming, tapping her fingers on her knees. Frank was glued to her, his almost-twin-sister with eyes and hair like him. They grew up leaning towards each other, partners in crime.

Your littlest one was a miracle. Born when you were told you had two years left. Well, you squeezed out another five. Alby took his first breath in hospital, under those fluorescent lights. Too risky at home, with the potential complications. And, without the help of Aunty. The anxiety of sickness was born into him, disguised by the light of hope. He cried whenever away from your bosom, was clingy and colicky. But the sweet, caring soul in him. He did his best. They all did. Look at them now.

Your sister is walking down the hallway towards your door, but your kids won't have a bar of it. They aren't ready to share what's left of you. It's Rose who notices first. She's down the hallway in a flash, arms folded, chin jutting out.

'No.'

'Rose, love, out of the way.' Lisa's not messing around. You can see the grief in the squint of her eyes. She always got mean when she was sad.

'No.'

'Move.'

'No.'

Suddenly Frank's beside her, hooking his elbows out defensively.

'You can't go in,' he says with a voice that wants to sound strong but cracks in the middle. Rose leans her back against the door, folds her arms across her chest. Screams for Eddie. Screams and screams and screams for him. Then there's Joe, scurrying down the hallway with his glasses slipping down his nose, Steve barrelling through like he's in a rugby match, throwing your dad and brother-in-law out of his path, and Eddie, walking as if the hallway is made of shards of glass, wincing with every step. He sees the kids, a human barricade against your bedroom door.

'You can't go in,' he says, in a voice hoarse from grief-sounds. It's a surprise to hear him speak up. He was always quiet with your family. Up above the treetops, you smile.

'Don't you be so self—' Lisa starts.

'No,' repeats Eddie. 'Not yet.'

Everything is hushed, except the sound of your mother, wailing in the lounge room.

Elena. Elena.

Elenaaaaaaaaa.

A nearby pink-and-grey starts up a screech along with her.

There's a silent moment, sucked in breaths. Then—

'Fuck off,' says Frank.

Your sister slaps him. The sound echoes into the evening, startling the pink-and-grey overlooking the scene alongside you. The sun is setting low over the paddocks. And now you have to turn away. Because the moment unfolds and caves in on itself, the endless tug-of-war of time. Down there, they're hurting, wailing, hitting, crying. Shouting, struggling, silent. It's about you, but it's also about them. About everything that has ever led them to this moment, everything they're carrying on their backs and in their hearts. You touch them gently, one by one. Each of them hurting from different places. All of them loving you. Then, just as Eddie stands at the kitchen sink, holds a glass of water to his lips and catches your reflection in the window, you're gone.

1. Rose

the morning before you left i cooked eggs
in the kitchen with lemon oil, the way you liked.
i thought the smell of buttered toast might make you stay.
you couldn't eat it and neither
  could i
so it sat on your dresser for a while until the smell
made us sick and dad threw it off the verandah
to the chooks.
i sat beside you gripping your hand, my nails
making crescent moons in your paper skin.
i tried to hold your eyes in mine but you
drifted, already leaving, beside me.
outside the boys kicked the soccer ball against the wall
it thudded over and over again, an angry little denial
that today was any different. they wanted you to come
to tell them to stop, to say lunch was ready
but instead after an hour dad came and screamed
at them and
alby cried so then dad cried too
and they all came and piled on the bed
sweaty and smelling of grass and desperation.
you stroked alby's forehead with your eyes closed.
'my beautiful boys,'
    you murmured, your hands searching for dad's face and
wiping the tears you found there.

'my beautiful rose.'
i didn't want you to touch me in case it was goodbye and yet
i couldn't let go of your hand.

outside the chickens ate the lemon eggs.
strange, how they didn't recognise them as their own.

2. Frank

one thousand nine hundred and
thirty-seven days since the final diagnosis
the doctor said you might leave us
today.
between then and now,
one thousand nine hundred and
thirty-seven goodnight kisses
three hundred and eight days in hospital
hundreds of beers pinched from the fridge
seventy-two beach trips
fifty-seven potato bakes
five birthday cakes
and you,
slowly slipping.

the house felt different
once we knew you were leaving.
we spoke in whispers
our fingertips traced the wallpaper
absently searching for something
to hold onto as we walked
down the hallway towards your door.
we were already breaking.
you were already leaving
cracked open, light pouring out of our chimney.

you argued about it.
one final argument.
you wanted to die at home.
dad thought it would be better in hospital.
'i don't want one more tube up my nose,' you said.
'i want to be in my house, with my people.'
dad, kneeling beside you, closed his eyes.
'i'll see if a doctor can come to be here when it happens—'
you took his words from his mouth; 'no doctor.'
'what if i—'
'nope.'
'i'll make us some toast,' dad said.
'yes, good,' you replied.
we hovered, rotating ourselves from hallway,
bedside, patch of carpet near the door, kitchen to make tea
i even picked you flowers, ripped them from the earth
roots and all.
i stumbled on the others a few times in the laundry
tears dripping down their noses.
something about the hum of the washing machine
the smell of laundry liquid
undid us more than the glare of hospital lights.
dad cleaned spew and piss and shit
made cup after cup of your favourite rosehip tea.
he blew on it softly to cool it
took it away a few hours later, still full.
his eyes were full of you.
and you, you just lay there
the late sun warming your face
weighing your eyes closed.

it was a brief moment

a flutter of eyelids
while the sun made shadow pictures
on the bedroom wall
and your heart
stopped
beating.

3. Rose

I don't remember sleeping. Only the moment the sun rose, and there we were, crammed into the lounge room, aching eyeballs and throbbing heads, cups of tea gone cold. An empty bottle of Nonna's limoncello on the coffee table, a plate of shortbread biscuits decorated with glacé cherries beside it, crumbs in the folds of the couch.

'Merry Christmas,' says Joe.

No one responds.

Alby pads over to the window, looks out into the garden. 'I forgot to leave carrots for the reindeer.'

Nonna reaches out, draws him to her. Speaks in Italian. She does that when she's upset. Like she can't translate her grief.

Steve pushes himself upright, goes to unpack the cars. Comes back with armfuls of food, some of it spoiled from the heat. Plates of fish, jars of tomato sauce, bowls of olives. Boxes of vegetables, loaves of bread. Aunt Lisa throws her arms in the air, runs laps around the kitchen, trying to save what would have been our Christmas feast.

Dad disappears down the hallway, closes the bedroom door.

There's no Christmas tree.

A few presents sit on the mantle, brought down from Perth. Grandpa hands one to Alby, who shakes his head, places it carefully back down.

I lock myself in the bathroom, splash cold water over my face. Sit on the edge of the bathtub, stick the heels of my hands into my sore eyes. Time has stopped. I might be in there for days, or just minutes. When I come out, the door to the kitchen is closed. I sit cross-legged in the hallway, watching through the knothole in the door.

Dad wants to bury you on the farm. Under one of the ancient eucalypts you loved to sit beneath with a book. Or scatter your ashes in your garden. I can hear his voice at the table, not much more than a whisper, as the others rise and fall above. Grandpa isn't having a bar of it and he's getting pretty mean. He's wearing a polo shirt with the collar ironed, ready for business. Hands clasped and moustache set in a firm line. Dad's still got his jammies on and he's running his hand through his hair. His face has wrinkles where once there were smile lines. Every now and then Aunt Lisa walks past the knothole, like she's stepping on and off set.

'Let her be in her garden,' Dad is saying. 'It's all I ask.'

We did up the garden after your first diagnosis. With the diagnosis came a note, in your handwriting, stuck to the fridge.

Less have to, more want to.

Us—in the garden. The years you were raising us kids, the flowers had wilted and drooped, the weeds and grass growing wild and tall. We went to the nursery in Albany, walked along the aisles smelling mint, rosemary and thyme, softly stroking the leaves of furry lamb's ear. I stepped my feet in your boot prints, sometimes I rode in the trolley. You made friends with one of the gardeners, Peter, who must have noticed the way you picked things up and gently put them back down. Mainly we were dreaming, not buying. Doctors are expensive. One day Peter came out with a tray of plants, and some packets of seeds. He lifted a bag of soil onto your empty trolley.

'You'll be needing this.' He laid his gift carefully on top. He wheeled the trolley out to the car, even though you tried to stop him, shaking your head, laughing. Peter gave us a long list of specific planting instructions.

'You let me know which ones are your favourite,' he said to me with a wink.

You cried on the way home.

The next day when I got home from school, you were in the garden with dirt up your forearms and peppered across your cheeks.

'I need a helper,' you called, straw sunhat falling over your eyes.

We planted daisies and lavender, sunflowers, poppies and cornflowers. That was the first year our old rosebush blossomed, thriving in the fresh soil we dug around its roots. The flower was a deep red, Papa Meilland, it was called. I would talk to it on my way up the driveway to the bus each day, 'Good morning, Papa M.' In the afternoon, 'How nice you are, Papa M.' One day I came home from school and the deep red flower was gone. I was heartbroken. Papa M's petals had fallen all over the grass and you took me outside to collect them in a hat. You made them into potpourri by drying them out and adding cinnamon sticks and aniseed stars, then you put everything in a little silk bag.

'Even death can be beautiful,' you told me.

Nothing about yours is.

A bang hushes the voices at the table and I smack my head on the door handle in shock. Out the window I see Frank on the driveway. He's throwing pinecones on the roof. They land like gunshots and the hot tin cracks and creaks. There's a shout from inside after the first one hits, but no one comes out.

Bang.

Bang.

Bang.

The banging is what it sounds like in my own head. Temples pounding, almost aching for an explosion, a release. Eventually, Steve marches out there and shouts at him.

'Get in here.'

In here, they've moved on to talking about the funeral. I keep watching the shitstorm through the knothole. Dad, Nonna, Grandpa, Aunt Lisa, Uncle Nic, Steve, Joe. They're crowded round the table and Dad's still speaking softly, gazing into the fruit bowl like the apricots might know what to do with your body. My cousins are sitting on the floor in the corner, fighting over a Barbie doll.

Nonna starts wailing and takes Dad's hands. Aunt Lisa pushes back from the table and bangs around in the kitchen. I can't bear it anymore, I creak the door open. Stand near the sink and start washing the cups. Frank's leaning against the pantry door and catches my eye for a second.

'The kids will just have to come to Perth to visit the cemetery,' Aunt Lisa is saying. She's shoving her hands up a chicken's bum, and her bangles clang against each other. 'Can't bury my sister in the garden, it's not the bloody nineteen twenties. What happens if the Russells kick you out? We going to dig her up?' She speaks too loudly, for the hushed kitchen. Pushes her sleeves up with her wrists, greasy hands held out in front.

Frank slams himself out of the kitchen.

Aunt Lisa pokes breadcrumbs, thyme and garlic into the poor old chook. Bile rises in my throat. I gotta get out of here. Soapy water drips from my hands, leaving splotches down the hallway.

Frank's in his bedroom, staring blankly upwards from the bottom bunk. I sag against the wall, knees bending, sliding down to the floor. We all shared this room when we were small, back when we could build a wall of Lego around us and live in our own world for a while. Back when we'd use the bath as a jump for our toy cars and make them fly through the air, and you would come and sit on the edge of the old tub and laugh. Our room was a crowded mess of bunks, but to us they were boats at sea and the sound of sheep outside the window was the foghorn of a faraway ship. Sometimes, Frank and I would pinch the salt shaker, lick our hands and stick salt to our bodies. Stand in front of the fan for a full-blown ocean effect. Steve and Joe would be sailors and we were pirates, stealing their stashes of marbles, footy trophies and cereal box toys.

Sometimes the room felt too small for all the growing and pushing and shoving my brothers were doing, especially when Alby came along. I would curl up into a ball under one of the bunks, like a pebble holding tight as waves crashed overhead. Punches were thrown and book pages torn, names shouted and fingers pointed.

Occasionally, I was the puncher, the finger pointer, the breaker.

Once I spat in Joe's Sea-Monkeys because no one would listen to me.

They all died. He cried, but I cried more.

I pick myself up off the floor. Without looking at Frank, I climb onto the mattress next to him. His name is carved in jagged letters on the bottom of the top bunk, where I used to sleep. I close my eyes, turn my face into his shoulder. I expect him to push me away, but he doesn't. I hold my breath and count to ten. Then twenty. Thirty. Forty. We drift into sleep while everything keeps changing around us.

father christmas doesn't come
but the doctor does
and someone else
with shoes that click
and a smile that says
sorry.

dad gets us to wait outside
and we sit in a line
on the dead grass.
i know the cicadas are singing
but i can't hear them.

then dad comes to the door
'rose,' he says and he looks at his hands.

in your bedroom he has laid three dresses on the bed.

the blue one with wooden buttons
you—standing with the other parents
at the school assembly.
me—holding my certificate finding
your eyes
in the crowd. you let me skip afternoon maths
and we ate ice-creams from the petrol station
peters vanilla dripping on our legs.

the red one with the bow at the back
you—eating spaghetti at the italian restaurant
your curls in a low bun, a few strands around your face

us—fighting over the last piece of garlic bread
me—hoping i look like you one day.

the ugly brown one from aunt lisa
big white spots
a sticky-outy skirt
you—nodding, smiling, twirling
then winking just for me.

in the wardrobe i find your green one
threadbare, sunlight spilling
through the holes.
you—in the garden
weeding singing pruning
you—next to dad on a grassy riverbank
you—holding my head to your heart
you—living.

the nurse has washed your body
gently closed your eyes.
i hover by the bed while she
dresses you
it is not pretty, nor graceful
your tiny body looks
heavy.

i kiss your cheek and go

back outside
i know
i'll never see you again.

Boxing Day becomes New Year's Eve. Aunt Lisa and Uncle Nic pack up my cousins, Nonna and Grandpa and head to Perth to plan the funeral. Dirty plates pile up in the sink and we eat Christmas leftovers with plastic forks to save washing up. Instead of writing New Year's resolutions, we work on your eulogy. I wish someone told me what this part would be like. The part where we have to get up and get on with it, without you. That I'd need to slice tomato and cheese, mash curried egg and mayo. I cut roses from the garden and put them in old brown beer bottles from the back of the kitchen cupboard. Thorns tag at my skin, but I barely feel them. I pack the flowers into Steve's kombi, along with the big plate of white sandwich triangles. It's one of the strangest things I've ever done—make finger food for people farewelling you.

People seem to be extra hungry or not hungry at all. Aunt Lisa kept cooking and cooking while she was here. We've got tubs of casserole and spaghetti sauce and tins of biscuits coming out of our ears, but I just can't touch them.

We don't celebrate New Year's Day, but on the second day of 1979, we celebrate your life. We hold a service at the local church for anyone who can't make it up to Perth for the funeral. Jenna sits next to me and squeezes my hand. Her dad has polished our school shoes. I had trouble tying my laces earlier, couldn't decide whether or not to double knot. Seemed important. No tripping up now. Alby's on my other side, pressed up to me, sitting up tall. The pews are lined with the people from round here—farmers and their families mainly. Hands with chalky dirt embedded under fingernails are clenched in laps. There's the school mums, the baker, the florist, the chemist, the town doctor, teachers from the school. Feet shuffle a little, this way, that way, and settle in stillness.

Dad stands at the microphone. He looks strange, out of his pyjamas. He must have lost weight; his head and hands are too small for his clothes. He's a man of one good suit, and he's wearing the same one he married you in, in this very church. I've seen the photos. The image is so sharp it catches in my chest, has to be rushed out of my mind. Dad's doing the same thing. Remembering and swallowing. Feeling and blocking. Trembling. He opens his mouth.

Swallows.

Blinks.

Breathes.

Clears his throat.

I can't keep looking at him, so I look around the room. Even that fireman, Eric, is here. He put out a fire Frank lit in the shed, years ago. The old magnifying-glass-in-the-sunlight trick. We knelt side by side, the tips of our heads touching. The flame caught us by surprise and we smacked heads, shrieked and laughed. But then the small flame became a big flame and the big flame started eating the carpet and running up Frank's sleeve. I tumbled down the ladder shouting for you and Dad to come, come fast, come real fast.

Steve gets up and stands beside Dad, one hand on his shoulder. Speaks into the microphone. I can't make out what he's saying, as if the microphone is stealing his words, jumbling them into some strange language. Dad looks like he's having the same problem.

There's a slideshow: a picture of you in your late teens, hair chopped into a blunt curly bob, just longer than your chin. You're in a chequered dress, and Grandpa's camera is round your neck. Your socks are poking out of too-big boots. I know this shot, it's from your first trip to Albany. You'd finished secondary school and it was summer holidays. You'd leave Nonna and Aunt Lisa in a world of baking and ballet and join Grandpa on his botany trips. Bump along in the old cream Austin, the one that's still parked in Grandpa's garage in Nedlands. The back seat would have been overflowing with piles of books, pressed flowers spilling out from between their pages. Every now and then, Grandpa would see something of interest and pull over sharply to the side of the road. You'd grab his pocketknife, hobbling behind him in those too-big boots, crunching over eucalyptus leaves and sticks to where he'd be standing, leaning over some brightly coloured orchid that looked like it was poking its tongue out at you. He'd hold his hand out for the pocketknife and ever so carefully cut the single stem, putting it in his top pocket until you got back to the car, where he'd rest it on tissue paper. Grandpa would test you on their scientific names. I wonder if your tongue tangled on their lengthy syllables like mine did when you tested me.

Diuris setacea.

Caladenia flava.

Thelymitra cornicina.

Steve's still making strange sounds at the microphone, but the rest of the room seems to understand him. Except Dad, who looks like his own mind keeps throwing up images, memories, taking him back to the start of something that is finishing now.

Acacia microbotrya.

Eucalyptus wandoo.

You would sketch pencil drawings of the specimens on your knees as he drove, bumps creating markings that you disguised as an extra leaf or flower. When your pictures were especially good, Grandpa used them as part of his work. They were usually the ones you did sitting at your desk, rather than in the passenger seat of the car. The bumpy car ones you gave to Dad, rolled up and tied with brown string. *Wattle in Williams, for you*, is the one I nicked out of Dad's shoebox and taped on my wardrobe door.

Steve has stopped talking. Is Dad supposed to say something?

My throat feels dry just looking at him.

'I loved her,' he says. 'Sweet Elena.' His voice cracks on that bit and he grips the microphone. Then he bows his head and steps off the stage. His legs don't stop at our pew though, they keep going straight past us and out the doors of the church. I get up and march behind him, my school shoes echoing on the stone floor. There he is, bending, hands on knees, dry-retching into the dying grass. He doesn't even look at me, just lowers himself onto his back and lies there, looking at the sky.

You told us about the first time Dad asked you out. The year after you met him at the Emu Point Jetty, you took up a teaching prac at the primary school in Albany. Wondered if you'd bump into him. Hoped you would. He spotted you one afternoon. Leant against the fence and watched, as you unlocked your bike and watched him back. He spoke quietly and you had to step closer to hear him, the man of few words that he was even then.

'Come fishing?' Dad asked. 'I know a spot with real nice shells.'

'I have Saturdays off,' you said, swinging your leg over your bike.

'Can I pick you up?'

'Meet you here at nine o'clock,' you said, and rode past him, down the street, without looking back. I've stored these stories in my mind, repeated them over and over. The more the cancer stole you away, the more I told myself who you were.

I offer Dad my hand and he takes it. It's difficult to get him standing, but we manage. Back down the aisle, our feet puncturing the air with exclamation marks. Everyone looking at us. I drop Dad at our pew, take my place at the microphone. Joe has finished reading a prayer, and it's my turn now. Frank refused to speak, and he's the only one not looking at me. There's a piece of dead grass stuck in my stocking, itching.

I swallow.

Blink.

Breathe.

Blood pumping in my ears. Hands tingling. Throat choking.

My lips forming words. My ears not hearing them.

i hope there are roses up there,

mum.

As if once wasn't hard enough, we have to do it again in Perth. None of my clothes look right in my bag. Like I'm going on holiday, or as if I'm going to be a nun. I'd rather be a nun than say goodbye to you a second time. I tuck the yellow socks you knitted me in among the black and grey. We wore colour at the service, but Aunt Lisa won't have it at the funeral. She saps the joy out of everything.

Alby tries to pack his Lego into his cardboard suitcase. He screams at me when I tell him he can't and hurls a red brick that clips my right eyeball. I feel like dropping his entire collection into the toilet. Frank doesn't pack anything, walks around slamming doors and breathing down my neck. He's looking for a fight, I can feel it. I haven't got one in me.

Dad and Steve do though.

In the laundry, the place it always comes undone. Dad's putting a load of washing on when Steve says, 'That won't be done in time, Dad.'

'Time for what?'

'We gotta go soon.'

There is a long pause.

Then Dad says, 'Do you think we really—'

'You've *got* to be kidding.'

Another long pause.

'God, the last one was just so *hard*—'

'I'll be in the car.'

Dad shouts something then. Something I've never heard him say before. Then Steve is slamming the kombi door and calling him an old bastard and sitting with his hand on the horn. The sound goes on and on. After what seems like minutes he jumps out of the van and stands up against the laundry window, talks to Dad through the flyscreen. His voice is firm but calm, like a parent coaxing a small child. Then there's Dad, whose voice has raised a few notches, higher and pitchy with panic and sadness. Whatever happens on either side of the window, Dad comes out and gets in the kombi. Somehow, though, he ends up in the very back with his knees up around his ears, and he cries.

Steve wordlessly stops the van in Kojonup. Joe opens the door and Dad climbs out, brushing himself off as if he's been out in the paddocks, but no chalky dust or grass seeds fall. Clears his throat, rubs his eyes.

'Right,' he says.

We reorder ourselves. Alby in the very back, me between Frank and Joe in the middle, and Dad in the passenger seat next to Steve.

'Orright, old fella,' says Steve, and fires the ignition. The two of them talk quietly, while the rest of us sit, numb and silent. The paddocks blur brown out the windows, and bugs collect on the windscreen.

In Williams we stop for a pie. We sit on the riverbank and pass the tomato sauce, scalding our mouths on the steaming gravy. Dad lies back, folds his arms under his head.

'Oh, Elena,' he sighs.

We roll into Perth at seven o'clock, fidgety from the long drive and dreading pulling up at Aunt Lisa's. She meets us in the driveway, a glass of chardonnay in her hand, ice tinkling around in the glass. We're just sitting there, looking at her from inside the van until she taps on Dad's window.

'Coming in, or what?'

She's made beds up for us, and I'm in with Amanda and Sofia. Their room is strewn with dolls and tiny pink outfits. I throw my bag down on the mattress and avoid the girls' eyes.

There aren't enough chairs at the dining table so we eat outside, cross-legged on the grass. Uncle Nic's had the barbecue going, and there's chops and sausages and white buns with tomato sauce. They are talking about tomorrow. Tomorrow we will wear this, say this, bring this. So and so is coming tomorrow. Do you have the flowers for tomorrow. Don't forget your good shoes for tomorrow. I look around, and us Tetleys are all the same. We chew slowly, swallow gingerly, gaze off in odd directions.

Dad's drinking a beer with Uncle Nic, looking as if he'd like to fall into the glass and drown.

I don't sleep much that night. It's still hot when I flop into bed, and the fans are pushing warm air around. I lie there and listen to Amanda and Sofia plan their outfits. Aunt Lisa comes and stands with one hand on her hip in the doorway. The girls try on dress after dress, looking at themselves in the mirror like they're getting ready for a fashion show. I'm going to wear a black dress I found in your wardrobe.

Sofia is matching her earrings with her dress, and I hate her. I tuck my knees up to my chin, pretending to be asleep.

'What are you going to wear, Rose?' asks Aunt Lisa.

'Black dress.' I keep my eyes shut.

'What black dress?'

'One of Mum's.'

'What? Show me.'

I roll over, away from Aunt Lisa. 'It's in the kombi.'

'Go get it, love.'

'Nah. Sleeping.'

Later in the night I go downstairs to get a glass of water. It's past midnight, and I don't expect to find Aunt Lisa at the kitchen table, drinking wine in the darkness. Her mascara has run down to her chin.

'Sit with me, Rose.'

It's the last thing I want to do, but I lower myself into a chair.

It's like the lid is off and there's no putting it back on. Aunt Lisa talks and talks about how you and her never quite saw eye to eye after Dad came along. Says you were too good for him. I tap my bare feet against each other and wait for her to stop, but she doesn't.

'You're a perfect mix of both of them, Rose. You think you see everything. I haven't had it easy either. All you Tetleys are like that. So caught up you never even see what someone else might be feeling. What I might be feeling.'

I get up and go to the sink, turning the tap on full blast. I can't even be bothered getting a glass, stick my whole face under the stream.

'Get a glass, Rose.'

I ignore her.

'Our parents were devastated when your mum moved away from the city,' Lisa keeps on. 'I had to be the responsible one. Your mum? Too busy to come visit. As if I ever wanted to go down *there*. Elena only wanted to go walking, go fishing, be in her garden. Not to mention Eddie hanging about with that boong, Bert, or whatever his name was.'

Aunt Lisa stops for a moment, to gulp her wine.

'When I did come down, Elena hardly even looked at me, always had to have her hands busy. She never asked if *I* was okay.'

The tap is still running and I'm staring out the window into the night.

'She was sick,' I spit.

'I had three miscarriages,' Aunt Lisa hisses. 'Three. Didn't tell her about any of them.'

A fly buzzes, butting against the glass. Vaguely, I notice the reflection of my dress hanging neatly from the doorframe. I swallow. 'You've got kids.'

'Yes, but I wanted more. A tribe of them.' She waves her arm, as if I'm responsible for having four brothers. I turn from her reflection to face her.

'And now she's gone,' Aunt Lisa says. 'No second chances, just like that.' She refills her wine glass. Puts the empty bottle down.

'I'm going back to bed,' I say. Each step up the stairs feels heavy.

* * *

Dad and Steve go in the limo, but the rest of us catch the train to the funeral. On one side of the line there's the Claremont Showground, deserted at this time of year. A lonely speedway car screams around a neighbouring track. The graveyard is just up the road. Guess it's convenient if anyone crashes.

I feel like a stranger. All the faces seem familiar, the same dark curls and sharp noses, but they lack context against the black hangings of the church and the sickening smell of boronia. Nonna's wails ring in my ears. She's twisting her hands in her lap. Grandpa sits completely still beside her. I don't speak. Neither do the boys. Dad manages a mumbled 'sleep in peace, my love' into the microphone. It annoys me that he says 'sleep'. You're not exactly having an afternoon siesta, are you? I can't stop thinking about your body, lying in the jarrah box at the front of the room. I want them to close the lid. Before the service started, people gawked and sobbed over you. You'd have hated that. I stay seated, all of us do. Jaws set. Looking straight ahead. The inside of my cheek has a permanent raised bit and I bite till it draws blood. The pain drowns out whatever Aunt Lisa is saying at the microphone. She holds it like she's going to belt out a song and I hate her more than ever.

Suddenly, Frank, Joe, Steve, Dad, Uncle Nic and Grandpa are standing. They move as one towards the dark wooden box that holds you. Dad and Steve lower the lid. And then it's on their shoulders. The men carrying you. The men you made, the men you loved, and the man who helped make you.

It hits suddenly, like a kick in the guts. I feel hot and angry, alone. Aunt Lisa catches my eye, but I don't hold her gaze. I feel like pushing the pew over, shouting at the people around me who didn't have to watch you fade. I squeeze the stem of one of your roses, so that the thorns puncture my palm. The priest is saying something, something about in the hands of God. I think God should give you the hell back to us.

dirt falls
on the coffin
the earth
reclaims
you.

The wake is at Aunt Lisa's house. There are cartons of beer, and ice buckets with wine, roses in vases and dozens of photos tacked onto the lounge room wall. Most of them are from before we came along. You as a baby, you and Aunt Lisa walking to school, you and Nonna sitting at Cottesloe Beach, you and Grandpa among the wildflowers. One of you and Dad on your wedding day. There's a few of us, but they're crammed together down one side of a pin-up board. Photos I've never seen before, and none of the ones we have in our big old photo album at home. A table is set up underneath with half a dozen candles and a leather-bound book and pen. Dad's there, blinking at it all. I know Aunt Lisa will keep the book once the guests have written in it. It makes me want to throw it in her swimming pool.

Everyone seems too fancy. They're all in nice tailored black clothes, shoes that tick-tack across the marble floor. I watch Dad fighting with the tap on a water cooler, turning it this way and that, not a trickle coming out. He's got his farm boots on with his suit, forgot his good shoes. I press the button on the tap down. Cold water flows into his cup.

'Ta, love,' he says. His eyes are wide and stunned, like he's got no idea what to do with himself. I can't help him with that, so I head for Steve, who's rummaging around in an ice bucket for a beer. He winks and grabs two, motioning for me to come with him behind the garden shed. We sit in the dirt, leaning our backs against the green tin.

'Fuck,' says Steve.

'Mhmm,' is the best I can manage.

There we are, sipping and sighing, sipping and sighing. We start a few sentences, but don't finish any.

'I just—'

'Do you—'

'I can't believe—'

'It's like—'

'Yeah.'

Alby finds us a little while later and sits himself down next to me. He's quiet, fidgety, chewing on his sleeve. It doesn't take long for Frank and Joe to show up. They walk around the side and sit down, as if hiding behind the garden shed in the dirt is an obvious place to be at your mother's wake. Frank stands up again. Sits back down. Stands back up. Kicks the dirt. Smacks the side of the shed.

'Cut it out, would you,' says Joe.

Frank ignores him. Steps back and examines the shed. Swings his arms, gets his foot up on the side of the fence and uses it to launch himself onto the roof. Seems fair enough, actually. We follow suit, the five of us sitting on the garden shed roof, watching the scene unfold beneath us.

Dad and Grandpa are sitting on white plastic chairs under the lemon tree, smoking cigarettes. Nonna is still wailing, her face puffed up, mascara down to her chin and lipstick smudged. Relatives fuss around her, dabbing her face with tissues and passing cups of tea, glasses of wine. Dad looks up for a moment, as he's tapping his cigarette into a pot plant. Gives me the tiniest of smiles. No one else has noticed us.

We sit there, skolling beer to numb the edges. Joe keeps shaking his head, screwing up his eyes as if he can blink it all away, then opening them again and looking disappointed. It's pissing me off, but I don't have the heart to tell him to stop. Steve goes off for a while, comes back with a bottle of whisky.

'Pass it here.'

'You've already had a sip.'

'Pass it *on*.'

The sun sets and the moon rises. Alby falls asleep with his head on my legs. No one seems to miss us and the one person I miss won't be coming back. At about eight o'clock Amanda spies us.

'Hey!'

Heads turn in our direction. People point and voices rise.

'Get off the bloody roof,' hollers Uncle Nic.

We scramble down, one after the other. A bizarre giggle rises in my throat, but a raw sob follows straight behind. Aunt Lisa is already shouting at us before we even step into the yard.

'You want to fall off the roof and kill yourself at your mother's wake?'

'Yes,' says Frank at the same time Steve says, 'Just leave it.'

I can't tell if he's speaking to Frank or Aunt Lisa. But then he says, 'Go pour yourself another wine, you old hag.'

Everyone falls silent. Uncle Nic pushes himself forwards, puffs his chest out.

'You watch it, Steve, you prick.' He's drunk, stabbing his finger in the air.

Steve heads inside, slams the door.

So, the funeral brawl isn't a myth.

Aunt Lisa turns red and her hands tremble. Amanda pulls her by the arm, escorting her away from us troublesome Tetley kids. I go mingle with the mob in the backyard. Drift past a few groups, feeling out of place among great-uncles and great-aunts and second cousins whose names I only really recognise from birthday cards. Nonna has finally stopped crying, and she beckons me over. I sit down in front of her, leaning my back on one of the legs of her chair. She surprises me then, leaning forwards and stroking some of my stray curls out of my face. I feel clammy from sweat and tears and booze. We watch Alby climb the lemon tree and refuse to get back down when one of our great-aunties tells him to. Nonna clucks her tongue but leaves him to it. She sorts through my tangled curls with her manicured fingers.

'Beautiful hair,' she murmurs. 'You should grow it long again.'

I cut my hair with my orange school scissors about four years ago, when I was twelve. I remember I stood in your bedroom looking in the mirror for a long time. It felt very dramatic. I thought maybe it would make me feel something different, and then maybe I could be someone different too.

'Space Oddity' was playing on Dad's record player. It reached the countdown bit and as Bowie sang 'lift off' I grabbed my long dark plait and chopped it.

Only none of it was as dramatic as I'd hoped. The scissors were blunt, so I had to hack at it a bit, and 'Space Oddity' ended but I wasn't done and when I snipped the final strands of my heavy plait, I felt a big tug in my heart. I stood there, holding my hair in my hand like it was a living thing I had killed. You found me, with hot, angry tears on my cheeks. Gave a little laugh and said, 'Oh, Rose, what on earth did you do that for?'

Then you took me into the bathroom and neatened it up with a pair of scissors. I sat in front of you in one of our kitchen chairs and you leaned on it as you snipped. I caught myself in the mirror, and I looked different—my dark hair falling in wild curls around my chin. You were so thin behind me—your skin a sort of yellow, off-milk colour. You noticed my tears and started massaging my scalp like Nonna is now.

'That's enough of that, Rosie,' you said, and smiled at me in the mirror. It had been so long since I'd had that much of your attention for myself. I remember wanting to hold you there, close the bathroom door and sit in the bath with you, lavender petals and steam.

'It suits you, Rosie girl,' you had said, crouching in front of me and looking into my face. 'Beautiful.'

'Beautiful,' Nonna murmurs again now, as if she's remembering with me. Someone passes us a bowl with Baci chocolates in it. They are sticky in my beer-parched mouth. Grandpa comes over with an old photo album with pictures of you when you were little. He calls for Joe, Steve and Frank, coaxes Alby down from his branch. Dad joins us, leaning on the arm of Nonna's chair. Memories and stories fill the spaces between us. It's a nice moment, in amongst the mess, until Dad makes a strange noise. His face is a funny colour, and he screws it up for a second before vomiting all down Nonna's back.

There's a long silence.

'Get in the kombi,' Steve says to the rest of us. I linger long enough to hear Dad making a gurgling sound from where he's kneeling on the ground. I can't tell if it's laughter or tears. I thread my way through the crowd, looking for Aunt Lisa. Tipsy, terribly sad, standing in front of her, I hold my hand out as if to shake hands. She takes it.

'Mum loved you,' I say.

Aunt Lisa gulps in air. I drop her hand and run to the kombi.

* * *

Steve drives us home. We arrive as the sun is coming up, and the phone starts ringing. Dad unplugs it and climbs up to the loft, which has been my bedroom for the past few years.

'I can't sleep in there, love, not anymore,' he says to me.

I peek around the door into your room. I can't sleep there either, so I climb into my old bunk above Frank's in the boys' room. Alby squeezes himself in next to me.

We sleep for about three days.

4. Frank

I can't be anywhere. Can't sleep in the bedroom. Can't breathe in the kitchen. Feels like there's no air inside the house. After one whole day of staring at the beams of the top bunk while the house sleeps around me, I get up and start running. First I do laps of the house, then the block, then the paddocks. I trace the gravel track at the base of the property, along the firebreak, until I'm not even sure where I am anymore. My legs ache and my chest is on fire but I run and run and run till I can't feel anything. My feet bleed in my socks and my head spins.

I wind up near Tunney, knees up under my chin on the side of the road. Try to catch my breath. Won't be making it back home tonight, but I'm not bothered. I scout out a tin bus shelter and climb on top, watch the sun sink lower in the sky. I've got a sick feeling in my belly, and it's not only because none of us have really eaten since the funeral. It's a clear night—Joe would name the stars if he was here. The Southern Cross, Orion's Belt, The Saucepan. When it gets really dark, I climb down and curl up on the bench, waiting for it all to be over or, at least, for sunrise.

The sky is pink when I stand on the side of the road and stick my thumb out. It doesn't take long. A truck driver chugging a choc milk picks me up in a storm of dust and bad country music.

'Rough night.'

I'm not sure if it's a question or a statement. 'Yeah.'

'Ah well.' The driver wiggles the volume up on his tape player and whistles along, terribly out of tune. The vibrations of the truck make my eyes droop, and I pinch myself to stay awake.

'Here's good.'

It takes a while for the truckie to brake. I hobble down the driveway, aching for a cup of tea and a feed.

I try to be calm. Put the kettle on. Grab a mug. Try to draw my breath in through my nose, out through my mouth. Like you would, sitting upright in your bed, your swirly-patterned shawl around your shoulders. Just breathing. I hated it. I wanted to see you fight, to know you were fighting till the end.

An End to Cancer was a book you were reading. It sat in a pile with all the other ones, that told you things that might keep you alive. Things like not eating red meat, cutting out sugar and shoving coffee up your bum. An enema, it's called. Fancy word for giving yourself the shits. You and Dad would sit there in bed, toast crumbs and steaming cups and piles of books. No one really eating the toast. Pages turning and fingers tracing words that gave hope, but they didn't work, Mum, did they? You still wasted away to nothing, to a tiny sack of bones and even your hair, even that slowly fell out, littering the pillows with the last thing you had left.

Blokes used to stare at you in the street sometimes, but in the end, people looked away when we passed them. They'd give us a quick glance, their eyes drawn to the pain and ugliness of it all, then they'd dart their gaze to the gutter, to the sky, anywhere, anywhere else but you. Inside your shrinking face, your big dark eyes stayed the same. Proof you were still there, trapped in that crumbling body. I couldn't watch you die, so I'd stay outside most days. Kick the soccer ball, go for a run, smoke a billy in the shed till my own eyeballs didn't look like mine anymore.

Try to breathe.

Try to breathe.

In.

Out.

Pour the steaming water into the cup. No teabags left.

My breath catches in this tight place in my chest and if I let myself feel that place too much, the pain is blinding. The walls close in around me and my feet stick to the lino floors. The others move like they're in a library, politely stepping around each other, muttering 'yes', 'no', 'thank you', before retreating back to wherever they've holed themselves up.

No one leaves the farm, and the summer holidays drag and stretch forever. Alby and Rose are off school, Steve barely seems to step out of the kombi, Dad's been in the loft for days and Joe keeps walking the paddocks, weaving himself around the dry grass, the balga trees, the gums.

I walk into the room Joe and I share with Alby and pull the mattress off my bunk. Grab a couple of blankets, and stuff some of my clothes into an old milk crate. Drag the fresh air into my lungs as I march up the driveway, away from the house. I arrange my things in the corner of one of the sheds, up on the hill. Sit there for a bit, my bum sinking through the foam mattress to the cold concrete. Fingers drumming on knees. Too quiet in here.

Up on the road, a worker leans on a shovel, tapping one dust-covered boot in time to Springsteen booming out of his cassette player. A grader bumps along the gravel, startling nearby birds.

I know how to walk real quiet. Without the leaves even rustling. And that's what I do, right up to where his radio cassette player is sitting in the gravel, next to a ham sandwich. I wait till a line of cars come, and the traffic-man is busy with his two-finger wave and nod of the head. I lean down and lift the cassette player, grab the sandwich for good measure, and back away into the shrub. Once I'm through the scratchy leaves and paperbarks that block our property from the road, I run towards the shed. I put the cassette player on the workbench beside Dad's tools, turn it up. 'Born to Run' thrums out of it. Yes. That's a nice touch.

Dad used to keep spanners and hammers and bits and pieces nicely polished and in the right compartments of his toolbox. Now they are smeared with grease and dirt, left wherever we've put them down. We tried to keep up with farm work after Dad gave up, started sitting beside your bed all day. He hasn't stepped foot in this shed since you started dying.

I collect a few tools, wipe them on my shirt, place them in the right component of the toolbox. But there's too many, and I am so tired. I lie on the mattress and fold my elbows behind my head. Remember the sandwich, unwrap the clingwrap. The ham is warm and sweaty, but my stomach growls in appreciation. It's gone in a few gulps. Feels heavy and sickening in my gut. I lie back, looking at the beams in the roof, covered in spider webs. I turn the knobs on the radio to drown out my thoughts, and to remind myself there is a world beyond this shitty shed, this crumbling farm, these shadow people.

you're dancing in the light
weaving in and out of the roof's beams
a late sunbeam
in the dust and darkness.

is this what i've become
a madman, seeing his mum in
rays of light
as rats scuttle and spiders spin webs?

'i didn't want to leave,' you say
your curls billowing
as an evening breeze strokes my face
'i didn't want to leave.'

but you did
i shout at the tin roof
you did leave
and look what you left.

I close my lips around the bit of hose I've stuck in an old plastic water bottle. Light the bud sitting in the mouthpiece.

Inhale.

The smoke fills my lungs, calms my thoughts. Gets rid of you. Just Frank in here. Just Frank.

Exhale.

Hours become days, maybe weeks. I find my favourite Bob Dylan cassette, *Blood on the Tracks*, and Zimmerman keeps me alive. There are some old magazines of Steve's in dusty boxes near the lawnmower. Flick through *Tracks* until the pages seem too bright, the sun reflecting off the newspaper. My head pounds and my eyeballs feel dry and heavy.

I put the magazine down beside an empty beer bottle and wank for a bit but I can't bloody get there. I smell like a sack of shit, so around lunchtime I go down to the house for a shower. You'd never believe there are six human beings living under this roof if you didn't know. It's so quiet. Rose passes me in the hallway and her eyes call out to me. I feel her ache in my own body, and it scares me. I can't go anywhere near her, hurting like that. I close the bathroom door and blast the shower. Let the water fill my ears, drumming on the top of my head. After, I stand in front of the fridge in my jocks. It's grim in there. I find the end of a block of cheddar and a bruised Granny Smith. Smuggle them back to the shed before I see anyone else.

* * *

At the wake, Aunt Lisa told me to lift my game. Grabbed my arm, her stupid manicured nails sticking in, and said, 'You're going to have to lift your game, kid, I tell you what.'

What does that even mean?

'Get a job, do some work on the farm, anything,' she'd said, emphasising every word as if I was stupid.

Lift your game.

My coach said that to me once. One of the first games I played on Steve's team, back when everyone still loomed over me, before I grew. I was just subbing in, and I might have been small, but I was fast. Strong. I had the ball and I was streaking ahead, but this huge bloke came at me outta nowhere, his shoulder knocking the air out of me. I went flying, clutching the ball to my chest. Landed in a heap on the grass and the dickhead grabbed the footy out of my grasp, sticking his boot into my ribs as he went. I wanted to shout at coach to give me a bloody break, couldn't he see I was out of my league? Can't Aunt Lisa see that too?

No one knows how to deal with this shit.

There are food smells coming from the house. That'll be Rose or Joe. I'm starving, but I can't imagine sitting at the kitchen table. I lift the shed door and step out into the evening, the smell of the sheep hitting me. Those poor fuckers should have been shorn in spring. They're shuffling around with last year's wool hanging off them. We better get our shit together soon. The gravel still holds warmth from the sun but the weeds are nice and cool under my feet. The dogs run up to me, jumping on my legs and licking my arms, reaching for my face. I push them down but give them a whistle, so they fall into step behind me. We walk together along the fence line, right down to the karri trees. I don't mind the company of Libby and Jacko. The kelpie tangles herself in my legs, while the border collie sprints on ahead. Past the hive, the bees catching the sunlight. There's the massive gum we used to climb when we were kids. There are some old plastic chairs with weeds tangling around the legs, and a deflated footy lying in the grass. I nudge it into the air with my toe and the dogs leap for it. Libby's teeth get stuck in the shrivelled plastic and I have to rip it out of her mouth. I throw the ball as far as I can, towards the dam. It falls pathetically short and the dogs tumble over each other, racing to get it.

I climb the tree, branch by branch. My feet know which places to step, and my hands reach instinctively, knowing the best places to hold. I used to climb up and down and up and down this damn old tree, jumping out and landing in the dry grass. I'd dare myself to go higher and higher and higher, and sometimes I didn't land so well and I'd get hurt. So many times, Steve had to piggyback me up to the house and you had to inspect my body for broken bones.

The first time I broke my leg, the ambulance didn't come, and Dad was in Albany for the day getting parts for the tractor. You drove the Kingswood to Mount Barker, with me lying down in the back, the others crammed in around me.

We were so little back then. Steve had his hand on my shoulder, and kept saying, 'You'll be right, mate.' Joe would occasionally pat my arm, and Rose, who was crouching between the front seat and me, looped her fingers around my sock. Every now and then she'd put a soft kiss on my broken leg and I'd yell at her to get off, but I didn't mind really.

I bloody loved the attention that came with a broken bone. At the hospital I got to go on a wheelie bed, and they set my leg in plaster and gave me jelly to eat. Joe drew a war scene on my cast, with bomber planes and people in parachutes. When I went back to school, my friends signed their names with coloured textas.

You bought me a colouring-in book because I couldn't muck around with the others, but I didn't like colouring in very much. I gave the book to Joe who sat beside me and coloured the pictures in neatly, while I smashed our toy cars into each other and waited for my leg to heal.

The weeds have grown up, over our scrapwood shelter. There's a plastic soldier, nestled between two branches, the kind made of green plastic that people gave us in party bags, or we used to buy a stack of from the toy shop in Albany. How's he stayed there all these years? I poke him with my toe so he falls into the tall grass.

* * *

The smell of washing powder hits me as I swing in the back door. It's a shock to see two bodies sitting at the kitchen table. Dad and Alby, playing cards. Joe is standing at the bench, rolling mince and spices into balls on a tray.

'Rissoles,' he says to me.

'Okay,' I say.

'Mrs Mengler bought too much mince, gave us some.'

'Okay.'

'Might go to the shops tomorrow.'

'Okay.'

'Bread and eggs and stuff.'

'Okay.'

Joe puts one perfect ball of minced meat on the tray, starts rolling another. 'Wanna come?'

'Nah.'

'Okay.' Joe says it this time.

I sit in the lounge room, waiting for the food to be ready. Alby comes in and sits next to me, leans his head on my arm. I shift back.

'Wanna play cards with me and Dad?'

'Nah.'

I flick the TV on but there's only static on the screen. I turn it up pretty loud because I don't want anyone to talk to me.

'Turn it down, will you, Frank?' Dad calls from the kitchen.

I ignore him.

Alby sighs and gets up off the couch. I turn the volume up louder. Dad comes in and pulls the door shut.

I turn the TV off and sit there in darkness.

When dinner is ready I grab a handful of rissoles off a plate and sit out on the verandah. Joe looks at me but doesn't say anything. He and Steve sit at the table with Dad and Alby. There's the occasional murmur of words, but it doesn't sound like they're saying much. Rose either isn't home or isn't eating. After a while, Joe comes out and sits on the steps, but we don't talk.

I leave my plate with the others in the sink and head back up to the shed, lying there in the darkness. There's a couple of blowflies buzzing around so I turn the lamp on to draw them to the light and smack them when they land on the workbench below it. I chuck AC/DC in the tape player and turn it up loud. Smoke a joint and fall asleep.

* * *

In the morning I go down to the house to find more things to keep me alive. I pull an old copy of *Playboy* from under the mattress on the top bunk and a blonde with huge tits and a tiny waist straddles a motorbike and winks at me. I think of how Katie Adams winked at me when I pulled her blue-and-white striped t-shirt over her head, and she had no bra underneath. Her breasts were warm in the palms of my hands and her undies were low cut with red polka dots. Her hip bones poked out deliciously, calling me to hold them.

I'm sitting on a tattered beanbag in my old room, flicking through the magazine pages. Alby's bouncing the basketball against the wall outside. It thuds over and over again. I bang on the window. 'Bugger off, Alby!'

The thudding stops momentarily, then starts up again a little further away. There's a half-drunk beer beside Joe's bed and I reach over and down it. It's warm and flat and pretty gross. I close my eyes.

rose comes and stands in the doorway of my old bedroom and
looks straight in my eyes, the only one who still does that.
she stands there, a footy under her arm and one of steve's
old shirts hanging loose round her shoulders.
rose tetley.
one of the boys.
she keeps her hair short now, cuts it herself, all jagged.
but her eyes are round and deep and brown and pretty
and they look at me, with this *look* in them,
this question, and, mum—
she looks so much like you i
hate her.
'wanna have a kick?'
she's balancing on one leg and
leaning on the doorframe.
her voice is casual but her eyes say
please.
and mum, i can't,
i can't even look
at her.
'nah,' i say.
she looks at her socks and
she's wearing those ugly yellow ones you made
and i see a tear roll down my sister's cheek
and it breaks me
and it feels good
at the same time.
to see someone, feel something
feels good.
her shoulders hunch in but she tries
again

'maybe in a bit?' she asks.
'fuck off, rose,' i say.
she sucks her breath in and looks at me.
it takes a lot to get to rose, but i know how.
and mum, i can't stop because
i can hurt, through her hurt.
hurting her makes me feel
something.
and i don't say anything else, but i just look
into her eyes and try
not to see you
until she turns
and walks away.

then i feel sick.

i think about summer when we were just kids
when we would run through the paddocks
chasing that ball. rose was good—
she could run almost as fast as me,
which annoyed me, back then.
and you used to say
'just let her win sometimes, frank,
she's only little.'
and sometimes she would win
all by herself,
but i'd tell her i went easy on
her and she'd get so mad—
she used to hit me with strong fists
and we'd tumble in the dirt.
back then, grazed knees were something

to be proud of,
you'd sit us on the laundry sink and clean
us up with dettol on cottonwool.
we were the troublemakers
rose and me. joe would have had his nose in
the national geographic and
steve was already bigger—riding motorbikes
catching waves. alby wasn't with us yet, back then.
back then.
i hate rose for thinking i can be
like that again, like her brother frank again.

how can anyone be the same, after this?

alby comes in later with a cereal box
on his head. 'i'm a robot,' he says
and i punch his robot head.
i can hear him crying in the lounge room.

mum, i think i've become a
monster.

On Friday, Dad finally gets in the car and goes somewhere. I have no idea where he's going, but he drives up the driveway really slowly, as if he isn't sure he wants to leave. I climb onto the roof of the shed and sit there, sliding my sock feet across the cool tin. I think about Max and Will and wonder what they're up to. Wonder if they'll call.

I haven't really talked to anyone since you actually started dying. You were sick for so long. Years. As long as I can remember. But there was a point when the rules changed. Doctors let us all into your hospital room at once, despite the 'two visitors at any one time' sign that hung on the door. Every day became the same. The beeping of the monitor, the nurses coming in with clipboards. Once, close to the end, the woman with the food trolley gave us each a hospital meal. Seven plastic trays with plastic cups of apple juice and a plate of overcooked roast. Think it was a Sunday.

It's easy to fade into the background. Sometimes, I'd say I was going to my apprenticeship at the mechanic in Mount Barker. Instead, I'd sit in the park all day. Smoke anything I could get my hands on. Baccy, bud. Lean against tree trunks and wish my way out of here.

I was good at cutting ties. Snogged Will's girlfriend at a party. He stopped calling after that. It made it easier, not having to tell anyone what was going on. Max tried a few times, rocked up at our place once on his dad's dirt bike. I couldn't have it, couldn't bear watching you die, let alone someone else watching me watch you die. I set the dogs on him, made them chase him up the driveway. Shook my fist for good measure. I remember him turning, his foot slipping off the pedal before he caught himself, the way he shrugged his shoulders in confusion before hooning away. They were at the funeral. I glimpsed them standing together at the back of the church, wearing their dad's suits, but I pretended not to see them.

I slide down the tin and jump off the roof, landing in the weeds. I can't be here anymore, just can't. Down at the house the keys for the Land Cruiser are hanging on the hook behind the door. I leave before

I can bump into Joe or Steve, the wheels slipping on the gravel as I mount the hill. The creases in the seats are filled with sand and I try really hard not to think about the last beach trip we had with you. My foot is heavy on the accelerator. 50. 60. 65. The faster I go, the less my thoughts can catch up to me.

I stop in Barker at the park, sit underneath my favourite tree. People walk past me with their plastic bags of shopping, their dogs on leads, their kids in prams. How can everything look the same as before?

In the shops the lights are clinical and mean. I shove an apple and some barbecue-flavoured chips in my pockets, bum a cigarette from a young couple out the front.

Inhale.

Exhale.

It's like all I can do these days is try to remember to breathe. Smoking makes it easier. Back in the car I hit the highway again. On and on, till houses take the place of dry paddocks, streetlights replace trees. Albany feels the same, yet different. Like when your best mate gets a haircut and you don't know if you like it. Down York Street, the town hall shows the time as nine o'clock. The clock on the dashboard says two o'clock. Haven't got a clue if either are right. I drag the Landy through town, take the scenic route along the headland past Middleton Beach to Emu Point. Pull up at the docks and just sit there.

Inhale.

Exhale.

Bare feet along the jetty, heel to toe. The smell of salt and fish guts, the breeze on my face. I sit on the edge, swing my legs.

Fuck, everything just hurts.

Back in the car, the radio turned up loud. Pink Floyd. I lose myself to guitar madness till paddocks take the place of houses, and trees replace streetlights. I'm turning down Will's driveway before I know what I'm doing. It's dark now, yellow light gleaming from one of the sheds. A dozen cars parked around it, and the beat of loud music rattling my door. I sit there for ages, my head against the steering wheel, wondering what I'm doing there. Then suddenly, there's Max stumbling up to the car, pulling my door open.

'Frank,' he says, and his freckled nose and blue eyes are so familiar and so normal my throat feels tight. 'Where the bloody hell have you been?' He pulls me out of the car and drags me towards the shed. Drops me on an old sagging couch and throws a beer at me. I feel cramped by the bodies around me. Want to crawl into a dark corner.

'Willy,' Max calls, 'look who the dog dragged in.'

Will rolls over on his skateboard, a joint hanging lazily out of his mouth.

'Well, well, well,' he drawls. 'Nice to see ya, mate.'

I don't say anything. The air smells sweet like tobacco and marijuana. The music is loud inside my brain. Some girl I've never seen before comes along and grabs Max by the shirt and they fumble their way outside into the darkness.

'Who's that?'

'That? That's Tilly. Where have you *been*, man?'

Have they forgotten?

Sean, a guy I vaguely remember from school, asks if we want to play pool, so we do. Or I try to, but my arms feel heavy and it's like my head is under water. Like everything else is happening above the surface, without me.

'What's wrong with you, mate?' Sean asks, when I accidentally sink his ball.

I slam my fist into the pool table. The balls smack into each other, and someone's beer crashes to the floor.

I try to steady myself, but the air is raw and scraping my lungs.

Max is on his way over, Tilly under his arm, and he drops her in shock.

'Shit,' she says, kicking an empty beer can.

Will actually laughs.

Max just stands there staring at me.

Sean drinks a lot of beer really fast.

I pull my jacket tight around me and head outside, Will and Max stumbling behind and Sean muttering something about giving us some privacy.

I get in the car to drive away, but they get in too, Max in the front seat and Will in the back, leaning forwards. I put the key in the ignition, but don't turn it. We sit there, each of us going to say something, then stopping.

'Sorry, about your mum, man,' says Max, hesitantly touching my shoulder.

'Yeah, sorry,' whispers Will, as if speaking softly will make it better. He reaches forward and squeezes my arm.

We sit in silence after that. Will lights another joint and we pass it around, sucking deeply.

'I'm going to go home now,' I say, starting the car.

'Okay,' says Will slowly. 'Are you sure you're okay?'

'Yeah,' I say. 'I'm okay.'

They get out, the two of them, wide-eyed and fumbling. They stand together and watch me drive away. I see them out of the corner of my eye, but I don't look back.

* * *

Sleep in the car that night. Parked up near the shed, windows down. Mozzies bite my face and I wake up before sunrise, needing to piss. Stand on the driveway, pee on the gravel, watching it weave between the stones. I get back in the Landy, slouch back in the seat, stare at the sinking ceiling.

Dad pulls the door open midmorning. Grabs the keys out of my lap.

'Don't take the car without asking,' he says.

'Didn't expect you to need it,' I say, rubbing sleep out of my eyes.

'I don't,' Dad says.

'So what's the problem?'

'You need to lift your game,' Dad says.

Ah. There's that phrase again.

'Yeah, you're doing great,' I say, my sarcasm pulling Dad's eyebrows into a frown.

'Put the bloody car back where you found it,' he says, turning on his heel.

'I'll need the keys then,' I call as he marches away.

He throws his arms in the air. 'You can come and get them.' The kitchen door bangs behind him.

I honestly don't know what you saw in him.

5. Rose

A car in the gravel dust. White with the orange dirt that defaces all the cars round here. My salt snot-grief and sadness in the dirt. The passenger door opens and a sneaker hangs out, hesitates with a little side-to-side dance, then steps. I'm crouching, knees jammed up and aching, folded up like a frog and not going anywhere fast. She has a purple skirt with big orange spirals on it.

'Girl down here doing sorry business,' says Orange Spirals.

'Hmmph,' comes from the driver's seat, engine still running.

I close my eyes. Over there somewhere, down at the house, Dad and the boys are moving in silent circles round each other. Even though inside us, nothing is quiet at all. Inside us is screaming and yelling and lots of *why* being asked with big question marks. But outside, cornflakes pour into bowls and fingers rub eyes and things might seem quite normal except it's three o'clock in the afternoon.

So that's why I'm out here making tear tracks down my legs. I was walking along the road to Jenna's place, behind the Tenterden General Store. But when I got there, I realised I didn't feel like going in. The Bettses' dog, Pippa, barked and wagged her tail at me, but I kept walking past the fence and along the highway.

So. On and on. Flies in my nose and my ears. Tongue sticking to the roof of my mouth. Sticks scratching my legs and gumnuts trying to roll my ankles. My mind calling out names of native plants as I pass them. Mallee bush pea, moojar tree, jam wattle.

Then sharp suddenly, catching my breath, pulling my chest in. Everything too bright and too sore. My knees folding and my hands holding my head trying to keep it in, but everything, everything coming up like the dread of rising vomit.

Pain and relief at once.

The letting out of things.

Release.

Then this. This woman with her orange swirls, who looks down at me, says, 'Yes, that's right.' She turns to the flowering tree beside us, like nothing is wrong at all. 'Get it out,' she says, and pats my back three times, firmly. 'Real nice moojar tree out here, Herb.' She looks towards the car.

The driver turns the engine off and the radio cuts suddenly.

'Lemme see,' he mumbles, door swinging shut. 'That's Eddie's kid, that is,' he says like he's naming a species of rare bird. 'A Tetley, that one.'

I am. A Tetley. This one.

* * *

In the car, I rest my head on the window and the glass shakes right into the tense parts in my temples. Orange Spirals is softly singing a sad song. She winds her hair into a knot and holds it there with a bright yellow elastic band. Turns to me from the front seat.

'Take you home, bub?'

I shrug. Somehow, the driver knows where home is. He slows before the driveway, and they talk in quiet mumbles. He keeps glancing at me in the rear-view mirror. They both seem unsure about going all the way to the house. He's driving in a pattern of start, stop, deep breath. Start. Stop. Deep breath.

'I can get out and walk.'

'S'okay, love.'

Dad's sitting on the verandah in an old wooden chair and he slowly rises out of it as we come down the driveway. He hovers, half sitting, half standing, as the doors slam. The driver stands very still and straight. He inhales with his eyes closed and his nostrils flaring. Dad stands all the way up, then looks over at the rosebush, as if something has caught his attention among the dead heads.

Orange Spirals looks at my dad for a long time, then around her at the dying grass, the weeds, the dogs tumbling in the dirt. I reckon she gets a waft of that dead sheep smell that's been hanging around, cos then she gets back in the car and winds her window up fast.

'Eddie,' the driver says, opening his eyes.

'Eddie.' He says it again.

Dad's still looking in the garden bed. I'm standing with one foot on the verandah step and one on the gravel, wondering who these people are and why Dad won't look at them.

Instead, he looks at me.

'We picked your girl up, Eddie,' says the man. 'She in the dirt.'

Dad nods, slowly, still looking at me.

'Sorry about your missus,' the man goes on. 'Bub's missing her, hey?' He nods in my direction.

Dad's eyes on mine. My chest on fire again and heaving.

'Thanks for the lift,' I mumble.

Joe comes out the front door, a book under his arm. He hesitates, seeing this man, this woman in the car. Then he sees me—ragged, frayed at the edges, crumpling. Joe's eyebrows jump up his forehead. He grabs my arm and pulls me into the kitchen.

I sit at the table while Joe puts the kettle on. He's always making tea, like it fixes everything. Out the front door Dad is slowly walking down the verandah steps and towards the man, who hasn't moved from the driveway. They stand together a moment, then walk back to the steps, sit side by side. Each movement is painful, slow. Dad scuffing the gravel, the man tapping his leg with his fingers. The woman, still in the car.

'Who are they?'

Joe is fiddling with the toaster while looking absently out the window. 'Dunno. They seem familiar.'

Dad has his head tilted towards the man, they are talking quietly. Then Orange Spirals winds down her window and starts screeching something. Suddenly Dad and the other man are standing up and everyone is shouting, throwing their arms around. Orange Spirals opens her door, leans out and scoops a stone out of the gravel. She lobs it into the air and it arcs onto the roof, clanging around the hot tin like a .22.

Joe jumps and the toaster backflips off the bench. Hot tea splashes down my legs. Alby comes running into the room, Lego pieces still in his hands.

We stand in the doorway and watch as Steve strides across the yard. There's a moment of hesitation, then he runs to the car and kisses Orange Spirals' cheek through the window. Her face rearranges from a crumpled frown to a beaming smile. She throws her arms around Steve's neck and holds him for a long moment, and there's only the muted sound of faraway sheep.

Then Steve pivots on his heel to face the man, who is standing by the steps with his hands swinging awkwardly at his sides. Steve marches up to him, catches the man's right hand mid swing, and shakes it.

Dad shoves his own hands in his pockets.

Eventually, the man pulls his hand from Steve. He lowers his head to our brother, murmuring something, then turns to Dad. He moves his head—nodding or shaking?—and then he's in the driver's seat and they're gone.

Dad stands out on the driveway awhile, hands still in pockets, head tipped back at the tall gums. When he comes inside, he avoids our questions and climbs straight up the ladder to the loft.

* * *

Steve tells me their names when we cross paths, cooling ourselves by the fridge. We all do it. Open the door and stick our faces inside, or our feet, or as much of ourselves we can fit in there. It's the closest thing we have to air-conditioning.

'How d'you know them?' I ask, rotating my arm above the eggs and butter.

'Who? Old Patsy and Herbert?' he opens the freezer and sticks his face inside.

'Is that their names?'

'We go way back,' says Steve.

'Yeah, but how?'

He grabs a handful of ice and drops it down my t-shirt. 'Just do.'

He's out the door before I can ask anything else.

I peel an old banana and bung it in the freezer. When we were kids, you would dip bananas in melted cooking chocolate and freeze them. We'd eat them out on the front verandah, sticky hands and chocolate spread over our faces.

No chocolate in our pantry anymore.

I sit out on the front steps in the sun while I wait for my banana to freeze. My bones feel achy and tired but I feel lighter, like I left a small piece of sadness behind in the dirt.

I'm about to go inside when Jenna wanders down our driveway. Pippa is panting and wagging her tail, pulling Jen's arm out of her socket. I am so relieved to see my friend. The feeling shocks me a little, so I keep sitting where I am. Jenna's skinny legs walk right up next to me. I know the curve of her knobbly knees as if I'm looking at my own. There's the silver scar on her calf from the time we pelted our bikes down the hill near the tennis club, and there's her wine-stain birthmark, on her left knee, the size of a Tic Tac. I lean back on my hands.

'Stranger,' I say, squinting my eyes against the sun.

She frowns and drops to her knees in front of me, letting Pippa's lead go slack. Pippa races off to find Libby and Jacko and the lead trails behind her in the dirt.

'Your bloody phone isn't ringing.'

Shit. We never plugged it back in. I pick at a scab on my knee. A fly buzzes around, keen on the fresh blood. Jenna brushes my hand away, then places hers on my cheek. She tips my head so our gazes meet. That painful feeling starts kicking around in my chest again, so I pull away. She sighs, and crouches back on her heels. Picks up a stick and traces patterns in the dirt.

'I've been worried,' she says.

'Want a juice?' I say.

In the kitchen I remember we don't have any juice, and we haven't had any juice since you last bought some. I pour us two glasses of water, and Jenna gets the ice tray out of the freezer and plops two cubes in each of our glasses. My banana has gone brown. We go out the back and sit together in the hammock.

'Cheers,' Jenna says, as if we are sipping fancy cocktails. Our glasses chime as we click them together. Jenna tucks one knee up to her chest, making the hammock tip. She's looking at me intently. I'm not quite ready yet, so she traces her patterns on my back until I am.

The words tumble and feel strange in my mouth, as if English isn't my first language. I tell her about the funeral, about Aunt Lisa, about Dad spewing on Nonna. My sentences start and stop, wrap around each other and fragment. At one point I swallow a fly and Jenna smacks me on the back till I hack it up and we both giggle, the weight of the conversation making us hysterical. Then Jenna clears her throat, and her face turns serious again. I wipe my eyes and keep going. As I'm talking, I realise I don't know where to stop. There's no end to the story.

It's still going.

It still hurts.

I don't know what comes next. My mouth starts saying those words.

Jen wraps her arms around me. Squeezes. I close my eyes.

The cicadas are screaming and the wind is flapping the clothes on the line.

Frank bangs through the back door and tips the hammock up. We end up on our hands and knees on the peeling wood of the verandah. I spit a few swear words and sit up. Jenna laughs, even though we both know it wasn't funny. She brushes herself off and with a kindness that is more than Frank deserves, she hugs him.

'Hope you're okay,' she says.

Frank steps back. 'Uh, yeah,' he says, and heads straight back inside. Jenna sits back in the hammock and extends her hand, hoicking me up next to her. The sun warms our backs and the flies keep buzzing and the cicadas keep singing. We lean our heads towards each other and swing slowly back and forth as the verandah beams creak.

* * *

I watch Jenna's back get smaller and smaller as she walks up the hill, headed home. In the kitchen, I'm shocked to find some half-mashed potato in a pot, fish fingers in the oven. A Cat Stevens album spins on the radiogram—must be Dad. Where's he gone? Back on the verandah, I call his name until he comes loping up the paddock with the dogs.

'Needed some air,' he says, not looking at me. I finish mashing the potato while Dad fiddles around in the cutlery drawer.

Steve's buggered off somewhere, but the rest of us sit together for once. As we eat, Dad keeps tapping his fork on his beer can, eyes on his plate like there's a television in his potato goop.

'Dad.'

Frank's been mute lately, so our heads jerk up.

'Who was that, before?'

'Old friends,' he says after a long pause, punctuated by the hollow tink of his fork on his can.

'What kinda friends ditch stones on your roof?' It's a bit rich coming from Frank.

Another pause. Tink. Tink. Tink.

'Those ones, I guess.'

'They boongs?'

Dad slams his can onto the table and we all jump. That's not like him.

'Don't use that word,' Dad says. 'Ever.'

Frank holds his hands up in surrender.

'They're Noongars,' says Dad.

'Why they sniffing round?'

'Get me another beer.'

We sit before the rubbery fish fingers and cold potato. Dad's story is slow and stilted. He's a man of few words, and this takes time.

When he was young, he worked on a farm out Cranbrook way, where a Noongar family were camped. One of the Noongar kids, Bert, was about his age, and they worked together as farm hands. Some of Bert's siblings were taken away by something Dad calls 'The Department' but Bert got to stay cos the farmer said he was such a good worker. His folks moved on to another farm eventually, closer to Mount Barker, but Bert wanted to try his luck somewhere else.

'Decided to go with him, to Albany. It wasn't long after the fire. And well, I liked the bloke.' Dad's knocking back cans of beer and he doesn't look any of us in the eye. His folks died in a bushfire when he was nineteen. He doesn't talk about it. Swallows the story down with booze. Keeps going.

Dad and Bert at Emu Point, fishing with crappy hand reels, bringing in fish after fish. Every day for a week, both of them there, filling buckets. The reek from the Whaling Station hanging over the town. Then Derek, a man with a fishing boat needing more men. Him asking Dad, not even looking at Bert. Dad saying he wasn't going without his mate. Times being tough, Derek scowled and told them to get on the boat.

And so. Dad and Bert back then. Getting lucky, a good team.

'Bert was their son,' Dad says, nodding his head out towards the driveway where our strange visitors stood earlier.

'Your Mum and I even lived with him for a while, in a fishing shack near the docks. Steve was a little tacker.'

‘So, what happened to Bert?’ I ask.

Dad pauses, hesitates, then drains his beer can. ‘That’s enough for now,’ he says.

I put the kettle on, but no one wants tea.

Dad climbs up to the loft and puts the door down, locking himself in.

* * *

The days all look the same—no one gets out of bed until nearly lunchtime. Except Alby, but he has learned to be quiet. He sits in the lounge room, carefully making Lego cars. He doesn’t like using mismatched colours, instead he rummages through the old box of Lego to find all the red ones, all the yellow ones, all the blue, so he can make perfectly coloured cars.

As the sun hits the centre of the roof of our house, making the tin crack and creak, we creep out of our corners. We meet in the kitchen, rubbing our eyes. I watch my brothers move like strangers, clumsy elbows and feet getting in the way.

Grief has made us awkward.

Dad opens the paper, same as always, and begins the activity that will consume his entire morning, often re-reading the exact same articles. He traces each word with his finger, nods at the same names in the sport section, and, when it’s a new paper, he takes the crossword out and carefully folds it for later. Steve grabs his keys off the kitchen bench and mumbles something about going somewhere. Joe cooks himself some eggs from the chooks. He does it slowly, purposefully, sprinkling some thyme from the garden on top.

When did we become so careful and slow?

I feel like smashing something, waking up the men around me. Instead, I make a cup of tea and some vegemite toast, using the end of the loaf and eating quickly, perched on the old wooden stool. When you were around, one of us kids always had to sit on it, because there weren’t enough chairs at the kitchen table.

Frank stumbles in later, smelling of cigarettes. He nods at us, like we're people he knows from the pub. He opens the fridge, stands with one hand on his hip, closes it again.

'Well, shit,' he says, and walks out.

Dad looks up from the paper, peering over his glasses. 'Did someone say something?'

I cough, shake my head at him, and am about to shut myself in the hallway and call Jenna, when Alby patters into the kitchen in his pyjama pants.

'Can we do something fun, Dad?'

Dad doesn't even hear him.

'Da-ad.'

I pick lint balls from my jumper and hover in the doorway. Dad stares at Alby, like he's forgotten about his youngest son.

'What do you want to do, mate?'

Alby opens his mouth a few times and shrugs. 'I dunno, just anything.'

Dad looks sort of frustrated and sad all at once.

I bang my dishes in the sink and, wiping my hands on my jeans, retreat into the hallway, where the old cream-coloured phone squats squarely on the dog-eared phone book, the spindly legs of the old side table sticking out on a funny angle. I sit on the floor and pick at a toenail as the numbers click and the phone begins to ring.

'Come round,' Jenna says, giving me permission to get the hell out of my house. I grab a yellow flannelette shirt and head out the back door.

* * *

One night, Dad climbs down from the loft with grim news.

'School tomorrow, Rose,' he says gruffly, putting the kettle on the stove.

What? He can't be serious. I know school goes back tomorrow, at least for normal people. The school holidays have gone in a blink, but I feel like all we did was hide in different corners of the house. It's supposed to be

Alby's first day of year one. I didn't expect Dad to send us. Not yet, anyway. He's pale and hunched like he hasn't been outside in days. How can he expect me to go to school when he's barely left the loft?

Alby lifts his eyes from a picture book to focus on Dad. 'School?'

'Yep,' Dad says, searching for the matches.

'No way.' My heart is thumping and I feel hot. I march down the hallway and hesitate, sick of sleeping in the boys' bedroom. That's it. I climb the ladder to the loft and grab some of my things. Dad watches me climb back down, balancing my jewellery box, wilted pot plant and a bunch of records under my chin.

'Where ya going, Rose?'

'You plan on giving me my room back anytime soon?'

Dad steps backwards, mumbles something.

'Right,' I say, and walk past him into the room you shared, closing the door. I can hear him fidgeting around on the other side of it for a while, before deciding against whatever he wanted to say, and retreating.

the faded walls are full
of memories
the time dad filled the room with flowers
on your birthday
the way he knelt beside your bed
you, too sick to sit up but
trying anyway.

the smell of vomit from the time alby was so
sad he spewed on the carpet
who knew grief created so much bile?
you, telling him to wash his face,
get the mop
too tired to be sad.

all around me your clothes
your jewellery your drawings your smell
i'm not ready to get rid of anything so i
hang my clothes beside yours in the wardrobe
get lost staring at the empty shape of your dresses
a wire coat-hanger where you once stood.

i rip
the sheets off the bed, throw them in the corner.
fresh, mismatched linen from the cupboard
fight with the fitted sheet
fold and tuck the top one
shake out the doona
win the battle—just.

stick my patti smith poster above the bed
put the runaways *queens of noise* album on your dresser
my plant on the windowsill
a touch of me
among pieces of you.

bare feet on the dry grass
a handful of lavender
to scatter around the room
windows open to the night

mine

          yours

ours.

I wake in the night to Alby standing in the doorway. I lift the blanket up so he can wriggle in. His breath on my cheek as he sleeps.

Sunrise paints the room pink. I lie there, heart hammering at the thought of being trapped at my desk in a neat row. After all this? How can I go back to being Rose Tetley, B-grade student of Mount Barker Senior High School?

Alby opens his big brown eyes and looks straight at me.

'Mum was going to take me, for my first day,' he says. 'I don't want to go anymore.'

I stare at his hand, clasping the blanket up to his chin. Those fingers are still so small.

'Come on, mate, up you get.'

I fix Alby some cereal, iron the creases out of my crumpled uniform. Alby and I in the bathroom—he brushes his teeth, watching my reflection as I try to tame my curls. The sad girl in the mirror grabs the toothpaste tube from her brother. She looks older than I remember.

'Grab your pencils and put your shoes on,' I tell Alby. 'We'll go in a minute.'

Dread, deepening with every step up the ladder to the loft. I stick my head in, clear my throat. Dad's awake, looking at the ceiling.

'Morning,' he says without looking at me.

'If you're making us go to school, you need to drive Alby,' I say. 'It's his first day. He can't take the bus.'

'Why not?'

'He doesn't even know where his classroom is. Mum was going to take him. You need to take him.'

'He did kindergarten there, he'll know his way around.'

'He's five years old,' I say.

'Yes, he is,' Dad says.

When I don't respond, Dad finally looks at me. 'I'm just not up for it,' he says. 'Why don't you take the ute. Drop Alby off then you can drive it on to your school.'

I'm not even supposed to drive on the roads yet without a licence. It's beside the point that I do behind Dad's back. The teachers would seriously bust me for driving it to school.

I climb down the ladder without a word.

'Have a good day, love,' he calls after me.

Joe's in the kitchen, washing Alby's breakfast bowl. 'I'll take him,' he says. He gestures up to the loft. 'I thought that might happen. Want me to drop you as well?'

'Nah,' I say. 'I'll take the bus.'

Alby in the doorway, drowned in a too-big shirt.

'Looking good, mate,' says Joe. 'Let's go.'

* * *

I trudge up the driveway to the bus stop, scuff my feet in the dirt waiting for the bus to pull in. I sit second from the back, our usual spot. Everyone stares. No one says a word. When Jenna gets on, she marches down the aisle.

'Mind your own business,' she snaps to the drongos gawking at me.

The trip seems faster than usual. Jenna bangs on about her all-time favourite song, '48 Crash' by Suzi Quatro. I have forty-eight headaches and we haven't even got to the school gate yet. When we do, I notice how young everyone looks. I feel like a withered old lady, as they mill around in groups, voices pitching with excitement or hushed in gossip. Jenna talks to people I don't really know, and it hits hard and sharp as I realise that while I spent the end of year eleven by your bed, school life went on without me. Jen pulls me in by the elbow, but I feel mute and awkward, nodding my head as she talks, without really listening to the conversation. In class, she absent-mindedly goes to sit beside Tess, instead of next to me. But then she sees me stiffly sitting on my own, shakes her head as if surprised at herself and slaps her books on the desk next to me.

'Sorry, muscle memory,' she murmurs in my ear. I guess her muscles have forgotten the decade she's spent sitting beside me. Now the classroom feels different, as if she is a part of it in a way I have never been and never will be. Jenna taps her foot against mine and smiles.

Mrs Watkins smacks her ruler on the desk to quieten the class. I notice her notice me and hope she doesn't say anything.

'Nice of you to join us, Rose,' she says, as if I spent last term taking a holiday in Bali.

All eyes on me again. Jenna shakes her head, 'unbelievable,' she mouths at me. Mrs Watkins starts with a current affairs quiz, barking out the questions as if she's talking to an army. I answer three out of ten. Mrs Watkins starts going around the class asking for answers. I gaze out the window, wishing myself to nothingness.

'Number two, Rose?'

I glance down, hoping an answer will have appeared on my page.

'Don't know.'

She keeps looking at me.

'I don't know,' I repeat.

'Try number three then.'

Is she for real? 'I'm sorry, Mrs Watkins, I don't know.'

Mrs Watkins shakes her head. 'Perhaps your friend can help you out?'

'Mark Edmondson,' Jenna says, looking at me apologetically.

'Good,' Mrs Watkins says, with an air of impatience. 'Tom, number four?'

I gaze out of the window again. Jenna draws a heart on the margin of my page. I have no idea what's going on in maths either, but at least Mr Davies doesn't single me out. Instead, he dumps a stack of papers on my desk at the end of class.

'Time to play catch-up, Rose,' he says. 'Sorry for your loss.'

'Thanks,' I mutter.

'Welcome.'

When the bell goes for lunch, I walk straight out of the classroom and Jenna jogs alongside me.

'I can't believe, like what on earth, bloody idiots ...' Jenna's breathless sympathy annoys me, so I say nothing as we walk lap after lap around the oval. Eventually Jenna links her arm in mine and offers me half her vegemite sandwich, like always. I shake my head.

'Go on, Rose.'

My mouth feels dry and the bread gets stuck in the back of my throat. Jenna smacks me on the back. 'At least it's not a fly this time,' she tries to make me smile. I do, specially for her.

* * *

Joe's in the carpark when Jenna and I walk out the school gate. He beeps the horn and the kids around me snicker.

'Rose.' Joe waves his arm out the window. Alby's sitting in the back, his nose pressed up against the glass.

'What are you doing here?' I open the passenger door, drop my school-bag in front of the seat.

'Thought I'd pick Alby up, so figured I'd come grab you too.'

It's a nice gesture, but it annoys me. I just want things to feel normal.

'Does Jenna want a lift?' Joe asks.

'Totally,' she says, climbing in next to Alby.

I turn to face my little brother. 'How was your first day?'

'Okay,' he says.

I reach back and pinch his cheek. 'Hey. Did you have fun?'

Alby shrugs. 'I miss Mum.'

Jenna puts her arm around him, and he leans into her. Joe turns the radio up and Leonard Cohen accompanies us home.

* * *

I get through most of the week just trying to smile and nod at the right time. Lunchtime laps of the oval become a regular thing. I feel like I can't sit still, can't stop in case someone asks how I am, or even worse, what happened. I never really know what's going on in class, but the teachers act as if that's my fault. I wonder if they expected me to be reading up on politics or Pythagoras' theorem in between passing you a bucket or calling your friends to tell them unless they come quickly, they would probably never see you again. Jenna gives me her notes and at night I stay up late, trying to read through them, but the words blend together and my mind wanders. None of this seems to matter anymore.

* * *

On Friday afternoon I get home aching for a cold beer. Dad's either in the loft or in the shed, I've barely seen him all week. Frank's watching TV, and Joe is cleaning the windows as if his life depends on it. Soapy water is running down his arms and he keeps going even when the windows are so clean I can't see the glass. I sit on the arm of the couch and Frank frowns, like it annoys him. Steve's banging around outside cleaning the kombi, and the sound of Johnny Cash drifts through the open window. Is Steve singing along? I stand in the doorway and watch my oldest brother moving about in this strong, sure way. I'm not sure how he's doing it. The rest of us are like jars with firmly screwed lids.

Steve catches my eye and wanders inside, poking his head around the door.

'Alright, well that's enough of that.'

Frank moves his gaze from slightly left of the television set, to rest on Steve's face. 'Enough of what?'

'We're going back to the docks. Tonight.'

I stare at him. Sometimes even just looking at each other is so painful I can't breathe. But Steve smiles like it's all decided. 'Grab us some beers, will ya Rosie?'

I drive the ute to the bottle shop in Cranbrook. Old Greg Smith looks at my boobs the way he always does. When he gives me my change I wonder if he cares that I am only sixteen, and that I am going to drink this sixpack with Jenna, while my brothers shoot cheap whisky and rum—bottles they've pocketed from this very store. With the lazy way he keeps one eye on a TV in the corner playing the footy, I don't think he cares that I'm underage, or that the price of this sixpack wiped my collection of coins I've found under the couch and rattling around the washing machine. I go to school with his daughter. She gives me crazy eyes when I get on the bus, and she always sits at the very front. I think they are religious. I think her mum still packs her lunch.

'Thanks, Greg,' I say as I step out the door, the shop bell ringing.

'Catcha, Jenna,' he says, without looking up. We've lived here my entire life and he still doesn't know my name.

* * *

Back home I stand in my undies and stare at my clothes. I don't feel like wearing any of them, so I go into the boys' room and rifle through Frank's t-shirts—all black with different band names on them. I choose Led Zeppelin, which is so long on me it's almost a dress. In the top drawer of the dresser I find a box of yours. It has your lipsticks and powder brushes and a few odd earrings. I wonder what happened to the other ones—where are they now? Did you lose them in the shower, down the drain? Or is one stuck in your old yellow scarf that's been in the hand-washing pile for years? I choose your deep red lipstick; 'plum' it says on the bottom of the tube. I'm not really sure how to put it on—it creeps out the corners of my mouth, and smudges when I try to pout. You hardly ever wore lipstick but when you did it was neat and between the lines, like the way you taught us to colour in. I wipe it off, then reapply a little.

'Where are you going?'

I drop the lipstick. Shit. Alby.

'Just out with the boys,' I say lightly. 'Why don't you get your train set out?'

'No,' he says, his voice cracking. 'I want to come.'

'I'll give you twenty cents,' I say. 'Dad'll still be here.'

'He doesn't talk anymore,' says Alby.

'I'll put a record on for you. How about *The Jungle Book*?'

Alby storms off.

I set the record player up for him and leave twenty cents on top of it.

I've got the cold beers by the door, ready to go, when at six o'clock Steve jumps in the kombi and hammers his hand on the horn. Joe and I are there in moments, sitting side by side with eyes that feel tight at the corners from all the rubbing and holding things in. After beeping half a dozen more times, Steve goes inside to get Frank, and we can hear their voices rising over the crackling of the kombi's radio. Then there's a thud, a crack, a scuffle on the grass beside the van, and Steve's lifting Frank into the backseat by the back of his shirt. Steve's got a graze above his jaw, and both of them have tousled hair.

Frank hisses from between his teeth. 'Arsehole.'

Steve cranks the radio and ignores him. Dad's sitting on the verandah, gazing off into the distance. We wave at him, but he doesn't see. Alby chases the kombi up the driveway, but we leave him in the dust.

'Poor kid,' says Joe.

'Don't think about it,' says Steve.

in the kombi steve speeds a lot
frank lights his joint and joe
picks your lipstick up off the floor
he puts some on looking in the rearview mirror
and i feel a bit weird about it
and frank punches him and calls him a
faggot
even though he isn't
and even though he is older
and even though it was really mean joe
doesn't say anything he just
wipes it off with the back of his hand
and steve passes him a beer
from the esky beneath his legs.

in the kombi jenna opens our beers
with her teeth and frank
can't stop looking at her so i pull
on the back of his seatbelt
just a little.
jenna can get my mouth wagging
the same way cheap gin does
she gets my heart defrosting
the same way a joint does
better
better than both, really.
she doesn't mind if we talk about that time
you went loopy on painkillers
opening and closing the curtains
singing to yourself.

she didn't mind the time i came and
cried
and couldn't stop.
she just sat behind me and tried
to braid my curls. her mum
had to untangle my hair
with a wet comb afterwards
but it was so
much better than being at my place.
jenna reminds me of those
'press for help' buttons in hospitals
all i have to do is dial her number.

in the kombi steve plays the rolling stones
and the van sounds like its wheels are going to fall off.
in the kombi i close my eyes
and breathe frank's joint smoke
it makes my bones heavy and warm
and laughter rolls out
from inside of me.

in the kombi we speed towards albany
towards emu point
towards the boats
the salt
the dark
the deep.

We pick up some of the boys' mates on the way. We're crammed in together, our knees knocking together and our elbows getting in the way. Frank's moved from the back and he, Joe and Steve are packed across the front seat. Frank's head bounces against the window, while Steve rides the breeze with a lazy hand out his.

At the docks we park the kombi near the Squid Shack and sit there for a moment, listening to the van's hum until Steve cuts the ignition.

'What'll it be tonight?' he calls over his shoulder.

'*The Rover*,' says Frank beside him.

'*Wind Dancer*,' says Steve's mate Shane.

'Don't mind,' says Joe.

'Never heard of that one,' says Steve.

'*Osprey*,' someone calls from the back.

'*Gypsy*,' I say.

Gypsy is my favourite boat. She is old and wooden and the people who own her have a whole shelf of different tea tins in the cabin, and tiny glass jars of milk and honey and coffee in the fridge. Sometimes when I go and lie in the little bed down there, it smells like oil and coffee, and I wish I could stay forever.

'Not *Gypsy*,' says Frank.

'Why not?'

'*The Rover*,' he says.

'*Wind Dancer*,' repeats Shane.

'What about *Neptune's Son*?'

'*Warrior*.'

Frank spills his beer. Steve tells him to watch his shit. The kombi is his pride and joy, bought with years' worth of savings.

These nights started out just us Tetleys, Jenna and Shane. We'd hang around the town, then the boys would meet some mates at the pub. Jenna and I would sit out in the beer garden, sipping pints, slowly adjusting to the bitter taste. We hardly ever paid for anything—there was one guy who worked the bar who would do anything for Jenna's smile.

But one time Frank got really drunk and yacked on the pool table and the manager found the spew in the corner pockets. He told Frank, Jenna and I not to bother coming back till we were of age while he was at it. There's only really one good pub in Albany, so we had to find something else to do.

One night we were driving around listening to Bob Marley & the Wailers when Steve pulled up at the docks at Emu Point. We sat there, drinking more beer, then we overflowed into the carpark where we milled around kicking an old footy and Jenna and I ran out and danced along the jetty. It started as a dare.

'Jump onto that boat,' someone called from the carpark.

'Yeah, do it!'

Joe looked over his glasses as Jenna hoisted herself up and onto the deck of one of the boats tied there. Within a few minutes we were all aboard. Steve was setting up the tape player and Frank had his nose in the boat's neat fridge. That first boat was *Gypsy*.

'*Gypsy*,' says Jenna, grabbing another beer. The boys hesitate. I pull the thread on my sleeve and cross my fingers.

'Fine. *Gypsy*,' says Frank, eyeing Jenna.

Steve nods his head. The decision is made.

We carry our stuff onto the jetty. We've got Joe's cassette player, Steve's guitar, beer, rum, potato chips and some cheese Shane pinched from his mum's fridge.

On the boats we become different people. Steve finds some black sunglasses in the cabin and he looks like Gatsby. Joe's voice is louder than normal; he's talking about Hendrix to Shane and Frank, his fingers mapping out his words on Steve's guitar. Jenna's found a scarf in a box by the bed and she ties it round her head like Audrey Hepburn. Shane is wearing an akubra hat he's pinched from a hook and he could be a dark-haired Robert Redford. I admire him out of the corner of my eye, then get up and stand at the back of the boat and pretend we are moving, rather than tied to the docks beside *The Rover* and a neon light. The wind would rush through my hair, and I could sing as loud and as out of tune as I liked and no one would hear.

one rung at a time
frank is climbing onto the roof
silver body in the moonlight.
a pair of binoculars tied with a piece of rope
he tips them to the moon—a sudden interest
smashes them down again on the fibreglass
he's teetering on
                    the edge
opens his mouth wide
tongue stretched down to chin
    jumps
 into the black water.
the others squeal and follow
stripping t-shirts and jeans, socks and tennis shoes
climbing rung by rung
but i see
the monster inside my brother's heart
eating him inside out.

I climb up after Shane. He waits for me to pull myself up and we stand together on the fibreglass roof. He's found a silver coin in his boardies and he winks at me.

'Heads or tails, Rosie?'

'Heads.'

A flip, a slap onto the back of his hand.

'Tails it is. Go on, get!'

I love the sensation of falling. In that one delicious, quick moment before you hit the water everything stops and even your heart is weightless.

The water is still lukewarm from the setting sun. Joe has the rum, and we pass it between us, burning our breath.

'Frank, mate, pass it on,' says Steve.

Frank closes his eyes and takes a really big gulp.

'Frank—'

'Okay!' He tosses the bottle back to Joe. But his eyes have gone funny, dragging behind the rest of him. Thirty seconds later Frank groans bile and soggy Original Smiths out of his gut.

A few of the other guys snicker at him.

'Get back on the boat, you dickhead,' says Steve.

Something in Frank flips out. 'Don't tell me what the fuck to do.'

Joe and Shane swim out of the way of the vomit. I glance towards my oldest brother to see what will happen next. He looks so, so tired.

'Just do it,' he says.

The boys try to pull Frank towards the boat, but he throws them off and turns to Steve. 'I hate you for bringing us here,' he says. 'It's not the same.'

It happens really, really fast. Frank spits at Steve, and Steve lunges for him. Both of them go under, the water churning around us. They pop up in the shallows, chests above water, diving at each other. Then Shane's in there too, trying to rip them apart, and Joe is hopping from foot to foot calling out in the background. Jenna draws one hand to her mouth and the other around my shoulders and we shiver on the sidelines. My heart feels jumpy and panicky and my mind throws up images of both my brothers floating in the water, facedown. Ever since you died, I'm scared everyone is going to. Jenna holds my head to her heart.

'Just stupid boys, Rosie girl,' she murmurs.

'Don't kill each other!' My voice sounds hoarse. Something about it catches both of them. Steve glances my way for one heartbeat before he delivers a final blow to Frank's cheek, then turns and wades through the water towards the jetty.

Frank spits blood and sand and hobbles to shore, avoiding the jetty and climbing up onto the bank.

The rest of us breathe heavily, as if it were us pummelling and being pummelled.

One by one we swim back out to the boat.

Joe sits on the esky, tapping his fingers over and over again. He looks like he might cry. The tape player is at the end of its run and clicks off abruptly. He fumbles with a few cases, drops one, then gives up, sitting back and closing his eyes, his fingers still playing 'Chopsticks' on the esky.

Shane has copped a split lip and he pours rum on it, grimacing. He takes a few swigs himself then wanders over to the tape player, opening it and popping Lobby Loyde & the Coloured Balls in.

Steve comes back after a while and Jenna and I clean him up with a tea towel we find in the cabin. He's scored a whopping black eye, and it makes my tummy drop knowing Frank did that. It's pretty rare Steve comes away with battle wounds.

The music's playing again, the talking is happening again, a joint is passed around. But I can't shake the panicky feeling and the worry—where's Frank? I go to get off the boat and look for him, but Joe opens his eyes and simply says, 'Leave him.'

I hesitate, then sit beside him. We share a cigarette, passing it back and forth in silence. Joe and I have always been pretty easy like that. He's softer, quieter, where Frank, Steve and I are more hot-headed. You always said we inherited the Italian temper. Yours was rare, but fierce. Joe is more like Dad used to be—he reads books about the environment and saving whales. He has a gentle voice and when he rounds up the sheep, they listen to him.

* * *

Later, I sit on the edge of the boat, wrapped in a beach towel. I like to sit here, my body rocked as the water rises and falls. The boys are passing around a pipe and Jenna is dancing, wiggling her hips in a pair of old denim shorts. I hope Frank hasn't gone far. It doesn't feel the same without him.

He isn't at the car when we bundle in after midnight. We find him walking along the highway, out of town. He's heading towards home, with his head down and his hands in his pockets. Joe's driving; he doesn't drink as much as the others.

'Get in,' he says, pulling up alongside Frank.

Frank climbs in without a word. His dark hair is matted with salt and sand and his face is swollen and raw. He perches himself in the back in a nook between the fridge and an old mattress.

'There's some ice in the esky.'

Steve says it, without looking at anyone in particular.

For a while, no one responds, but after a bit Frank slowly opens the lid and prizes a piece of ice out, holding it against his temple.

Jenna squeezes my hand as we near her place. She kisses my cheek when Joe pulls up, whispers in my ear. 'Are you okay?'

'Yep.' I squeeze her back.

Joe waits until she gives him a thumbs-up before he backs out and we carry on. I wish I also climbed through her window and was getting into her bed with its sunflower blanket and Beatles poster on the wall behind it. The cat would plod down the hallway and nudge the door open, coming to rub itself up against Jenna, before purring to sleep beside us. Jenna used to think Meggie the cat was her mother's spy, prowling the hallway, making sure Jenna made it home to bed.

I wonder if you spy on us sometimes. You'd be sad at the state of us tonight.

I sigh, and lean forwards to rest my hands on Joe's shoulders as he drives, dropping my head against the back of his headrest. We are quiet now; tired from the energy it took to leave the house.

'Look at the moon, Rosie,' Joe says, pointing to the silver fingernail above the dashboard. I watch it all the way home, as we rumble back to reality.

under the covers
beneath the moonlight
a dream grabs me with cold
mean fingers
a ward full of hospital beds and hair
falling out in clumps of wispy strands
and you
eyelids flickering, a heart monitor playing heavy metal music
instead of beeping
your heartbeat.
me, desperately trying to turn the volume down until
it stops
everything is silent
and the nurse runs in and says
you killed her
and i try to turn the music back on,
but it won't play and the monitor is blank and you
won't open your eyes.

The weekend slides past us. On Saturday Frank goes fishing for jilgies in one of the dams and comes back with empty buckets and a foul temper. Steve tells Dad one of the fences needs fixing and the sheep need shearing. Dad shrugs at him and goes outside to stand on the verandah, a can of beer in his hand, using his toes to clear cobwebs on the balustrade. Steve fixes the fence, his arms moving in short angry movements. Dad ends up sitting on the verandah steps most of the day, flicking lint balls off his old pants. I see him water your roses then sit back down again, brushing his hands off like he's done a day's hard work.

I sit in bed, reading comic books and painting my fingernails Apricot Dream.

We eat baked beans on toast for dinner on Saturday, and for breakfast on Sunday. On Sunday Joe and I pull a few weeds from the orchard, avoiding your garden which needed it more. We don't talk much. Steve drives the kombi further away from the house and shuts himself in there. Alby jumps on the trampoline for four hours straight, then spews baked beans on the carpet. I clean it up.

And suddenly it's Monday.

Early in the morning Mrs Mengler from up the road comes over with a broom, a mop, and a plate of biscuits. Dad's in his dressing gown watching cartoons with Alby and I'm in the kitchen packing lunch for school.

'Morning, Eddie,' she says chirpily to Dad.

Dad rubs his eyes. 'Oh, hi, Margaret,' he says, shifting in his seat and fiddling with his dressing gown. 'Come in, if ya like.'

She's already in the door. 'Time to have a clean-up here, I think.' She slaps her plate of biscuits down on the table. 'You're looking a bit peaky now, Rose.' She eyes me from across the room. 'You'd better grab me a bucket, then eat a few of these.'

'Oh, it's alright, Mrs Mengler, I mopped the floors not long ago.'

Mrs Mengler pauses, then smiles down at me. 'I'm here to help, love. Grab me the bucket.'

I get her a bucket of soapy water and she starts to mop our kitchen floor. I look at her suspiciously. She's wearing a spew-coloured knit sweater, but I like the brooch that twists at her neck. I think you had one like that.

She chats to Dad about the cricket, her son Andrew, and her vegie patch. Her sentences string together and she keeps glancing at me out of the corner of her eye.

Dad stays very quiet, tapping his ugg boot feet together.

'Oopsie,' he says, when Mrs Mengler starts slapping our cushions together and dust makes her sneeze. 'I mean, bless you.' He's had to stand up to let her get to the cushion he was leaning on. He hovers behind her. 'You don't have to, really.'

Mrs Mengler stiffens. 'Oh come on, Eddie,' she says. 'Elena would want this cleaned up, set straight again.'

Dad flinches. 'Y'know, now isn't really a good time, Margaret,' he says. 'Got to get the kids to school and all that.' He eyes me eyeing the biscuits. I step away from the table.

'I know you mean well, and all,' he adds, drumming his fingers on his thighs.

Mrs Mengler is stacking up our dishes and banging around in the sink looking for the plug. She's tipped out the vase of flowers Alby and I picked for you. They were brown and even maybe a little mouldy, but we were keeping them.

Dad's in the doorway, standing where the lino becomes carpet. 'I ... I think I'd like you to leave, Margaret,' he says. His cheeks are a polite shade of red. I turn around to put the cheese in the fridge and when I glance over my shoulder she's gone, waddling up the driveway. The door slams, and the force unbalances the pile of biscuits on the table. Some of them cascade onto the floor.

'Pass me one of them will ya?' Dad says meekly.

The biscuits are warm and buttery. We laugh about it, but I feel confused, like there's something I've missed.

'Are you actually taking us to school?'

Dad looks up at me. 'Oh, um, Rosie love …'

I turn away and slip my lunch into my schoolbag. 'Don't worry about it.' I squash some of the biscuits in my pocket, feeling guilty without knowing why. Alby and I leave Dad and his ugg boots behind us.

Alby stumbles along, flicking through a picture book as he walks.

'I want to be a pilot,' he says, narrowly avoiding walking into a ditch. I grab the back of his backpack and steer him.

A pilot. How does this kid have the mental capacity to think of his future right now? Then again, he might be onto something. The world might make sense if you could see it from above. You could look down and see all the houses and their matching cars and the people coming and going, and you'd know. You'd know that person with the yellow scarf belongs to that house with the red roof and that silver car parks next to that spiky tree because that person couldn't afford a house with a garage.

You could watch the sheep flock together and know where the man and the dog are leading them, you could see the clouds coming in over the hills and you could say, 'Oh look, it's going to rain. How about that.'

You'd always know what was going to happen.

I'd like that.

Alby's forgotten his lunch and has to run back to get it. Up on the road a worker turns his sign from STOP to SLOW. A car speeds past anyway and the road worker gets mud in his face. He stands there and sips his choc milk like nothing happened. I've forgotten my bus money and instead of kicking me off, Mick, who has never said anything nice, ever, says, 'Don't worry about it, kid,' and wiggles his eyebrows.

Nothing makes sense from the ground.

* * *

In English, Mrs Parsons wants us to write about our childhoods. English is alright when we are reading books like *The Crucible* and *Frankenstein*. I like getting lost in different worlds. But today Mrs Parsons wants us to write about our own.

I tap my pen on the side of my desk thinking about getting Jenna to come over after school and bring a massive pizza with her. They have an amazing pizza oven out back of the Tenterden Store. I love the smoky taste of the woodfired flatbread, and the warmth of the pizza box on my knees.

'Having trouble getting started are you, Rose?'

I look up at Mrs Parsons' rounded body and wobbly chin.

'A little, yeah.'

'What's the biggest thing that's ever happened to you?'

Really?

'Sometimes putting it on the page helps,' she offers.

I keep my pencil tapping.

She sighs. 'You can do it now, or at lunch, Rose. Suit yourself.' Mrs Parsons walks back to her desk and sits down, shuffling papers with slightly raised eyebrows.

my childhood stopped the minute
you got the first diagnosis
red dirt on small brown boots, unlaced.
pale blue socks with stars on them,
one pulled up,
          the other down.
four kids on the back of a white ute
you sang songs that reached us
out of the open window.
'house of the rising sun'
haunted us
while this sun burnt our noses
and the road knocked our knees together
my brothers with grass seeds in their hair
joe curled up with the dogs
steve catching insects, his hands open to the wind.
a brown paper bag, four chocolate frogs
a reward—we had to wait a long time to hear the news.
none of us were hungry but you still sang
'somewhere over the rainbow'
we went to the show first, then to the doctor
you wanted it that way
bought us tickets for the ferris wheel
and the gaping mouthed clowns
i had fairy floss in my hair
when they told us the news.
the chocolate frogs melted through the bag
and it would take weeks to lose my
uneven sock tan.
four kids on the back of a white ute
fairy floss in my hair.

Outside the air is dry and thick. I gulp water from the drinking fountain, sharp and cold. My bones ache with tiredness. One step after the other up the ladder on the school's water tank, until I'm at the top, lying on the smooth, cool surface. The clouds above me are piercingly white, and I close my eyes. If we can't have pizza, what will I cook for dinner tonight? I try to remember the contents of the fridge this morning—a couple of bits of old bread, cheese—I think we still have some potatoes …

Just before the bell rings I climb back down out of the clouds and head for the bus. Jenna and I take our rightful place second from the back, unbuttoning our collars and opening the window.

'Where did you bugger off to then?' Jen asks, holding my face in her cool hands.

'Nowhere,' I say.

She kisses me, between where my happy-eye-creases used to be, and my temple.

I pull away, even though it was nice.

We stop at Kendenup Primary and Alby scrambles on with a few other littlies.

The old bus rumbles and skids along the dusty back roads, back to the place that doesn't quite feel like home anymore, and I tap my fingers, but not quite in time to 'Dreams' by Fleetwood Mac playing on the radio.

* * *

I'm chilling in my room when Jenna rings. I'm expecting her any moment now, her Dad pulling up in his clunky orange truck, Jenna jumping out onto the gravel, the dogs jumping on her in excitement.

'Rose, I'm under house arrest.'

'What, why?'

'Mum found my ciggies in my bag from Friday. I promised her I'd stopped after that time I accidentally left them in my dirty jeans and she found them in the wash.'

'Shit …'

'Yeah, she's pretty mad. I told her to rack off and she really didn't like that.'

'Damn.'

I hang up and raid the pantry for those potatoes. The afternoon sun is coming in the blinds and making it hard to see. Someone's been out in the orchard, picked a pile of fruit. Peaches and apricots. At least it's not all rotting on the ground. You loved this time of year. You'd bake pastries and cakes with the stone fruit, the kitchen smelling of tangy fruit and cinnamon. Dad must be out in the paddocks somewhere with Joe and Steve, and Alby's reading in what seems to be 'our' bedroom. I feel like slipping out the back door and disappearing for a while.

Instead, I rifle through your old cookbooks, standing on a chair to reach them on the top shelf of the pantry.

Frank has that look about him when he gets home. I'm chopping potatoes and onions for a potato bake.

'Hey,' I say.

He narrows his eyes and grabs a peach out of the fruit bowl. Juice runs down Frank's chin. He gets one of Dad's beers out of the fridge and sits at the table. On the fridge there's a photo of me and Frank, way back when. We are standing in the dam in our undies. Frank has one arm around me, and a jilgie in the other. A few moments earlier the jilgie had bitten my toe, so Frank pulled it off and held it carefully away from us.

'No you don't, you bugger,' he'd said. He made sure I got that jilgie when we ate them for dinner that night with sour cream and chives. In the photo Frank's head is tipped back and he is laughing. I have a few tears on my cheeks, but I'm laughing too. Only a year apart, we looked so similar. The almost twins. Our arms and legs are thin and brown, and it's hard to tell whose arm is whose, like branches from the same tree.

'I already ate,' he says, lolling back on his chair.

'Maybe you can have leftovers tomorrow.'

'Nah.'

'It's potato bake.'

'I don't eat potato bake.'

'It's your favourite,' I say, looking up from the onion I'm chopping.

'You're not Mum,' he says. And then he's gone.

The knife is in my thumb. Only the tip, but holy shit, it's in there. Blood spurts across the onion. I shove my thumb in my mouth and stand there, in the doorway, as Dad walks in.

'Smells good, Rosie,' he says. I grimace at him. There's nothing even on the stove yet.

'God, what happened?' he asks, noticing the blood.

'Nothing. Cut my thumb.'

He opens the fridge to get another beer, finding it empty. Grunts and closes it again.

* * *

That night I get up to pee and notice someone in the kitchen. Frank's in there, leaning over the stove. I can smell potato bake.

'It goes in the oven,' I say.

'Piss off, Rose,' he says.

I want to tell him I miss him and I wasn't trying to be you.

'Goodnight,' I say.

'Whatever,' says Frank.

6. Frank

The days start and finish with me on my mattress, elbows behind my head. Sometimes I don't go outside at all, just listen to the mice and rats scuttle around, the scrape of the trees on the tin roof. Outside, the sun hurts my eyes. I don't like being in the light, where things seem real. My ribs are kind of poking out of my chest and my skin feels like it's gone translucent, like if I stood in the sun you'd see straight through me. I slap the comic book shut, throw it on the pile. Sigh and stretch, look around. Wander over to the workbench, sit on the stool. It squeaks as the springs contract. My brain feels so hazy. I want to be better. Feel better. I can imagine you telling me to get it together.

'Got better things to do than waste away up here,' you'd say.

So I slowly sort the rest of Dad's tools. Feels good to get something done. Rose's muffled voice comes from outside. She must be walking the dogs round the paddock. I almost get up, imagine falling into step alongside her. Instead, I grab a stray pencil off the bench and start scribbling on the inside cover of the tractor manual. Gives my hands something to do. Something starts to take shape. Trees with gnarled branches and messes of leaves form around the words *John Deere, 4010, Tractor*. Stars and mountains and ocean waves follow, the lip of the wave curling around the trees' lower branches. Sometimes incoherent shapes, frantic, crowding each other. Then lots of shading, dark, creating space in shadow. It's loose and smudged and freeing, somehow. Not at all like your neat sketches of plant specimens, labelled in cursive writing. My leaves have jagged edges and others have curls, some of the roots grow up into the sky and some of the stars fall below the earth. Guess I never sat still long enough to give drawing a real go.

I draw till the pencil is blunt, and I can't be bothered sharpening it with the pocketknife. Instead, I roll a spliff and inhale deeply. I've left the shed door hanging open, and there are specks of dust falling through the light. A loud bang comes from up on the road. The joint slips from my lips and the flame nips my chest.

Fuck.

I stagger up the driveway, blinking in the sunlight. The smell of burnt rubber is sharp. I jump in Joe's faded yellow Hillman, the torn leather still holding some of the sun's warmth.

I see it as soon as I pull out of our driveway. A couple of hundred metres past our turn-off there's a green Corolla with the bonnet smashed in. There's a roo on the side of the road and a girl standing with her hands on her hips. As I pull up, I see it's Will's girlfriend, Vicky. She's poking the roo with her toe and it's twitching, its hind legs making circles in the gravel. She doesn't say anything to me, just cocks her head to the driver's window. Her sister is behind the wheel, staring straight ahead.

Vicky looks back at the kangaroo. 'It ain't very happy,' she says, blowing a pink bubble with her bubble gum. I drive back to get Dad's gun, and Steve and Joe get in on the action and come too. Bloody Steve even takes the glory and shoots the roo. Joe helps Alice out of the car. Vicky and I watch the roo's body fall still. She winces but doesn't say anything.

There isn't actually anything wrong with the car, except how smashed in the bonnet is. Kangaroos normally always take out the radiator, but this time somehow, everything is in one piece. Thing is, Alice won't stop crying and Vicky doesn't know how to drive. I drive Alice's car back to our place, with Vicky beside me, still chewing her bubble gum. The other two pile Alice into the Hillman and follow us.

It's getting dark, and we don't really know what to do—the girls' house is on the other side of Mount Barker.

'We could drive you?' suggests Steve.

Alice doesn't want to cause the bother.

'You could call your folks?' says Joe.

'Dad'll be at the pub,' sniffs Alice. 'And Mum's a nurse, she's working.'

Vicky rolls her eyes, as if the whole situation is a personally planned attack. Will's been dating her for ages now, but I've always liked her, even before we kissed. It was at a party a while back—she and Will were fighting about something. I'd holed myself up in the bathroom and was sitting on the edge of the bath, worried I should be at home with you. What if you slipped away while I downed cans of VB and pretended to watch the footy? I was sitting there counting the number of blue tiles on the bathroom wall, when Vicky stormed in. She had make-up running down her face and strands of her blonde hair catching in it. She slammed the door shut, locked it, and sat on the other end of the bath. I was so drunk I can't remember a word we said, except that we both cried. Strange, what beer and loneliness can pull out of you. What I do remember is Will banging the door down to find us making out. He shouted a lot, and I spewed in the bath. I woke up there in the morning, with my neck on a weird angle, and the tap dripping cold water on my cheek. I didn't hear from Will, or Vicky, for a long time after that.

Dad can't believe his eyes when we walk in the front door with the girls.

'I'll give you ladies a lift home,' he says, once Steve fills him in.

Alice and Vicky look at each other. Alice tucks her hair behind her ear and bites her lip. 'Do you think we could stay the night? Our parents work late,' she says.

'Oh ... of course,' he says.

The girls haven't eaten, so Joe rummages around in the fridge and makes a huge plate of toast with cheese and pickle, takes it out to the verandah. I grab a small triangle, feeling each mouthful land in my stomach. Alice takes tiny, bird-like bites that she swallows slowly, and Vicky eats two at once, slapped together like a sandwich. Alby comes out and asks them lots of questions, like which football team they like, and what their favourite book is. Rose sits on the gate with her back to us and I lean in the corner, listening. Alice doesn't like football, and she reads books I've never heard of. Vicky doesn't like books, and she supports Subiaco, because her grandad used to play for the team.

I retreat back to the shed.

Halfway through the night there's a tap on the shed door. I can't sleep, and I've been drawing again, found some nice white paper in a dusty box. Must have been yours. The silverfish have chewed holes through bits of it, but I don't care. I put my pencil down and go over to the door. Vicky's standing there, in an old pair of Rose's pyjama shorts and a Rolling Stones t-shirt of mine.

'Rose hogs the bed,' she says, looking up at me.

'So do I,' I say.

'I don't mind,' she says, stepping around me and into the shed.

I stay, looking out into the night, wondering what on earth is going on, but also too tired to care much about anything.

Vicky walks around, tracing her finger over things, frowning slightly. I keep the door open, so she can leave whenever she's ready, and go back to drawing. She comes and stands behind me, her head tilted to one side, brushing my shoulder.

I keep drawing. Feel self-conscious. Wish I had chucked the pencil aside and picked up a comic book. Probably seem insane. Probably am. I draw a sun with black glasses and a doobie hanging out of its mouth.

I try to ignore the fact that a few months ago, if there was a girl in my room I'd have been cracking jokes and trying to get her clothes off. Anyway, I don't want to make things worse with Will, so I stay quiet. She keeps wandering round, picking things up, putting them back down. There's a bucket of shells and smooth pieces of glass you collected from our beach trips to Albany. Vicky runs her hand over them, holds a conch shell to her ear, and traces her thumb over a piece of glass. I watch her out of the corner of my eye.

Eventually, she seems to get tired, and sits in the centre of my mattress.

'I like all the lost treasures you've collected,' she says. 'Reminds me of the tip shop.'

I look over at her.

'Like, in a good way. I go with Dad sometimes. I found a nice vase once.'

She's holding one of my empty whisky bottles. It's a small one, some expensive brand I pocketed in Albany. It has leaves carved into the glass. I like that one too. I don't know what to do but I feel tired, so I go and sit on the bed next to her. I roll a joint and light up, blowing the smoke away from her. The tape player's sitting on the floor where I left it, so I reach my leg out and nudge the on switch with my toe. The Doors are in there, and 'Back Door Man' is halfway through. Vicky rests her cheek flat on my shoulder and sighs.

'Sorry about your mum,' she says.

I stiffen—other than Jenna's hug the other day, no one has touched me in a long time. I go to move backwards, but she takes my face in her hands and kisses me. I can feel myself recoiling and the embarrassment draws me back in. I don't want her to think I'm a freak. We both know she's hot. I should want this. My hands go to her hips, and I drink in her warmth.

After what feels like a lot of kissing, she flops back and lies down beside me.

'Me and Alice were escaping,' she says, looking at the cobwebbed roof.

'Escaping what?'

'Life,' she takes the joint from me—somehow I managed to keep a hold of it through the kiss.

'What were you gonna do?'

'Run away to Perth. Get a job in a café or a petrol station, or wash dishes, or clean.'

'Why?'

'Why do you sleep up here?' she shoots back at me.

I look up at the roof above us too. I can hear the rats and see part of the night sky through a gap in the tin. I don't say anything.

'My dad hits my mum,' she says, after a while. 'We don't want to be there anymore.'

I take the joint from her and blow smoke at the roof. 'What about Will?'

'What about him,' she says.

'Did you tell him you were running away?'

'Nah.'

I go and get the last of my whisky, pass it to her. She takes a big swig.

'Are you still gonna do it?'

'Do what?'

'Run away.'

'Maybe.'

Her hip is poking out the top of Rose's pyjama shorts, and I trace it with my finger. The top of her knickers shows little cherries on them.

We fuck quickly.

Afterwards she curls herself against my back and says sleepily, 'I'm glad I found you among all the lost things.'

* * *

In the morning I wake to stale bubble gum in my mouth, and no Vicky.

Lie there, listening to the sheep baa. Wonder what to do with my day. Those poor bloody sheep. What have Joe and Steve been doing out there all these weeks? They must have fixed the same fence a dozen times. I guess if Dad pulled his finger out and we rallied together, maybe we'd be okay. I hope the Russells don't kick us off the farm.

I waste another hour, trying to muster the energy to do some mowing. There's no way I can tackle the sheep on my own. 'The Family Farm,' Dad used to call it. Steve, Joe, me and sometimes Shane have helped out for as long as I can remember. You and Dad didn't seem to mind me dropping out of school, so long as I kept on with things round here. But honestly, this is not where I want to be for the rest of my life. Drenching sheep, shearing sheep, moving sheep from one paddock to the next. Steve loves it in a way Joe and I don't. I thought I wanted to be a mechanic, even started an apprenticeship, but I'm not so sure anymore.

I grab a handful of old crackers from the house and head down to the bottom shed, where I know the lawnmower needs fixing. It's about to get dry, real dry, and if we don't keep on top of the grass it's going to be full of snakes. I tell myself that's more important than shearing. I lie under the mower and try to get the bloody thing started. I've always been good with engines and cars and things—Dad used to joke about how I break everything inside the house, but I'm good at fixing things outside it.

This time though, the mower just won't start.

It's a huge industrial-sized one that Dad bought for dirt cheap off the council. It makes mowing the paddocks a dream—when it works. I unscrew the spark plugs, clean them, and refit them. The air filter seems okay and so does the carburettor. I'm covered in grease and when I go to sit up, I smash my head. I take the socket I was using and throw it as hard as I can into the paddock.

I'm so fucking sick of this place.

I sit on the mower and try again and again to start it. When it still won't start I throw a couple more things into the paddock, then climb into the cabin of the old tractor that's taking up space down here. It's been broken-down for what feels like years. I rest my head against the steering wheel and close my eyes. The sheep reek, even though I'm nowhere near them. The whole place stinks of them, all the time. When I was little, if I didn't want to go to bed, Dad would take me out into the paddock and we'd count them. He'd hold me up, leaning on the fence. Three hundred and one, three hundred and two, three hundred and three, until I got so tired and sick of sheep that I wanted to sleep.

As much as I hate it here, I can't imagine being anywhere else.

'What the hell are you doing, Frank?' Steve's standing in the doorway of the shed. He throws a stone at the cabin of the tractor to get my attention. It bounces off the window and lands at his feet. I crick my neck. My temple starts pulsing like crazy. I gaze over Steve's head into the paddock and try to wish myself away from here.

'Hey,' says Steve. 'If you're just going to bloody sit there, I could do with a hand in the top shed, mate, I'm trying to get ready to start shearing.'

From where I'm sitting in the cabin I have to look down to make eye contact, because the tractor seat is pretty high up. I imagine starting up the engine and running him over.

'I'm having a rest,' I say, winding up the window.

Steve throws his hands in the air and walks away.

After a bit I climb back down and have a look at the lawnmower again. I'm about to go and get the tools from the paddock when Dad comes in.

'What are you up to?' His voice is warmer than it has been.

I crane my neck from my position on the floor. 'Trying to get this damned thing going.'

'No luck?'

'Nah.'

He hesitates, then leans down next to me. Shimmies in and lies under the mower too, looking up.

'The carbie needs to be tightened,' he says after a moment. 'Pass me the spanner, will you?'

I crawl out from under the mower and glance out at where it fell in the paddock.

'Haven't seen one down here,' I say.

'Yeah, in the toolbox over there.' He points to the almost empty toolbox in the corner. I rummage around in it pretending to look, then give up and walk slowly towards where I threw it, in the grass.

'Where you going, mate?' Dad asks, sitting up. I shrug at him and pick up the spanner and a couple of other bits I threw. I sidestep back towards the shed, trying to hide the tools. Dad's looking at me funny so I end up just holding the spanner out to him. I start to laugh because I think maybe we can laugh about it. But Dad doesn't laugh at all. He doesn't even crack a smile.

'You have a terrible temper, Frank,' he says. Then he leaves.

I wish the lawnmower would tip and crush me. I wish the tractor would catch alight and the shed would burn down with me in it. Why the fuck can't Dad see I'm doing my best? I feel you rolling your eyes at me, saying, *This isn't your best, Frank.*

* * *

Around lunchtime I head back into the house to forage for food. Dad's watching TV, but he doesn't have the volume on. I grab the box of cornflakes on my way through the kitchen and pour some into my mouth. The dryness makes me cough. I lean over by the sink in the bathroom and throw up. Two mounds of orange muck clog the plughole.

What a piece of shit.

I can't even look at myself in the mirror. My whole body aches and feels brittle, as if someone could snap me.

I used to be so much better than this.

I was as strong as Steve, played footy in his league. I spent every weekend I could fishing in Albany, dragging bream and whiting in on the line. Me and Will and Max would road trip in Max's beat-up ute, and once we had our catch for the day we'd swim out into the river and float on our backs. We climbed trees and made rope swings, drank beers from the treetops and dove from the highest branches. I remember the way it felt, diving from the paperbark trees—that rush, as you fall. Sometimes we'd light a fire in a tin drum from the farm and sleep in the ute or on the riverbank, under the stars.

Back then I always got in trouble for doing things too much: drinking, smoking dope, laughing. But I didn't stay in trouble for long, because when I laughed, it usually set someone else off. God, we felt invincible, like there was nothing that could take us, nothing that could knock us down.

The other day Alby begged me to kick the footy with him and after twenty minutes I felt like I was going to collapse. I get into the shower and close my eyes so I don't see my body reflected in the mirror. I turn the water all the way to hot, so it burns.

I stand there for a long time, until the water runs cold. Dad bangs on the door and tells me to get the hell out of there, but I don't. The cold water pricks my skin and I feel almost alive.

'Shit, Frank, the tanks will run dry!' Dad says angrily through the door. His voice is higher pitched than it used to be.

'Fuck off, Dad.' My own voice sounds more like a scream than a yell. I hate the way it sounds—broken in the middle.

Dad shoves the door open and throws a towel at me. His eyes are a bit wild. I see myself in them. I feel exposed, small and pathetic. Dad looks surprised at himself when our eyes meet. He apologises and shuffles out the door.

I slam the door behind him and sit on the edge of the bath.

We are shadows of the men we were.

I take the shaving razor from the sink.

you're everywhere, mum,
everywhere. you're in the potato bake rose makes for
dinner, because she makes it the way you taught her.
you're in the worn welcome mat that sits at the door,
and the way alby parts his hair in the centre.
you're in my bitten nails and the raw skin next to them
your voice in my head saying *don't do that, frank.*
your voice is in my head a lot. in the beginning
it said nice things to me like *i love you* and
i didn't want to leave.
but now it tells me what i'm doing
isn't good enough, that what i'm doing is
wrong.
i expected better, frank.
i thought you were better, frank.
can't you be better, frank?
i can't tell where your voice ends and mine starts
but i'd like them both to be quiet
i'd like you to leave me alone
even though
i miss you.

The razor blade is not that sharp—I think me, Steve and Joe have been using the same one for a while. I have to push pretty hard to draw blood.

I do it on my thigh, and the blood runs down my leg. I sit there, my head throbbing and my hands shaking. I don't get up because I have nowhere to be.

With the blood comes a release. I've never done this before. I feel kind of sick, but also a bit excited. Adrenaline pumping through my veins. The pain feels right.

But the high doesn't last long. By the time I walk back up to the shed, I feel tired, achy, as if I've run a marathon. I sleep, my hand resting lightly on my thigh, where I've wrapped paper-towel around the cuts. I wake with a jolt a few times, lifting my hand to see blood on my fingers. My leg pulses. Fucking idiot.

* * *

My feet make orange clouds in the gravel dust as they hit the earth. I'm fast, just my toes lightly touching the road. Woke and needed to run again. My leg feels sticky, blood making my shorts cling to my thigh. Don't think about it. The sun is hitting the shrub, turning the green almost silver. I'm at the Tenterden shop in no time. Past the shop, Jenna's dog barking behind me.

'Hey!'

I keep running.

'Hey, Frank!'

I slow. Stop. Turn.

It's Jenna.

'Yeah?' I say. 'What?'

She's standing in her yard, arms folded across her chest.

'Oh, uh, just thought I'd say hi.'

I'm standing outside her gate now. 'Hi,' I say.

'Where are you going?'

'Dunno.'

'Okay. Ah, enjoy your run.'

'Thanks.'

Past the Tenterden shop, past Jenna's dog, still barking. Round the bend, on and on. Jenna Betts. She's a nice chick. Like another sister. But not. I find myself slowing as I come back past her place, but she's not in the yard. I jog home, grab some nets from the shed and head for the dam.

Jilgies. That's what I feel like.

Maybe I'm okay today.

* * *

There aren't any jilgies. Or none that get in the bloody net anyway. I wind up in the shed again, staring at the tin roof. Another day in here. I draw a bit, smoke a lot. Alby comes in at some point, must be after school, with a pack of cards. I'm high as a kite, giggly. He flinches when I laugh too loud. I've scared this kid. Makes me sad. Love his guts. I fuck everything up.

'Again,' Alby says, already dealing another hand.

'Nah mate, I'm knackered.'

'Come on.'

'Nah.'

Alby keeps dealing. I wipe my arm across the bench so the cards scatter on the dusty concrete.

'Dickhead,' Alby mutters. Never heard him say that before.

'Piss off, Alby.'

He does.

* * *

Later in the evening I go up to the Tenterden store, in search of comfort food. Walk out again with a packet of Twisties. It's not stealing cos the

Bettses would give them to me if I asked. I'm lying on the mattress, tipping them into my mouth when I hear Joe and Steve outside the shed door. They throw it open—you have to really push it, and then it keeps rolling up once it's up halfway. I can see their legs first. Steve's are more muscular. He has his brown farm boots on, and Joe has tennis shoes with thin orange laces. I watch their feet step closer to me because it's easier than looking at their faces.

'Hey, mate,' says Steve. 'Have you seen the jumper leads?'

I lick my finger and trace it over the packet, getting all the powdery yellow stuff. 'Nope.'

They start to look over the other side of the shed, shifting things around, but I feel like they are looking at me.

'What do you even need them for?'

'The battery went flat on my car,' Joe says.

'Piece of shit,' I mutter.

'What the hell.' Joe's looking at the shelf in the corner, near my mattress. It's got a couple of bottles of spirits on it, that I've collected over time, stealing them from the bottle-o. There's whisky and rum and tequila. I've finished almost all of them. There's also a bong and a jar with quite a lot of weed in it. Steve grows his own, down behind one of the shearing sheds. I dug up one of the plants and put it in a pot round the back of my shed.

My pocketknife is next to the bong, and a roll of toilet paper. They probably think I'm shitting in the bush, which I am, because sometimes I hate going in the house so much I avoid it at all costs.

But the toilet paper is there because when I got back from running, my thigh was really gushing and I had to hobble down to the house with my hand over the cuts and grab some more toilet paper to clean up the mess.

I'm not sure what Joe has seen that bothers him, but he crouches down next to my mattress and asks me what I'm up to. As if we've bumped into each other in the park, walking our poodles.

‘What does it look like?’ I say.

‘Not much,’ he says slowly, his eyes hovering on another line of empty spirit bottles he’s just spotted. I put them on the windowsill because the light shines through them all different colours. It’s like having a stained-glass window.

I grit my teeth. ‘Can you piss off?’

Joe steps backwards, but Steve comes closer. He whistles low as he runs his eyes over my grog collection. ‘Mate,’ he says, really drawing it out.

I don’t want them here. This is my place. I screw up the Twisties packet and stand up.

Steve’s not happy. ‘What the fuck? Have you been digging up my green?’

‘Nope,’ I say.

‘Unbelievable.’ Steve points a finger at me. ‘You need to get it together.’

My fists respond automatically, but Joe shoves Steve out of the way. ‘Let’s leave him to it. Jumper leads aren’t here.’

I lie there trying to nap, but there’s no way my body will give me the sweet relief. I sip the dregs of some of my booze bottles, hoping for sleep but instead scoring a pulsing headache. I take a couple of puffs of mary jane, and then a couple more. Eventually the shed starts spinning. It feels better, takes the edge off. At least I can breathe as the world tips sideways. Suddenly I want to be out of the shed, doing something, anything. I don’t trust myself to drive, so I limp up to the road and stand there with my thumb out. Some old cobber picks me up in a black ute, the cab full of cigarette smoke. Something about the smoke, the jerky way he drives and the piercing singer on the radio bring bile rising up my throat. He ditches me just before Mount Barker.

‘Spew in the gutter, dickhead, not in my car.’

I take his advice.

The walk into Barker takes me about half an hour. When I get there, I wish I was back in the shed. The streets are quiet, except for a couple of people walking their dogs as the sun sets. I hang around the petrol station, trying to decide what to do. Find myself inside, flicking through trashy magazines. There's a fat middle-aged lady with a visor on behind the counter, her curly hair sticking up over the top of the cap. She's chatting to a skinny chick at the till with braces and long dark hair. I pretend to read a motoring magazine, while listening to them talk. There's something about the warmth in their voices, the comfortable way they move around each other. The skinny girl is dancing to some pop song on the radio and the older lady, whose name tag reads Brenda, starts to wiggle her hips. They both snap up straight and stifle their giggles behind the backs of their hands as a woman with pink sunglasses on her head shepherds her kids in the door. The family seems to fill the shop, helping me fade further into the background.

'Kate, check on those pies will ya, love?' Brenda has her professional tone on now.

The skinny chick heads out back and returns with a steaming tray. Slides the fresh pies in beside the Chiko Rolls and wedges. I catch a waft of the warm pastry smell, and suddenly I'm starving. I wait until the family go to the counter to buy an armful of ice-creams and pay for petrol. Kate goes out the back again and Brenda is busy serving. I slide the glass door open and grab a pie, tucking it under the bottom of my t-shirt. I'm good at this stuff. I have quiet fingers and a poker face. Normally.

One of the kids looks straight at me.

'He's stealing,' he says, tugging on his mum's sleeve.

I beeline for the door, sticking my head down. The skinny chick pokes her head from out the back. 'Oi, ya dickhead,' she hollers.

'You'll be payin' for that,' Brenda says.

I'm almost out the door when the woman who threw a stone on our roof the other day walks in. She clocks me straight away.

'Tetley boy,' she says.

Any chance of a quick getaway is gone now. The whole room knows my last name.

'You know that kid?' Brenda asks.

'What's he done?' the woman asks. 'Frank, innit? He's a good kid.'

I stare at her.

'We'll sort it, bub,' she says, then turns to Brenda. 'Your service boy won't serve us.'

A man is sitting in a white Valiant at the front of the queue. A bloke is refuelling the car behind him.

Brenda glances back to the woman. 'Sorry,' she says briskly. 'You'll have to wait your turn.'

The woman shuffles on her feet and puffs up her chest. 'We pulled up first. This lady here also got served before us.' Her finger stabs at pink-sunglasses-woman who quickly busies herself, handing the ice-creams round to her children.

Brenda doesn't say anything, just fixes her mouth in a straight line. The door chimes as the man steps inside.

'You causing trouble, Patsy?' his voice is friendly.

'Your wife thinks you should be served before everyone else,' Brenda says.

The man smiles awkwardly. 'Well, we were actually here first, missus, but we're happy to wait.'

'We are *not*,' spits Patsy. 'The petrol station isn't the only place we were first.'

The family hurry for the door.

Patsy plonks her handbag on the counter, fishes around in it. Slaps a note down. 'I'll pay for whatever he got.'

'He stole a pie,' drawls Kate, smirking.

Patsy turns to me.

'Want sauce?'

I'm still standing in the doorway, wishing I could vanish. The hot pie is burning the side of my stomach, where I've tucked it under my shirt.

I blink, then shake my head.

'Course he does,' says the man.

'Go fill up yourself, Herbert,' Patsy says, grabbing a sachet out of the big jar and sliding a silver coin to Brenda. Then she turns on her heel and grabs my elbow as she walks out the door. I try to shrug her off, feeling pissed off and choked up all of a sudden.

'What you doing, you silly bugger?'

I frown.

Patsy opens the car door. 'Get in.'

I shake my head and start to back away. I have no idea who these two are. I just want to eat my pie.

'Let him be, Patsy,' Herbert says.

'Where are you going then?' Patsy gets in the front passenger seat. 'Look like your mum, you do.'

My eyeballs feel dry and scratchy and my head's still spinning. Herbert fills up and pays. All I want is to be in the shed, in darkness. But for some reason, there I am, getting in the car. Herbert nods at me, then gets in the driver's seat.

'Eat yer pie, love,' Patsy says.

So I do. It's still steaming hot and it burns my tongue, but it tastes real good.

'Give him another feed when we get home,' she's speaking to Herbert, tilting her head towards me.

Herbert nods and taps his fingers as he drives, humming along to whatever song is playing in his head.

* * *

I've already decided before we get to the house that I won't go in. I don't really know who Patsy and Herbert are, but I have this strange memory of Patsy handing me a juice box. The straw wouldn't go into the little foil hole, and I remember the satisfaction when it finally went through, juice spurting out the top. I don't know where we were, or what was going on.

Maybe I made it up. Everything feels a bit off. I'm embarrassed, exhausted, and my head is thumping. I feel like I'm hungover, already.

But then we pull into the driveway, and I know the house. There's the bright blue door among the chipped white weatherboard. A wind chime tinkles as Herbert opens the front door. I know the worn rug, lining the long hallway. There's something familiar about the wallpaper and even the smell. It makes me feel uneasy, and I stumble over the doormat.

'Something else to eat, Frank, love?' Patsy calls from the kitchen. I follow her voice into the room. Herbert looks at me closely. I feel like he can see straight through me. There's something about him, about both of them. They feel powerful, like they know stuff.

'Pie filled me up,' I say. 'Thanks anyway.'

'How's your old man?' he asks, buttering his bread.

'Uh, he's okay.'

I can't stop thinking of the screech Patsy made when she threw a stone on our roof. I was impressed with her aim, watched the whole thing from the shed. She reminded me of myself, throwing pine cones on the roof. I know it feels good, making a bang like that. Patsy passes me the bread anyway and smiles warmly.

'You were a deadly footy player, you were,' she says. 'Right back from when you were little.'

I want to ask how they know me, and why I know this place. But I'm really uncomfortable. The kitchen isn't big enough for all of us. I've forgotten how to hold myself, how to speak, what to say.

'Right,' I say, stepping backwards. My plate crashes to the floor and I turn and run down the hallway, the blue door slamming behind me.

* * *

I hitch a lift home with a woman who starts driving again before I can even close the door. There are beer cans tinkling around my feet and sun-bleached parking tickets jammed between the dashboard and the windscreen. The woman is chewing gum and wearing sunglasses even though it's dark. I tell her three times that we're getting near my place and she still drives past it. I'm just thinking I'll have to jump out while she's driving when she screeches to a halt. She doesn't say anything at all, keeps chewing her gum with a robotic jaw. I slam the door and jog back to our driveway, skidding on the gravel.

The walls of the shed are starting to feel like home. I listen to the branches scrape on the tin roof as my breathing finally slows.

* * *

I run again in the morning. Helps my mind, but I can't go so far anymore. Puffing. Skinny legs. I slow down at the Tenterden store. Hug the fence line and wind up round the back, behind the water tank. Stuff this, I don't think I can do it today. Pull my tin out of my pocket, roll a joint. Light up, inhale. Cough. The smoke is sharp in my lungs. There's a rusty tap on the side of the water tank, and I stick my mouth under it. It blasts down my front, wetting my t-shirt. Damn. Sit on the grass, leaning against the concrete. Light back up.

'Hey.'

It's Jenna. Again.

'Ah. Hey.'

'Whatcha doing?'

I raise my eyebrows, sucking on the joint. Stay silent.

'You are on my property. So I'm entitled to ask.' She grins.

I offer her the joint. 'Here. Rent.'

She shakes her head.

I keep sucking.

'Actually,' she says, leaning against the water tank. 'Can I have some? For later?'

'Some green?' I squash the roach out in the dirt.

'Yeah.'

'Um. Sure. I guess so.' I open the tin and break her off a decent bud. 'Do you know what to do with it?'

'Of course.'

'Just checking.' I hand it over.

'Thanks,' she says, and before I know it, she's kissed me on the cheek and walked away, back inside.

Weird.

I walk home. Can't run after the doobie. Lie back on my mattress, pull the covers over me and close my eyes.

* * *

I can hear the phone ringing from the shed. It rings and rings. I swear I've never heard it up here before, but it feels like it's inside my skull. Eventually, I stagger down to the house to rip the cord out of its socket. I barge in just as Dad picks up. He plays with the cord as he speaks, wrapping it around his finger over and over until the tip of his finger turns a deep red. I don't know how his feet don't get hot in summer—he's wearing his ugg boots with his undies. I lie on the couch and switch the TV on. There's nothing on, never is. I turn it off and lie there, listening to the fridge humming from the kitchen and Dad mumbling.

He comes in after a bit, sits in an armchair and swings the footrest up.

'Who was that?'

'The Russells.'

The Russells own our farm. We've never had any trouble with them, but we've always worked damn hard. It's different though, without you. We can't get our shit together.

'What did he say?'

Dad taps his fingers on the arm of the chair. 'Asked if we got the flowers Mrs Russell sent.'

There's more, I know it.

'I'll get rent to them soon. Told 'em we've got shearing under control.

Better get onto it. Probably all ridden with footrot and flystrike.' His sentences are jagged, like he's struggling to get the words out. I know the feeling.

The Russells are from Perth. They've got money. Bought the farm with their inheritance but had no bloody clue about looking after it. Used to live in the neighbour's house, surrounded by peppermint trees. Our house was advertised for rent, and you and Dad were desperate for your own place. You said Dad went over in his best shirt, spoke with Mr Russell. Said he could shear the sheep, wean the lambs, fix the fences, mow the paddocks, anything he wanted. You moved in that weekend and the house was grubby, you said there were even weeds poking through some of the floorboards. There's a photo of you two in the kitchen, you in a t-shirt of Dad's, your legs bare and brown with summer. You're holding a beer bottle to your lips and looking at Dad. He's walking towards you, his arm reaching forwards. I think it was a self-timer shot that went off too early. You have paint on your arms.

You scrubbed the house, filled cracks with plaster, painted everything clean and white, except the kitchen, that got yellow. Thrifty, you were. I wonder if it was always you who kept things going, kept the gardens watered, food on the table, sheep sheared. Without you, everything is falling apart.

I want to tell Dad we need to shear and we need to do it now. Tell him I'll finish fixing the mower and we can get on top of the paddocks. Tell him we can call Shane and rally the troops to get it done.

But I'm so tired. I know what needs to be done, and also that I can't do it. What kind of bloke am I? I hope the Russells cut us some slack. They're kind enough, but it would take more than kindness to be okay with watching their farm fall to pieces.

the feeling of cutting has
become
addictive
almost like pleasure it offers
sweet

release.

i make deals with myself
i can make a mess of my thigh/ wrist/ rib cage
but for you
i have to stay

alive.

7. Rose

On Monday afternoon I get home to a big cardboard box by the front door. It has *The Good Samaritans* printed on it in red letters. I try to push it inside with my foot, but it's too heavy. I bend down and pick it up, leaning it on my hip as I squeeze in the door. The tape lifts with the tip of the bread knife. Inside there are cans of beans, Mills & Ware's Milk Arrowroot biscuits, shelf-life milk and some funny-smelling cheese. There's packets of pasta and rice, a loaf of white bread, eggs and Smith's chips. Milo, teabags, instant coffee. Even toothpaste, two bars of Pears soap and a box of tissues. My cheeks feel hot. Who organised this? Underneath everything is a piece of paper with 'Care package courtesy donations from your community' written in cursive on it. You used to donate to the Good Sammy's, cans of things we hadn't used from the pantry and sometimes old toys we didn't play with anymore. Chances are some of the baked beans were from our own pantry in the first place. I shove things on the shelves and in the fridge. I leave the box and the note on the table, so Dad can see what things have come to. That night, I find him making a Milo in the kitchen. He pours hot water in his cup and asks if I want one.

'Nah.'

I see the note in the top of the bin. I know that he knows. But he doesn't say anything.

school skirt rolled at my hips lets it swing
just above my knees the way jenna taught
me. white shirt too big
rolled at the sleeves, *frank* scrawled across
the tag in your handwriting.
the teachers talk monday
through to friday, wearing the chalk down to
dust on the blackboard.
and i try to remain here—feet beneath the desk
working my lead pencil down to a smooth
silver bulb. i fill pages but not a trace
stays in my mind.
the teachers talk monday
through to friday and i just try to remain
here, where the orange gravel dust stains our legs and
the summer burns our skin. here, where
the fan chugs in the background
circulating stuffy air and the water tanks run dry
and we have to buy bottled water from the canteen for
two dollars sixty.
here, where mrs watkins writes
rose
on the blackboard because she gets tired of
calling me back, asking me to pay
attention. here, where you once were
on friday afternoons, in the carpark
with our frayed beach towels thrown
over the backseat of the rusty white land cruiser.
the dogs licking our faces and you
with the windows down and a big smile.
you'd take us to the beach, and we'd stay there till dark

burning red as lobsters
our hair growing crispy with the salt.
dad didn't come—this was our time
with you. you'd pull in to the fish and chip shop
on the way home, and we'd eat in the car under
the streetlight, greasy paper and
battered fish, vinegar on hot chips.
here, where i have to clean the windows
my penance for trying to escape
here.
the teachers talk monday through to
friday and the chalk crumbles at their feet
like ash.

On Friday afternoon, I ride my bike to the Tenterden store to buy a Twin Pole with some coins I pinched from Dad's wallet. Jenna's dad smiles broadly as I walk in the door.

'Whaddya want, Miss Tetley?'

I slide the freezer open and grab an icy pole. He flaps his hands at me when I try to pay.

'Jenna's at her piano lesson, but she'll be around tomorrow,' he says.

I sit on the steps and the icy pole drips down my arm. Ants climb up my legs and I slap them as they get close to my shorts. My favourite orange-and-pink gingham ones—they're so old the elastic has given up and I have to keep hitching them up. I'm licking juice off my fingers when Shane pulls up in his old black ute, his dog Clyde next to him on the passenger seat. I try to look casual, leaning on the handrail and untying my shoelace so I can tie it back up as he swings out of the door.

'Hey there, Rosie girl,' he says. Only my family call me that, but we've known Shane so long that he's picked it up too. He's wearing a white t-shirt cropped at the arms and a blue flanno. He looks like a Tetley, and we treat him like one. I'm glad he's not my brother though. His dark curls are messy and fall in line with his stubbled jaw, which is jagged in a way that makes my lower belly twist.

'Oh, hey,' I say, leaning back on my elbow and squinting up at him in the sun. He walks past me into the store, the doorbell ringing as he enters. I can't decide whether to jump on my bike and pedal for home or stay and chat. I don't want him to think I'm waiting for him. Shane comes outside with a pie as I'm still deciding and sits next to me on the steps.

'Do you have a ciggie?' I say.

He grins. 'You smoke now, do ya?'

'Yeah.' I light up with his matches, cupping my hands around the cigarette.

'Been good, Rosie?'

'Yeah.'

He's got a thin silver chain round his neck. I don't really know any other boys who wear jewellery. Shane is just different. He never looks like he's trying to fit in, but he doesn't stand out obnoxiously either. His grandma used to be a cook at the Marribank Mission in Katanning, and some people say Shane's grandad was a Noongar man. Reckon they tried to run away together, but he got sent over to Gnowangerup. Shane's mum, Sandy, never knew her dad. They get away with saying he was Italian because Shane and Sandy kinda look like us. They can pass for Mediterranean—it's easier that way. I've heard you can cop a lot of shit if you're a Noongar, some of them sent off to missions, away from their families. Not sure why.

'Your old man hasn't called in a while. Managing okay on his own is he?'

Back before things went to shit, Shane used to work a few days a week with the boys at our place, helping out with the sheep, and he's good with fixing things.

'Nah,' I say, scuffing my tennis shoe in the dirt. 'Dad doesn't do much these days.' We sit there in silence, and I tap ash off the end of the cigarette onto some of those pesky ants.

'The tractor still broken down?'

The tractor broke down before you died, but the boys and Dad just left it. Weeds are growing around it now.

'Yep.'

Shane looks at me closely for a moment, then wipes his hands on his pants. 'I'm going to swing by, do you want a lift?'

'You don't have to come, I'm sure they'll get to it, they just ...'

Shane lifts my bike onto the tray of his ute. 'Let's go.'

* * *

When we pull up, I don't know whether I should go with Shane to the tractor, or head on down to the house. We walk down the driveway and my feet skid on the gravel but I catch myself. Shane laughs. I wonder if the boys and Dad will be mad that I told him the tractor still isn't fixed. I don't want them to think I asked Shane to come fix it—we're too proud for that. I decide to skip the house. Dad will be sitting at the table or in his armchair and besides, Shane is chatting to me about Queen's new album and I'm going on about The Runaways. The bloke at 78 Records in Perth told me once he reckons Joan Jett is going to quit and go solo. Me and Steve have a bet about it. He reckons they'll stay together. I reckon she's more punk than the others will ever be. I can tell Shane's surprised how much I know. That's being a Tetley, though. We are all obsessed with rock'n'roll.

At the tractor, I feel clunky and awkward as Shane starts rummaging around under the cowling. Joe has appeared from somewhere and has a toolbox with him.

'Been meaning to get to this,' he says.

I leave them to it.

A few hours later, Shane pops inside and drops the keys on the kitchen table.

'Tractor's orright now, Ed, mate,' he calls, sticking his head into the lounge room. 'Give me a buzz about shearing, the sheep need it.' He doesn't give Dad time to reply—grabs an apple off our kitchen table and is out the door.

I watch him striding up the driveway. I wish we were going back to the docks again tonight, but after last time, I don't think we will be. I loved our Friday nights, creeping home super early on Saturday mornings. It was something we kept doing through most of your illness. Became part of how we coped. Throughout the week I'd either be at school or at your bedside. But most Fridays we'd go, leaving you and Dad in the evening light. Alby would normally go to a friend's place up the road. You'd joke it was your date night, and Dad would read to you or carry you out into the lounge room to watch a movie. I remember the first time you did that, Dad made popcorn so you could pretend you were at the cinema.

I think he ate most of it, but I saw how much it made you smile. I reckon you both preferred not to know what we were up to, and mostly we got away with it. But you could be a bit unpredictable, the sicker you got. One time you looked at us as we were about to go and said, 'Don't,' in a raspy voice.

'Don't what?' Steve asked, squeezing your hand.

'Don't go.'

We looked at each other, hovered in the doorway and beside your bed.

'Fine, get out of here,' you snapped. 'Drink yourselves to death. Glad you get the choice.'

The memory still hurts.

'Mum, we'll stay,' I remember saying, sinking down next to you.

'Get out,' you said, not looking at me.

'I don't want to go.'

'Yeah, Mum, we'll stay.' Joe was gripping the end of the bed tightly. I remember how white his knuckles were.

Dad was pacing, glancing from each of us to you, and out the window, his hands clasped behind his back.

'I want you to leave.'

I will never forget the way you hissed it, will never know if it was medication, pain, grief or genuine anger. Dad unclasped his hands and clasped them again in front of him.

'I think it's best you all go,' he said quietly. 'Go on.'

We walked mutely down the hallway. My jaw was so tight my ears started ringing. I didn't want to get in the kombi, but Joe grabbed my arm as I was about to turn away. We sat, Steve and Joe in the front, Frank and I in the back, in silence for a long time. Then Steve coughed and started the engine, punching off the radio as soon as it came on. None of us said a word, and that time, Steve didn't pick anyone up. He drove straight past Jenna's and Shane's. I sobbed in a way that I had never sobbed before, and never have since. My chest heaved and my shoulders shook. It was one of the last times Frank showed up for me. About a month before you died, he closed right up and stopped letting me in. But that time, as I lost myself in the kombi, lost myself completely, Frank was there. He scooted himself across to the middle seat and took me in his arms. He rocked us gently, back and forth, and when his t-shirt got wet through, he took it off and mopped my face with it.

Steve pulled over somewhere between Barker and Albany, into a truck bay. Joe jumped out, slid the van door open and Frank lifted me out. I crouched in the gravel and my brothers crouched with me. Suddenly there we were, lying in the dirt, holding each other. It got dark and we stayed, on our backs by then, looking up at the sky. At some point a car pulled into the same spot, a woman and a young boy with a small white dog. They moved around us carefully, looked at us like we might be dangerous. Their dog pissed under a paperbark, then so did the boy.

When they pulled back onto the highway, one of us started laughing. It rippled through us all, that hysterical laughter. There were no clouds that night, and Joe pointed out stars and planets, told us about galaxies beyond the Milky Way. I imagined being somewhere far, far from earth. Lifting up, out of my body and rising above the gum trees, higher and higher till the highway looked like a ribbon, then faded to nothing. We got back in the kombi eventually.

I felt so tired, like I wanted to sink into the backseat and never stand up again. When we pulled into the driveway, Steve kept driving, down to the bottom of the property. He parked up beneath a marri tree and chucked Bob Marley & the Wailers in the tape player. We had beers in the esky ready for our night on the boats, and we sat in the back, the door open into the night. Steve passed a pipe around and Joe shuffled the cards. I fell asleep, my head on Frank's feet. His toes are long and slender, like yours. Steve drove the kombi back up the driveway eventually. I woke up as he lifted me up and piggybacked me inside. The house was silent, and as soon as we were under the roof, the spell was broken. We fragmented again under the pressure between the walls. I miss how close we felt in the kombi that night. And I desperately miss Frank.

I go up to the shed to try talk to him when he doesn't come down at dinner time. I'm nervous as I walk up the hill, planning my words. My throat feels tight. Music is blasting out of the shed. He's lying on the mattress and his eyeballs are so bloodshot the whites are almost completely red.

'Frank.'

He looks round vaguely, sees me, then simply looks away again. He's under the covers and a tape is playing so loudly I can't even tell what band it is.

'Frank.' I hit the eject button. Never seen that tape deck before.

'WhaddyadoingRose,' his words slur together. He looks and sounds like a stranger.

'Checking on you.'

'Go way.'

'No.'

'GO WAY.' He shouts it, like an angry child. I find myself falling backwards, slipping over the gravel. When I get back to the house I want to tell Joe, or Steve, or Dad, that something's wrong. But I can't. I don't want to get Frank in trouble. Instead I fill an old milk bottle with water, take a few sausages and a couple of pieces of bread, and head back to the shed. I feel dread with every step. Scenes of walking down our hallway, unsure how we'd find you, flash into my mind. At the shed I flick the light on, feeling jumpy, and the fluorescent glow flickers.

'Arghhhh,' Frank throws his arm over his eyes.

I crouch by the bed with the plate of food and the bottle of water.

'Please eat.'

Frank rolls away from me, hunched in a ball. I gently touch his shoulder.

'Eat.'

He starts shaking, and first I think he's crying, but then I hear his laugh. He's laughing. I stand up quickly. My face feels hot. I kick the milk bottle over by accident as I run out the door and it rolls along the concrete and nearly trips me up. I reach down, grab the bottle and gently roll it back into the shed, so it stops near Frank's mattress. Down at the house I stand by the front door, breathing deeply, looking at the moon. It's a while before I can walk inside.

That night Joe and I watch a weird horror movie that's on TV. A drowned bride becomes a vampire, her dress clinging to her body as she rises out of the lake, bloodthirsty. There's a corpse in a bass guitar case, townspeople turning to vampires, knives being brandished, and teeth bared. I wake up at two in the morning, my neck on a funny angle and my mouth hanging open. Joe is asleep beside me, his head rolled forwards. I tiptoe into my bedroom and lie awake until the sun rises.

* * *

That morning I make a strong coffee and stand outside, just to the left of the kitchen window, leaning against the house where no one will see me. I can't be Alby's mum today, can't face Frank again. I put my cup down on the verandah balustrade. That's it. I'm not even going back inside. I head straight for Jenna's.

Her dad is making bacon and eggs, I can smell it from up on the highway. He smiles when I knock on the door.

'I'll put another egg on.'

After breakfast we sit on Jenna's bed, listening to Suzi Quatro and reading Mrs Betts' *Women's Weekly* magazines. They're pretty boring, all about cooking, cosmetics and the Royal Family. Jenna likes the horoscopes though.

'Celebrate what is good today, and show compassion to others, especially those you value most. Today is a good day to pursue romantic interests but be sure to keep an open mind and heart.' Jenna sighs.

‘Maybe you should tell Jackson how you feel,’ I tease. We met Jackson at Kendenup Primary, and he was one of the few students who came on to Mount Barker Senior High with us. Jenna has always had the hots for him. His family have a farmers’ market stall in Albany on Saturdays and sometimes we go so Jenna can sweet-talk his mum and smile at him while she pretends to be very interested in their string beans and carrots.

‘Nah, I think I’m off him,’ she says, pulling at a thread on her bedspread.

‘What?’ I say. ‘Since when?’

‘I dunno, recently.’

‘Why?’

‘Just over it. I mean, he has a pet frog.’

I raise my eyebrows at her. ‘You have the hots for someone else?’ I lie on her mattress and walk my legs up the wall, stretching them out. Jenna doesn’t say anything. I roll and look at her. She’s scratching a mozzie bite. Looks at me, watching her.

‘Nah,’ she says.

‘Tell me.’

‘No one.’

Mrs Betts calls to say lunch is ready and we wander into the kitchen. She’s made egg and bacon pie and she gives us both a slice and plops some cherry tomatoes on the plate too. Mr Betts comes in from the shop with three cans of lemonade. He gives one to each of us with a wink, then goes back to look after the till. Mrs Betts commandeers her magazine and pours her lemonade into a wine glass. I feel like I’m on holiday.

* * *

I spend the weekend at Jenna’s place. That night we eat pizza that Mr Betts cooks on the wood fire out the back. I sleep well beside Jen, listening to the rhythm of her breath, the cat keeping my feet warm. In the morning we walk Pippa along the road to the tennis club, round past the cemetery and back. It feels so good to be away from my place that I stay till it starts getting dark on Sunday. Mr Betts drops me home about seven, and I walk up to the front door reluctantly. I head straight for my room, jumping into bed with my jeans on. I listen to the house move and settle around me. Alby opens my door around nine o'clock and I close my eyes, pretending to be asleep. I hear him sigh and close the door again. Wonder if Dad did anything with him. Contemplate getting up and grabbing him, but I leave him to it. Stay where I am, curled into a ball, until I fall asleep. It takes a while because the thought of school fills me with dread.

Monday is hard. Jenna chats with Tess at recess and I stand beside them but have absolutely nothing to add. Jenna looks concerned and tries to include me in the conversation, but I keep forgetting to listen.

'Yeah,' I say, offbeat. 'Same.'

They both pause, laugh awkwardly and then keep talking. At lunch Jenna does laps of the oval with me, but as we walk she says we should try doing something else.

'We could go sit with the others, behind the hall,' she says. This is where the 'cool' kids sit, and we've never been one of them.

'They aren't that bad,' Jenna adds. 'I sat with them sometimes, while you were away.'

Her words hurt, for some reason, but I don't say anything.

'Okay, how about we play footy with the boys even?'

I roll my eyes.

'Or what about—'

'You can, Jen,' I interrupt. 'Do whatever you want. I'm happy walking.'

Jenna looks hurt. 'It's just we've walked around the oval like seven times already and lunch is only halfway though. I'm getting dizzy. There are other things we can do, Rose.'

'You go do them, then,' I snap. 'I'll be here.' I don't expect her to actually leave.

'You sure?' she asks uncertainly.

I want to say no. 'Yep,' I say.

She kisses my cheek and walks away. I keep walking round and round, determinedly not looking anywhere but straight ahead. My heart hurts. In class I expect Jenna to sit with her new friends, but there she is, in our spot, same as usual. She leans her shoulder on me. I flinch, feeling angry and hurt even though I know it's unreasonable.

Tess gets on our bus that afternoon.

'She's coming over to my place,' Jenna says in my ear. 'So I'm going to sit with her. But you can come over too if you want.'

Something is stuck in the back of my throat and I cough. 'It's okay,' I splutter. 'I've got plans.'

Jenna frowns at me. 'You're welcome at my place, Rose, always.'

'Thanks,' I say, and then I sit in our seat without her.

All the way home I lean my head against the window, watching the paddocks streak past. When we get to Jenna's stop, she turns to me. 'Sure you don't want to come?'

'I'm sure,' I say, raising my hand in a wave.

'See you tomorrow,' Jenna says, and Tess smiles.

* * *

That evening, I sit in the kombi with Steve and take swigs of his beer. He's got a real nice set-up inside. When he's parked up, he folds the seat down and lays a few wooden beams and a mattress on top. He's sprawled on the bed, gently strumming his guitar. I lean against the mattress and listen, my head half-heartedly in *Frankenstein*. Later I sit on the kitchen bench and eat a carrot. I can hear the hum of the television, and Dad snoring in front of it. He never watched this much TV while you were around. I cut some carrot and slices of cheese and put it on the arm of the couch next to him in case he's hungry when he wakes up.

* * *

At school Tess sits on the other side of Jenna. Jenna reminds me of the gaping clowns at the Albany show, turning their heads from side to side. She turns from Tess to me, Tess to me trying to keep us both happy, feeding us both conversation. I wish she would stop. When the bell goes, Jenna grabs my arm.

'Come sit with us,' she says, smiling.

It hurts that 'us' means something other than her and me. I shake my head.

'Rose,' she says, her nails digging into my skin. 'Please.'

Her hand falls as I pull away, but as I walk towards the oval, I regret it. I guess it's not fair to expect Jenna to spend her free time forming a sand track around the edge of the oval. On my own my thoughts catch up with me. To drown them out, I try to remember the lyrics to Queen's 'Keep Yourself Alive', my feet walking to the beat.

Back in class, Tess sits between Jenna and me. She tries to talk to me, asks me how I am, what I did on the weekend, what pizza toppings I like.

'We had a Hawaiian last night, but we added olives,' she tells me.

'Okay,' I say. 'I'm trying to listen to Mr Bennet.'

Jenna's eyebrows jump up into her fringe. I can't tell if she's mad at me or not. The three of us work in silence until the bell goes. On the bus Jenna sits next to me. We don't talk, but she holds my hand until she gets off at her stop.

* * *

The next morning the bus pulls into Jenna's stop, but she doesn't get on. I stand up to try see where she is and notice her leaning out from behind the shelter. She's waving to me frantically. The bus is about to leave, and she's still not getting on. I look around. Alby is playing cards with some of the boys from the primary school and he doesn't see me throw my bag onto my shoulder and squeeze out the door, just as the bus pulls away. Jenna pulls me behind the shelter, and we fall into the tall grass.

'What the hell?' I sit up and stare at her.

She smiles widely and loops her finger in one of my curls.

'Where's your uniform?' I ask, pulling back and looking at her. She's wearing pale denim flairs and an old white cropped t-shirt. She looks like Stevie Nicks.

'I thought we needed a day off,' she says. We are still on our bums in the dirt, and she flops onto her back. I feel clunky, unsure where to put my body. I never feel like this around Jen. She pulls my shoulder and I fall beside her. The clouds are shifting above us in the summer wind.

'I've got us some weed,' she says, turning to me excitedly.

'Where from?'

'Secret.' She taps the side of her nose.

I undo my tie, loosen my collar and sit up. I'm happy about skipping school, but Jenna never keeps secrets from me. I'm about to ask again, but she speaks first.

'Wanna go by the creek?'

We throw our schoolbags on top of the bus shelter and climb over the fence into the paddock. The sheep scatter around us and the morning sun bakes our heads. We walk to the edge of the paddock, through the twisted paperbark trees, where a creek runs through the weeds.

'Let's do it here,' Jenna says. 'I want to be near water when we're high.'

We sit beside the creek and Jenna pulls an old tin out of her pocket.

'Can I see?'

She opens the tin and passes it to me with a huge smile, proud of herself. 'I nicked some papers from the shop too.' The buds are dark green and remind me of a herbal tea you used to drink. I've smoked green with the boys a bunch, but we've never done it like this, just us. I've watched my brothers roll so many times, so I take the papers and Jenna picks the buds into smaller pieces. I pack the joint and tear some cardboard as a filter, rolling it into an S shape, the way I've seen Frank do it. Bits of bud keep falling out the end, and my fingers feel big and clumsy. Jenna tries to help, getting in the way. I swat her hand away.

'Okay,' I say, licking it and sealing the paper together. It's lumpy and poorly rolled, but Jenna's pretty pleased. We take our shoes off and hang them from a tree branch. Jenna balances out along a log and sits with her bare toes dangling in the stream. I follow her, sticking one arm out like a trapeze walker, the other holding the joint carefully above my head. I sit beside her and Jenna lights up, holding the joint between her teeth, eyes gleaming. The smoke smells like summer evenings, like my brothers, like Friday nights, like adventure. I can feel myself thawing out, the air between Jenna and I becoming easy and light. We are just us, like normal, away from the strangeness of school. We pass the joint between us, arm in arm, swinging our legs. The flies swarm around us, trying to land in our eyes and mouths.

'Bugger off,' Jenna says, swatting them away.

The smoke burns the back of my throat and I cough, choking as I laugh at the same time. Jenna slaps my back a little too hard and I overbalance, falling into the stream with a splash. Cold creek water seeps into my clothes, choking in my nose and mouth.

'Rose!' Jenna stands on the log and peers into the water. She hesitates, then peels her t-shirt off and throws it onto the bank, her jeans, bra and undies landing beside them. She twirls like a dancer, then lands beside me in the stream. We drift lazily on our backs, fat smiles on our stoned faces.

'Let's get boyfriends and hitch to Perth,' says Jenna.

'Or even Melbourne,' I say. 'I've heard they have bowling bars where you can drink pina coladas while you play.'

'We'd need some fakies to get into clubs in the city,' says Jenna.

'And we'd need better clothes.'

'Where are we going to find the boyfriends?'

'Anywhere but here.'

I strip my wet uniform off, and we lie there, basking naked in the sun. The moment feels golden.

'Thank you,' I say.

'What for?' Jenna turns to me, twigs in her hair and water droplets in her eyelashes.

I think for a moment. Hold the air in my lungs until I feel like I might explode. Jenna reaches across and holds my face in her hands, the way she always does.

'I love you, Rose Tetley,' she says. 'I can see the clouds in your eyes.'

My heart throbs in a painful way. No one says that anymore. You used to tell us you loved us every night. I haven't heard those words since you died. I push Jenna backwards slightly.

'You're so baked, Jen.'

She groans and sits up. 'Oh my god, I'm so hungry.'

'Mmm same. I feel like a burger from the Barker pub.'

'With chips and a milkshake.'

'I want a milky bar too.'

We swim to the edge of the creek and Jenna pulls her dry clothes on.

'What are we gonna do with you? Your clothes are wet,' Jenna says.

'We could create a nudist colony,' I say, wringing out my sodden uniform. Jenna is the only person I feel comfortable seeing me naked. It's all the years of baths and running around in front of the sprinkler when we were small.

Jenna laughs. 'Or we could go in the back way to mine and grab you something. I reckon we should go somewhere.'

'Where?'

'Who cares? Just somewhere.'

We head back towards the road. A butterfly lands on my shoulder and we stop, staring at it dreamily. Jenna reaches her finger out and touches it. The butterfly lifts her wings together and they merge into one; tie-dyed patterns of deep orange and red mesmerise us.

'She's beautiful,' Jenna whispers.

'There's another,' I say, as one lands on Jenna's forehead.

We stand there in awe. I can't tell how long we've been there for, when a blowfly buzzes around our heads, unsettling the butterflies as we swat it away.

'We must go on.' Jenna salutes her hand to her forehead like a soldier. I giggle and march behind her. When we get close to the road, I wriggle back into my wet uniform.

'Let's hope Mum is in the kitchen or something, she'd bloody boot my arse if she found out about this,' Jenna says, as we arrive at the bus shelter and grab our bags down. A car zooms past and honks at us. I blush but Jenna gives them the finger. We duck behind the fence and walk back along through the paddocks, the reeds tickling our legs. At the back of Jenna's house we lurk behind the water tank, checking for any sign of Mrs Betts. We dash for the verandah and creep in the back door, tiptoeing into Jenna's room. The sound of the vacuum cleaner drifts from the front of the house. Jenna opens her drawers and throws me a pair of denim shorts, a bright yellow stretchy t-shirt and some dry underwear. I still feel spacey from the joint. As I pull my leg through the tight denim I knock the side of Jenna's dresser and a glass vase falls off the side. It smashes on the floor. I freeze.

The sound of the vacuum in the kitchen stops.

Jenna throws open the window and mouths 'quick!', her eyebrows rising up her forehead. There are footsteps coming down the hallway. I lunge for the window as Jenna jumps out before me. We land on the dry grass below and sprint for the cover of the peppermint trees near the fence. From there, we can see the shape of Jenna's mum in her room. She stands by the window a moment then turns and walks back out.

'Ohhh my god,' breathes Jenna in my ear.

'We woulda been dead meat,' I say, pulling the t-shirt over my head.

We burst out laughing, shoving our hands over our mouths in case

Mrs Betts hears. Together, we head for the highway, walking along the side of the road.

'Where do you wanna go?'

I look at the road stretching out before us.

'It's a long walk to anywhere from here.'

'Wanna hitch somewhere?'

A ute zooms past us, two kelpies on the back barking in the wind. It's only ten thirty.

We've got nothing to lose.

'Yeah, why not?'

We stand side by side at the Tenterden road sign with our thumbs out. A white Ford Falcon passes us without slowing down, followed by a grey Commodore.

'Come on,' mutters Jenna.

A blue Corolla beeps but doesn't stop.

'Right,' Jenna says looking sideways at me. She slides her hands inside her singlet and pulls it up, stretching it over her tits. She pulls her bra down so her nipples are pushed out the top.

'Let's see if this helps.'

Jesus. I wonder what you would think of me now.

'You do it too, Rose,' Jenna instructs me.

I frown and reluctantly start to peel my t-shirt up, when a burgundy ute pulls up beside us, spraying our legs with dust. A man with a long red beard wearing a blue flannelette shirt reaches over the passenger seat to wind down the window. He has black sunnies on and a stubby of Emu Export in his hand. He whistles low at Jenna, eyeing her chest.

'Where ya headed, girls?'

Jenna pulls her singlet down. 'Where ya going?'

The man nods at the road before us. 'Albany.'

Jenna raises her eyebrows at me. 'We should try get the school bus home this arvo,' she says.

‘We could stop in Barker,’ I say, imagining that burger.

‘Ya coming or not?’ says the bearded man.

‘Can you drop us in Mount Barker?’

‘Yep. Get in.’

Jenna takes the front seat and I climb in the back, settling in among some crumpled clothes and a small white dog I hadn’t seen until now.

‘That’s Minnie,’ says the man, looking over his shoulder at me. ‘She bites.’

Jenna looks at me in the side mirror with her big-eyed look.

‘Great,’ I say.

He pulls out and we are off, roaring along the highway.

‘My name’s Maverick,’ says our driver.

‘Emma.’

‘Jane.’

‘What you two up to then?’

‘Escaping,’ says Jenna, turning around to grin at me.

The dog is baring her teeth at me, standing with her front feet pressing into my thigh.

‘Bugger off,’ I say, pushing her off me.

‘Oi,’ says Maverick. ‘She’s a sweetheart that one, really.’

‘I’m sure,’ I say.

Maverick cranks Kiss, ‘Hotter Than Hell’, and Jenna bops her head, her blonde hair bouncing with her. The dog retreats to the other side of the seat and Maverick winds down the window for her to stick her little head out in the wind.

‘There’s some stubbies in the back there if you want some, Jane, babe,’ Maverick says, winking at me in the rear-view mirror. ‘You two look like high school runaways.’

We laugh but don’t say anything. I reach into the esky and pass Jenna a stubbie of Emu Export. Crack mine open and sip the bitter beer, some of the froth pouring out onto my legs. My bones feel heavy and warm from the weed. I close my eyes and lean back. The music carries me.

When I open my eyes we are almost in Barker, and Maverick has his hand on Jenna's knee.

'Where shall I drop ya then, girls?' he says, his eyes lingering on Jenna's boobs again.

'The Barker hotel is fine,' Jenna says, shifting her knee so his hand falls sideways. Maverick pulls up and we jump out quickly, leaving our empty beer bottles rattling amongst the others on the floor.

'Do you ladies need a lift home later?' he asks with a wink.

'Nah, thanks,' Jenna says, tilting her chin up at him.

He speeds off, his little white dog yapping at us out the window.

We stand in the street for a moment, gathering ourselves.

'Well, that was an experience,' says Jenna.

'You okay?' My head still feels like it's disconnected from my body.

'Mmmm. Keen for a bloody burger,' she says. We traipse up the steps arm in arm. The barman looks us up and down. Jenna walks straight up to him and leans on the counter.

'Two burgers and two pints of Swan please.'

The barman pushes his hair out of his eyes. He looks at us some more, for quite a while.

'Did you hear me?' Jenna asks. 'I said—'

'Yep, got it,' he says. 'Should you guys be at school?'

'Clearly not, you drongo.'

He blinks at Jenna, then looks across to me. I shrug non-committedly. I haven't seen this barman before. I keep reading his t-shirt, which says 'goog' across it, with a picture of a cracked egg. I snicker and he stares at me. This is not going well. I glance around the room for Gary, one of Joe's mates who works here. Jenna is just getting in the barman's face, leaning up in her tennis shoes.

'You listen here—'

'Rosie!' Gary comes round the corner, holding a huge stack of beer glasses under his arm. 'How are ya, darlin'?' He waves the sullen barman out of the way and puts the order through himself.

'That's Derek. He's a bit dull up here,' Gary says, tapping his finger to his head. Next minute we are sitting out in the sunshine, two pints in front of us, shovelling hot chips into our hungry mouths.

'Gary is so cute,' sighs Jenna. 'Not my type, but cute.'

'What's your type?' I ask. 'No pet frogs?'

'No pet frogs.' Jenna smiles. 'Cheers to that.'

Our burgers come out, oozing with cheese and mustard. We sink our teeth into them and sit there in content silence.

'So long as we make it back in time for the bus, we should be sweet,' I say. We finish our burgers and do a runner. I feel kind of bad for Gary, so I toss some coins in the tip jar on the way out.

The rest of the day passes quickly. We browse in the Good Sammy's, trying on worn silk headscarves and tacky high heels. Jenna buys some peach-coloured socks that stretch up to her knees, and I buy a home-recorded cassette mix that looks like someone made it for their girlfriend. *For Ruby* is scrawled across the case.

The beer has made us tipsy, and we still have the munchies. We buy chocolate hedgehog slices from the bakery and take them to the park, eating them while lying on our stomachs on the swings. At quarter to three we walk towards our school, trying to stay far enough from the fence that the teachers and students don't notice us, but close enough that we can see the bus when it comes. We lurk behind the trees, and wave at Mick as he comes around the corner. He notices and slows, pulling up in the gravel beside us.

'What are you two up to then?' he asks, peering down from his driver's seat.

'Just let us on will ya, Mick?' Jenna pleads.

He taps his steering wheel, hesitating, but we jump on before he can reconsider. We sit near the back, slouched down in our seats. Mick pulls up at the school and kids start to file on. Nancy Smith gives us crazy eyes when she gets on but doesn't say anything. I can see Alby looking for me when he gets on at Kendenup Primary, and I shake my head, holding my index finger to my lips. He sits closer to us than normal and watches me out the corner of his eye, as if he thinks I might make a runner somewhere else. We're almost at Jenna's stop when we realise we should have brought our uniforms with us so we could at least look like we went to school today.

'I'm going to tell Mum it was a free-dress day,' Jenna mutters as the bus pulls into her stop. The wind pushes her hair in her face as she steps onto the gravel, and she turns and looks back at me and waves. I wonder if she knows she's what's keeping me here, keeping me alive.

Alby asks lots of questions as we walk down the driveway.

'I had a doctor's appointment,' I say, not looking at him.

'Are you sick?'

I know the alarm in his voice, and what he's afraid of. 'No.'

'So why did you go to the doctor's, then?'

'General check-up.'

'Did you wag?'

'Yep.'

'I won't tell.'

'No, you won't.'

We open the front door and I wait for Dad to notice. He's sitting at the table, tapping a blunt lead pencil against the newspaper, making a dull thwack sound over and over again. He smiles at us.

'How was school?'

I assume he's asking Alby, going to dish it to me later. Alby gives his spiel about spelling and learning about volcanoes.

'What about you, Rose?' Dad asks.

Is he serious? I'm wearing Jenna's clothes, and as I got off the bus I realised I left my schoolbag at her house. I look down at my empty hands.

'Uh, yeah, great,' I say.

He smiles again. 'Great,' he echoes, looking back down at the paper.

'What did you do today?' I ask, frustration boiling inside me.

I want him to look at me, properly.

I want him to notice things.

I want him to care that I didn't go to school.

I want him to shout.

'Me?' he asks, as if he's forgotten who he is.

'Yeah. You.'

'Oh. I pottered around here for a bit. Not much really. Cracked the crossword.'

'Right.'

Alby escapes down the hallway. I think about the boys, struggling to keep the farm afloat. About how it's been months, and Dad still hasn't moved. About that bloody care package from the Good Sammy's. I can feel this dull ache behind my eyeballs, and I'm starving again. I grab the box of Cheerios from the pantry and pour some into my mouth.

'Get a bowl Rosie, love,' says Dad.

Something in me flips. I tip the box up higher, missing my mouth. Cheerios spill down my front and all over the floor.

'Rose!' Dad says.

'You're not my dad anymore.' I turn to look at him.

His face cracks.

He's completely bewildered, his eyes magnified from his glasses. He doesn't say anything, just keeps blinking at me, as if I smashed something, or threw water over his head. I don't even know what I meant or why I said it. My knees are weak, and I feel like weeping all of a sudden.

'Sorry, Dad,' I whisper.

I grab the dustpan and broom and sweep up the mess. Turn and head for my room, closing the door behind me. I sit on my bed with my doona wrapped around my shoulders. My tummy is cramping and I can feel the greasy burger and Cheerios twisting in my gut. I want you to come in with your cool hands to my forehead, like you would when we were sick.

I must have fallen asleep. Joe knocks on my door as I'm rubbing my eyes.

'I've put some sausages on,' he says. 'And some potatoes.'

I don't trust myself to look at him without crying.

He turns to leave, then hesitates in the doorway. 'How was school?' he asks.

'I didn't go.'

'How come?'

'Jenna and I wagged.' I still can't look at him. Joe has always reminded me of Dad. I wish it were Dad sitting here with me now.

'What did you do?' Out of the corner of my eye I see him push his glasses up his nose.

'We got baked.'

'I'll put extra potatoes on for you then,' he says.

I bite the inside of my lip and try to remember how free and light I felt, only hours before, floating on my back in the stream.

We eat dinner together quietly. Frank's place is empty. No one comments on his absence. He'll come when he's hungry, or half starved, or wants more beer.

The potatoes are crispy on the outside and soft and steamy inside. Joe's cooking reminds me the most of yours.

'I think I want to move to Melbourne,' he says, standing at the sink and pouring a glass of water.

'What's that?' Dad's always a beat behind.

'I want to move to Melbourne,' Joe repeats, leaning against the kitchen cupboard.

We stare at him.

I can feel a knife in my ribs.

'What for?' asks Steve.

'Study, maybe.'

'Study what?' Steve again.

‘Anthropology, or biology, I think.’

‘What does that mean?’ asks Alby.

‘Yeah,’ Dad says, a fork of potato halfway to his mouth. ‘What does that mean?’

‘I want to learn about the world.’

‘Why?’ Dad puts down his fork, still with the potato on it.

‘You were interested in it too, once,’ Joe says, not unkindly.

‘What about the farm?’

‘I don’t think farm work is for me.’ Joe’s voice shows he’s thought about this a lot.

Dad picks his fork up again and puts it in his mouth, very slowly.

‘But the sheep love you,’ Alby says.

Joe glances at him. ‘And I love the sheep. So I don’t think I want to work in farming.’

‘You didn’t finish school,’ Dad says. ‘Dropouts can’t go to uni.’

It’s a low blow. We all know Joe only left to help out on the farm because Dad needed it. He loved studying—was top of the class.

Joe fills the sink with steaming water for the dishes, even though we haven’t finished eating. He doesn’t say anything for a while.

‘You’re a farm boy, Joe, mate,’ Dad says, more warmth in his voice. ‘A smart one, for sure. But you don’t belong in the city.’

‘Well, I don’t know if I want to be a farm man,’ Joe says, and leaves the room.

* * *

Next English class, Mrs Parsons tells us Mary Shelley wrote *Frankenstein* to deal with her childhood traumas. She says we are ‘holding a mirror to ourselves’ to see ‘what’s behind the monsters we write’. People are talking about vampires and werewolves, hooded figures and zombies. I sharpen my pencils and line them up along my desk. When Mrs Parsons looks at me, I push myself to standing and walk away.

If she calls me back, I don't hear it.

I swing into a toilet cubicle, latching the door behind me. I've read some of the graffiti on the back of the door, considered adding to it, when someone goes into the cubicle next to me.

'Rose,' says Jenna.

'Yep?'

'Stupid bitch has no idea, has she?'

'Nope.'

'Let's go sit on the water tank.'

Jenna's brought cigarettes—stole them last time she went shopping with her mum. The stakes would have been high and I know it. She's put a daisy inside the box, trying so hard to help, and here's me thinking she's a bad friend.

We smoke half of them, one after another, lying on our backs looking at the clouds. We don't say much, but I appreciate that she's there beside me, resting her legs on mine. Jenna likes English class. I guess Mrs Parsons has given up on us. She must be confused; Jenna and I normally get along quite well with the old chook. At the end of the period she comes out and stands at the bottom of the water tank.

'You'll want to come down now,' she says in a quiet voice that is anything but gentle.

We do.

She puts her hand out for the cigarettes. 'Shame,' she says.

We get a week of lunchtime detention, Jenna writing an essay on Mary Shelley, me cleaning windows. At least they've given up on trying to make me write. I know Jenna is putting a brave face on for me, but the only thing I care about is that she's in trouble too. This isn't her mess.

Jenna's mum picks us up, along with Alby. We could have caught the bus home, but she wants to talk to me.

'It's not the way to go about this, Rose,' she says, looking at me in the rear-view mirror. 'Things are hard enough for you already, without winding up in trouble at school.'

'Mum,' Jenna says, 'how exactly do you think you'd go about it?'

'What are we talking about?' I say.

'That's enough from both of you.'

'For the record, the cigarettes were mine,' Jenna adds defiantly.

'Can I have a cigarette?' asks Alby.

Mrs Betts turns the radio on.

When we get to my place, Mrs Betts turns around in her seat. 'I won't tell your father this time, Rose,' she says. 'But no more allowances.'

I guess you only get one get-out-of-jail-free card when your mum dies. She's sounding mean, but I remind myself of all the times Mrs Betts has had me over, fed me, tucked me in beside Jen. She's never once questioned me, all the times I've shown up at their house, hungry and sad. I feel bad for letting her down, and tangling Jenna up in this.

'Yes, Mrs Betts,' I say, getting out of the car. 'Thanks for the lift.'

* * *

I throw my bag down on my bed and turn, surprised to see Dad standing by the dresser. Didn't notice him when I walked in. He's clasping a pair of your earrings in his hand, staring down at them.

'Hey,' I say. 'Whatcha doing?'

He turns the earrings over in his palm. 'These were my mother's,' he says, softly.

'Oh.'

Dad never talks about his family.

'Gave them to your mum our first Christmas together,' he says, still staring intently at them. 'We were saving for our own place. I'd always kept these. Fire burned everything else, but these were sitting on the bathroom sink, black from smoke and I polished 'em up good.'

I stand beside him, look down at the opals set in silver studs.

'Your mum only wore them on special occasions.' His breath smells like beer. 'She liked to hear stories about my mum, thought they'd have gotten on well. They would've, you know, two of the best women I've ever known.'

This is a big speech from Dad. I wonder where it's going. Part of me hopes he'll give me the earrings, but most of me just wants him to keep on talking.

'You never speak about her,' I say, looking at his reflection in the mirror.

'Who?'

'Either of them.'

'Hmm.' He looks back at the earrings, closes his fist around them and drops them in his pocket.

'Better do your homework,' he says, already out the door.

* * *

Two days later, Frank goes missing. He might have buggered off before that, but it's not till Wednesday that we notice. As I walk up the driveway to the school bus, I bang on the tin shed. Normally, Frank bangs back, or shouts at me to rack off. This time, though, nothing. I don't think much of it, but in the afternoon on the way down the driveway, I do the same. My schoolbag is hurting my shoulders and I have a headache. I'm worn out, missing you. I want to sit beside Frank in the shed, share a joint and listen to some music. Maybe a round of Briscola, that Italian card game you taught us.

I thump on the tin with my fist. Again, there's no answer. I heave the door up, expecting him to throw something at me, but there's no one there. Down at the house, my question falls on blank faces.

'Isn't he in the shed?' Dad's sitting in the dark in the lounge room, eyes on the television, but it's not on.

Joe's been checking the beehives for honey. Comes in for a glass of water. 'Haven't seen him.'

Steve's driving the tractor along the driveway. 'Dunno,' he shouts over the engine.

That night, I fry eggs for dinner and tip baked beans on a couple of pieces of toast. Dad eats standing at the bench, Steve says he ate earlier, and Joe has a few mouthfuls of beans out of the pot.

'Any sign of your brother?' Dad turns halfway in my direction.

'Nah.'

'Wouldn't worry. He'll show up when he's hungry.'

I wrap a fried egg on some soggy bread in cling wrap. Bastard better be home soon.

* * *

In the morning, I bump into Joe, stickybeaking around the shed.

'Reckon he took off somewhere,' he says looking through his round glasses at me. 'Doesn't look like he took anything with him though.'

'You a detective or something?'

Joe doesn't laugh. He gets in his shitty old Hillman and winds down the window. 'I'm gonna go search for him,' he says. 'Want a lift to school?'

Alby's got a summer cold, poor kid. I jump in beside Joe.

Joe plays The Kinks but the tape keeps getting jammed. He smacks the cassette player with the base of his palm. I chase Frank's lanky outline in paddocks and front gardens. Joe slows as we get close to the school, and I look sideways at him.

'I don't wanna go. I'll help you.'

He bites a nail.

'Please.'

Joe slowly pulls back out of the drop-off bay. We park up near the bakery and search the streets, looking into strangers' faces.

'Where would he go, Rose?'

'No clue.'

'Come on, you know him best.'

Where the others saw chaos in Frank, I understood. We used to mess around, hitching places and finding our way home again. Frank taught me how to steal, just small things, a trinket here and there, a beer out of the fridge, a chocolate bar. He made me feel brave and wild. When he was angry, he let himself be. If he didn't like something, he said it. If he felt like a beer, he took one. And Frank would stop at nothing to make someone else laugh.

But he sucked himself in and pushed me out the more you faded. I've got no clue what's going on with him anymore.

We get milkshakes and sit in the park.

'Should we go all the way to Albany?' I suck the straw till it gurgles in the bottom of my paper cup.

Joe stirs his straw. 'Yeah, guess so.'

'Reckon he hitched?'

'Must've.'

Back in the car, Joe speaks really softly. I have to tilt my head to hear him.

'Think it's cos of Mum.' It's like a question, without the question mark.

I don't know how to respond. 'Isn't everything?'

The road opens up in front of us. I keep an eye out for a black t-shirt.

'Are you okay?' Again, his voice is a whisper.

I grip the handle above the window. 'Are you?'

Joe rummages in the glove box, pulls out a packet of gum. We don't talk anymore, just chew.

* * *

We can't find him. Not at the docks. The skate park. Middleton Beach. We cruise up York Street, 'doin' a Yorkie', the locals call it. On the way back through Mount Barker we pull into the shops. Might as well stock up on some food.

I'm eyeing off the punnets of strawberries when I notice her opposite me. That lady who threw a stone on our roof. She's wearing the orange spiral skirt again. She pauses for a second, punnet of strawberries in her hand. Then her face opens into a smile.

'Rosie, bub,' she says. 'How you going?'

'Um,' I say. 'Hi.'

On close inspection, the strawberries don't look so good.

'They're a bit scungy, aren't they?' Orange Spirals holds the punnet up close to her face.

'Yeah.'

She puts the strawberries back. Rummages in her bag. 'You been going to school these days?'

'Mostly.' I shuffle my feet. 'Just not today.'

'Good girl. Smart, like your mum.'

I feel myself going all prickly.

'You look like her, you do,' says the woman—Patsy?

I squeeze my eyes shut and open them again. Orange Spirals is still there, in the supermarket glare.

'I gotta find my brother.' I scratch a mozzie bite on my wrist.

'Course, bub. That him over there?'

I don't bother explaining that we're looking for Frank. Joe is holding a box of Weeties, his finger tracing the ingredients. He wanders over, nods his head politely to Patsy and passes me the box.

'Never knew how much sugar was in these.'

This is what cancer does to a family. Makes you think there could be a tumour hiding in your breakfast cereal.

'Bitta sugar won't kill ya,' Patsy cackles as I chuck the box in the trolley. 'You're the second Tetley boy, aren't you, love?'

'That's right.' Joe takes the Weeties back out of the trolley.

A shop assistant hovers near Patsy, looks her up and down, cranes his neck to look in her basket. Patsy fumbles around her bag. Pulls out her shopping list, holds it up to the light. Steps around the shop assistant as if he isn't there.

'Thanks for the lift, the other day,' I say, heading for the fridge. We need some cheese.

'No worries, bub. Have a good one, you kids,' Patsy says, still consulting her shopping list. The shop assistant clears his throat.

Cheddar in the basket. Some ham. Bread. We're done here.

* * *

Jenna calls in the evening and I tell her Frank's missing.

'You're kidding,' she says.

'Nah.'

Dad just keeps sitting in the lounge room in the darkness.

I sit out the front on the verandah, trying to think where he'd go. The pink-and-greys are screeching again, the perfect recipe for another headache.

I can see a human-shaped blob at the top of the driveway. The blob morphs into Jenna, and she jogs right up to me.

'Where did ya see him last?' she pants.

I shrug.

Jen frowns, doubles over, hands on her knees. 'Where would he go?'

'Dunno.'

'I told Dad,' she says. 'He's gone for a drive, to try find him. If ya want, he'll come pick us up, we can go too.'

Our dad should be the one looking.

'Didn't know you cared about Frank so much.' I feel hopeless, glum.

'Let's check the shed again, maybe he came back.' Jenna pulls me up.

He's not there. We shuffle around, moving boxes and looking under benches as if we're playing hide-and-seek. Frank was crap at hide-and-seek, always made too much noise.

'Dad'll be here soon,' Jenna says. 'We'll find him.'

We don't.

* * *

Steve rings the police in the morning. Been three days since we realised Frank was missing. Five since we've seen him. The cops aren't impressed.

'They reckon we should have called ages ago,' Steve says.

Dad repeats his mantra: 'He'll show up.'

It's hard to concentrate at school. Tess sits on the other side of Jenna, and they gossip all day. It really grinds my gears. Can't they shut it?

When I walk down the driveway that afternoon, there's music coming from the shed. It's The Doors, 'Light My Fire'. I break into a run, skidding on the gravel. There he is. Puffing on a joint, sprawled on the mattress.

I'm on him in seconds, my fist connecting with his jaw.

'What the fuck, Rose?' Frank shoves me sharply and my knee smacks the concrete.

'You can't just leave like that. Where have you *been*?'

Frank blows smoke in my face. 'Around.'

Down at the house I tell Dad.

'Told you he'd turn up,' he says, getting up. 'I'll go see him myself.'

I hope he busts Frank with that doobie in his hands. I hope he kicks his arse to Albany and back.

Steve rings the cops, lets them know.

Joe cooks sausages for dinner, and Frank stabs three with his fork and walks straight back up to the shed. Steve laughs, Joe shakes his head.

In the morning, Frank's gone again. This time, no one sends a search party.

8. Frank

I spend most days in Barker now. Some nights too, curled on the park bench. There's a few boys who stick to themselves on the other side of the park—some evenings they kick a half deflated footy around, but they're pretty quiet come nightfall. I befriend the skinny bald man who sleeps in the post office doorway. His name is Dave and he isn't as scary as he looks. I know how to walk the street swagger anyway. Let my arms swing at my sides like a stupid gorilla, stick my neck forwards, jut my chin out. Make direct eye contact with people who look like they might ask questions. Stare until they look away.

Back home they keep squinting at me, and I keep shrugging back. 'Been in the shed/paddocks/at Will's,' I say when they ask questions. So long as they don't call the police again.

Late afternoon, out the front of the shops, leaning against the wall. A man in a Claremont footy cap shuffles my way. I don't have anything for this bloke. I'm outta smokes and coin. I try to disappear into the shadows—I don't usually have to try too hard. This time, no luck.

'Frank,' the man says.

I peer under the brim. It's Herbert. Shit.

'Hi,' I say.

'What you up to, lad?'

'Just doing some shopping,' I say, pointing to the grocery sign.

'Hmmm,' mumbles Herbert. 'Getting late.' He rummages in his pocket, pulls out a cigarette. 'Don't tell Patsy.' He winks.

'Nah,' I say. 'Can I have one?'

Herbert doesn't seem to hear. He blows silver smoke into the night.

'How you holding up, Frank?'

'Good,' I blurt. 'Fine.'

'Must be hard without your mum,' he says, tapping ash. I frown. What does he know?

'Kids are meant to grow with their mothers. We lost two of ours. Two boys. Took 'em from us, they did.'

I nod, not really sure what he's talking about.

'Robbie died out at the mission. Said it was from pneumonia or something. He never was a sick kid.' Herbert sucks, blows, taps ash. 'And then George, they grew him up smart and snobby. Barely recognised us when he came back. Couldn't really see our boy in him either. Loved him all the same, but he stays away.'

I bite my nail, fanging for a smoke.

'And then we lost Bert anyway. Three kids, we lost. Patsy still cries for them in her sleep.'

As Herbert finishes his sentence, Patsy comes bustling out of the shops, weighed down with plastic bags. Herbert is quick to take them from her.

'Frank, what are you up to, bub?' Patsy smiles.

'Just about to do some shopping,' I lie.

'Better get in quick, they're about to close.'

I take my chance, and duck in the doors. I sulk around for five minutes or so, till I'm sure Patsy and Herbert have gone. They make me uneasy, those two. Like they see the parts I'm trying to hide.

The sun is going down and the streets smell like dinner cooking. Chops. Sausages. Spag bol. I look into backyards, walk with my hands in my pockets. At number six, a woman washes dishes, looks out her kitchen window. She has a big pink ribbon in her hair. At eight, a kid jumps on a trampoline, his head appearing and disappearing above the red brick fence. At ten, a dog snarls through the gate, and a man's voice yells *shuddup!* Across the street, a car pulls up at eleven and a man whistles his way to the front door. I loop back to the shops, scoping out a lift back up the highway. I don't feel like roughing it tonight. Out the front I find a bloke heading to Kojonup, who lets me catch a lift. Even gives me a drag of his cigarette. I'm feeling lucky.

I get home as the sun is fading low over the paddocks. I sit on the roof, swigging the last of my whisky. It's beautiful out here. I just don't know why the beauty hurts.

one afternoon as i sit on the mattress,
tracing patterns on the dirty floor with my finger,
jenna walks in. she brings the sunlight with her,
tangled in her hair. i reach my fingertips towards her,
hungry for,
starved of,
light.
she stops,
says something.

i can't hear her.

her lips stop moving.
hands reach
out towards mine,
our fingertips
touch.
we stay like that awhile,
me sitting, eyes closed,
fingertip to fingertip with jenna betts

jenna betts stands still,
and the sunlight keeps beaming
in her hair.

When she goes, the shed is dark again. I watch her glowing all the way down to the house. I've never seen a man glow like that. I can hear her voice, with Rose's slightly deeper one, as they walk past the shed again. I stand in the doorway, in the shadows. Watch them sit on the edge of the dam. Rose points at something, Jenna laughs.

I miss her.

Rose.

You.

Me.

Jenna leans her head on Rose's shoulder. I wonder what they are talking about. What could they be talking about? I don't remember how to do that. I lie on my bed and try to imagine what I'd say if Max or Will came over for me.

Their voices change suddenly.

'You're joking,' Rose shouts. 'No!'

Jenna's voice, sounding panicked, rising too. 'Rose,' she's saying, 'would you just *listen* ...'

It goes on and on. From the shadows, I watch as Rose storms off into the paddocks, Jenna chasing after her. They rarely fight, those two. It must be something big.

Jenna comes back in as she's leaving. I can hear her this time.

'Hey.'

'Hi.'

She wiggles her feet up and down and her big toe pokes out of the hole in her tennis shoes. We both look at it.

'Are you okay?' she asks. Her toes stop dancing.

'Yeah.'

'Okay.' Jenna keeps standing there, looking at me. I look at her back. I won't ask what happened. I shouldn't. But I wonder. She has tear tracks down her cheeks.

'See you soon,' she says eventually.

'Bye.'

My heart is pounding. I can hear it in my ears. I lie back on the mattress and put my hands on my chest, the blood pumping under my palms. What a thing it is to be alive.

Rose boots a footy at the shed after Jenna goes. The tin cracks like thunder and my ears ring. I lurch out of the door and there she is, on the drive, her hands on her hips. The footy is rolling back down the hill towards her. I watch her, willing her to do it again.

She does.

It slams onto the roof, bounces once, then lands on the gravel in front of me.

Neither of us say a word.

I pick up the footy, measure the distance between us. Boot it as hard as I can. Rose's hands reach to catch it but her fingers slip and it pounds into her stomach. She drops to the gravel, gasping.

I laugh. Turn my back. Walk into the shed and slam the door down.

* * *

I add another five-bar gate to my inner arm. The end of a nail, I have to push to tear the skin. One. Two. Three. Four. The fifth slash a diagonal line. Sometimes I save up the days and record them all at once. As Monday to Friday bleeds onto my shorts, I count. Two months since you died.

Summer keeps blazing and no one shears. I keep track of weekdays by noting when Alby and Rose march up the road to the bus, and the days no one gets up till lunchtime. You liked early mornings. You'd be out in the garden, pruning and watering and smiling at the flowers. By the time we got up, you'd be drinking your cup of tea on the verandah, talking to the birds. I reckon lots of the birds left when you did. Birdbath is empty. You used to scatter seed for them. Dad would laugh, point out that the birds always managed to feed themselves before you came along.

'Everyone likes breakfast made for them sometimes,' you'd wink.

Dad would get the hint, go put the toast on, reboil the kettle.

The thing is when I look forward, I just can't see anything anymore. Not working on cars, not fishing, not farming. I crave the adrenaline kick from surfing and skating, but don't have the energy to get up and go. Instead: Beer. Bong. Beer. Bong. Fading. Fading. Fading. When my Bob Dylan tape finishes, I flip it and start it again. His voice is the best tonic of all.

People stop checking on me. No one seems to visit. Don't hear Jenna's voice, or Shane's or even that pain-in-the-arse lady's, Mrs Mengler, who kept coming round eyeing Dad straight after you died. It's like the whole world has left us to rot.

* * *

Tuesday afternoon. Barker. The park. I know it's Tuesday cos I saw the Bulls at footy training on the oval. Coach was there, sprinting up and down the sidelines, jumping jacks in between the action. There's something not quite right about him. Doesn't Coach know there are bigger things going on than a bunch of twits chasing a piece of leather around? Then again, his mum is still alive. Comes along to every game, leaning on that walking frame of hers, wearing a knitted beanie in team colours, even through summer. Maybe it's her fault he turned out weird.

Anyway, Tuesday afternoon. I'm sitting in the park, leaning against my tree. Jenna walks past, with another girl. Tess, I think. She's hot, but not as hot as Jen. Her brother is on the footy team. They're sipping soft drink out of big cups, walking arm in arm. I look down, fiddle with my shoelaces. Pretend to check my non-existent watch. Hope she won't notice me, when—

'Frank,' Jenna calls.

I keep my head down. I don't want to be seen like this.

'Frank!'

Bugger it. 'Hi,' I say, looking up at them. I want to admire their legs, standing just beside me, but I determinedly squint into their eyes.

'Whatcha doing?'

'Just chilling.'

'This is Tess.'

'Hey.'

Jenna passes her soft drink to me, and I take it, flattered. I slurp away at her Fanta, while they make themselves comfortable, sitting beside me.

I try to think of something to say. 'How was, ah, school?' I pass Jen's drink back, flick my hair out of my eyes. Feel too exposed, shake my head so my curls hide my face again.

Tess rolls her eyes. 'Lame.' Then she leans in. 'How are you, Frank?'

I sit back, straighten my spine. 'Yeah, I'm sweet.'

'That's good,' Tess sighs. 'Poor old Rose.'

What?

Jenna shrugs and her eyebrows rise.

'We're worried about her,' Tess says, blinking heavily. 'Did you know at lunch she walks around the oval? Like, around and around?'

I frown. Imagine Rose, head down, hands in her pockets, pacing.

'Like, all lunch,' Tess presses. 'Round and round and round.' She draws a circle in the air beside her ear, stretches her eyes wide.

I don't think I like Tess.

I catch Jen's eye. 'Rose is great,' I say.

Jenna holds my gaze. 'Great,' she repeats slowly.

Tess leans back, slurps her drink, swishes her ponytail. 'Do you like ABBA, Frank?' she asks.

'Nah.'

The girls drift into banter about the latest hits. I lean against the tree, keep my ear out for Pink Floyd or Donovan, but it's all Barbra Streisand, The Bee Gees, Rickie Lee Jones.

'The Beatles are cool,' Jenna says. 'And Skyhooks. Dad can't get enough of them.'

Finally, she's speaking some sense.

'Velvet Underground,' I offer. 'You gotta listen to them.'

Jeez. They don't know Lou Reed.

Why isn't Rose with them? And what's she doing walking laps at lunch?

'There's Harry,' squeaks Tess. She whips her ponytail around with such ferocity I'm surprised she doesn't crick her neck. A guy I recognise from the grade below me wanders over, scuffing his feet in the grass as he walks.

'Hey,' he says, clearly eyeing up the girls. An internal battle tugs inside my chest. Most of me would rather die than see twits from school when I'm a sad sack of bones like this. The other part of me wants to punch this bloke's nose in for the way he winks at Jen, while leaning up against Tess.

'Woah, Frank, mate, I didn't recognise you.' He shoves his grubby, nail-bitten hand at me. I stare at it, then back at him. His nose is pink from the sun, his cheeks littered with freckles. His curls have blond tips like mine used to. Harry laughs, smacks my arm with his hand then withdraws it.

'Been getting any waves?'

'Nah.'

'Haven't seen you out there for a while, hey.'

'Yeah.'

Harry shrugs. 'Bit of a haul getting to the beach from here, I guess.'

'Yeah,' I say again, like that's all that is keeping me.

Before you died, I surfed a huge swell out at Parry's. One of the days the doctor said you might not make it. There were lots of them. You kept making it, despite the odds. Every day we were preparing to say goodbye, and you kept holding on. Got thumped that day. The ocean pushed and tore at me, and I fought it, daring it to take me. So it did, for a while. A ten-foot wave, onshore winds, choppy and unpredictable. It scooped me up, pummelled the shit out of me, rolled me over and over and over. I stopped fighting, I let go. Begged the ocean to take me. I wanted to go with you.

Instead, I washed up on the beach, chucking up saltwater. Half my board was strewn on the sand, the other thrashed around in the whitewash. The two pieces rest like headstones in the corner of the shed. There are so many cobwebs, I reckon a redback might have hatched a whole nest there. My fishing rod is part of the mess, webs hanging where fishing line should be. A graveyard of the things I loved.

Harry's chatting to the girls, cracking jokes and nudging their elbows, making them laugh. He reminds me of me, before all of this shit. The me I could have been.

'A few of the guys are up behind the shops,' he says, gesturing behind us. 'Wanna go?'

Tess is on her feet in moments. Jenna looks to me. 'Wanna come?' Her voice tilts in question.

I drink in Jenna's open face. She doesn't frown or narrow her eyes like I'm a difficult maths equation. Jenna's bright blue eyes. They remind me of who I am because I think she sees him. Frank Tetley. I'd like to ask her where she found him, and if together we can bring him back.

'Nah,' I say.

'You sure?'

'Yeah.'

The three of them brush grass off their clothes, sling their bags over their shoulders.

'See ya round.'

I watch them disappear down the side alley. I know the spot. We used to muck around there too. The school bus stops on the other side of the road and sometimes, when you or Dad couldn't pick us up till later, I'd meet Max and Will out the back where the skip bins squat and abandoned trolleys roll around. We'd waste a few hours messing about on our skateboards, smoke doobies, sweet-talk girls from school. I wonder if Harry will be locking lips with Tess or Jen. I wonder if Jenna is sweet on anyone. I wonder why Rose isn't with them. When I get sick of wondering, I mope my way over there, as if I'm headed for the shops. At the last minute, I turn, weave my way down the side alley and hover in the gutter, just before it opens out to the old staff carpark.

I can hear them. Guys talking shit about waves, the hollow scrape of a skateboard. I want to be part of it, but at the same time I hate them for having it. Normality. Connection. Whatever it is. I'm leaning against the wall, the heat of the bricks warming my back. One step away from joining them. I could go up to Jen, ask her if she likes Supertramp's earlier stuff. I reckon she'd like 'Dreamer'. I'm not a big fan of them, but I reckon she would be, and 'Dreamer' is their best track for sure. But what if she says, 'no' and the conversation grinds to a halt and I've pushed my way into a dumb high school hangout with kids who aren't fucked up, like me? Kids who surf enough on the weekends to burn their noses red. Kids whose parents pick them up from the bus stop. Kids who are younger than me, but way more on track.

I push off the wall to leave.

'Hey, who's that?' drawls some guy rolling lazily on a skateboard.

'Frank,' Jenna calls.

Harry untangles himself from Tess. 'Whatcha doing, mate?'

'Was he perving on us?'

'What a weirdo.'

'Be nice, his mum died, didn't she?'

My cheeks are hot. I can only look at Jen, the words and gazes of the others bouncing off me like angry bees. Then, it happens. Jenna frowns. Like I'm a maths question she can't figure out. Her eyes ask me the same question as everyone else. What *are* you doing, Frank? I turn on my heel, and before I know it I'm running. Running away. Like a scared little kid. I run and run, their laughter burning my ears. Through the park, up the street.

What are you doing, Frank?

Fuck off, Mum, I don't know.

I slow to a jog, look up at the marris that line the road.

'Frank!'

Oh, god. Jenna has followed me. I press my eyes closed for a moment, grind my heel into the dirt. Swivel to face her.

'Hey.'

'You okay?'

'Yep.'

'Should've stayed and hung out.'

I grimace at her.

Jenna stands on the curb, making herself the same height as me, levelling my gaze.

'Frank,' she says, softly.

'What's wrong with Rose?' I blurt out, desperate for the attention to be anywhere but on me.

Jen sighs. 'Same thing as you,' she says.

What's wrong with me? I want to ask.

'You're sad,' Jenna answers, as if she's heard.

'Oh,' I say, stepping back. 'The thing is, I, um, actually ...'

'Frank.'

I stop. Her frown is gone, and her face is open. Jenna is seeing me. My heart hammers.

Jen steps forwards, brings her lips to mine, one hand to my cheek.

It's not like kissing the other girls. It's not heated, or rushed, furious, or fumbling. It's gentle. Soft. Tender.

She steps back.

Before I've even thought about it, 'thank you' falls out of my mouth. The words hover between us. I watch the dappled sun lighting up parts of Jenna's face. Her lips are slightly open. She's standing very still.

'You're welcome,' she says.

And then I run.

* * *

An old woman gives me a lift from the highway just out of town. She's wearing a pink windcheater and oversized round glasses. Her fluffy grey curls give her a fairy-godmother appearance. When she puts the radio on,

I expect her to choose a classical channel. Instead, she twiddles the dials until a heavily distorted electric guitar screeches through the car. She nods her head along to the beat and drives slowly, the whole way to Tenterden.

I feel giddy.

Everything looks strange. As if things are standing two inches to the left of before. Not quite right. I feel disoriented. Pace the shed, hands in pockets. Remind myself of Rose. I walk laps of the paddocks till the sun sets.

When I'm sure Rose isn't going over, I jump in Joe's Hillman and drive to Jenna's. I park in the paddock across the road, behind the sheds. Jenna's sitting up in her bedroom, listening to The Easybeats. She stands very still in the light of the window for a moment, then she lifts the window, almost solemnly, as if this meeting were planned. It's not till now the reality she could have turned me away hits me, and the urge to be close to her surges through me. I climb over the ledge, landing with a small thud, pulling down my t-shirt, running a hand through my hair and trying to straighten myself up.

It's hot. She's got The Beatles centred above her bed, then ABBA, Queen, The Bee Gees and Ramones. Rose gave her the Ramones one. I was with her when she bought it from Mills Record Bar on Adelaide Street in Fremantle. The shop owner rolled it up inside a cardboard canister and we went to the haberdashery and bought a length of red ribbon. Rose rested it on her legs the whole way back to Tenterden, worried it might get squashed. It was for Jenna's thirteenth birthday. We ate hot chips on the Bettses' back verandah and had a water fight on the front lawn. All of us Tetleys went but I think Rose was disappointed, wanting Jenna for herself. The other girls from school were there and Rose didn't speak to them much. They were a bit funny with her, like they didn't understand my sister, standing there with her wild hair and one of Joe's old cut-off Kinks t-shirts. I don't know if Rose cared, but it didn't show if she did. She was quiet, sullen in a rock-chick way that made me proud. Jenna moved among it all gracefully, laughing at jokes and passing a bowl of liquorice allsorts around while we drank lemonade and beer disguised as lemonade.

Steve and Joe didn't stay long. They went home with you and Dad, but I stayed. The girls had started noticing me. I squirted them with the hose while they jumped on the trampoline, and Jenna's dad came out and told them to keep their clothes on, thank you very much.

Jenna pads over and closes her bedroom door, shifts the bolt across. I can hear the TV in the background, and her parents' muffled voices.

She looks at me with big eyes and I know there's a lot going on behind them.

'How are you?' she asks.

I take my shoes off, taking a long time on the laces.

Jenna's wearing turquoise pyjama shorts made out of that synthetic stuff that feels like silk, and a white singlet. She hits the eject button on her cassette player and the door opens slowly. She takes out The Easybeats and puts another tape in. The Ramones stalk the room. She's standing with her right foot on her left thigh, making a figure four with her legs. She pauses a moment, then hits eject again and puts Fleetwood Mac's *Bare Trees* in. She drops the case.

I wonder if I should leave.

She clears her throat.

'I like this one,' I say, looking at her glow-in-the-dark stars on the ceiling. The sun is still going down, so they aren't glowing yet. They're a weird, slightly fluorescent green colour, and I can see the Blu Tack seeping out from underneath some of them.

'You like what?'

'This song.'

'Do you want a glass of juice?' As soon as the words have left her lips, Jenna closes her eyes, like she regrets asking. I know she can't go and get me one. Her parents are used to having me over, but not without Rose, and not lately.

'Nah,' I say.

She nods.

She sits on her bed, leaning her back against the wall, her knees bent and her elbows on them.

I sit on the carpet, leaning my back against her chest of drawers.

We stare at each other.

Jenna scratches her nose. I scratch my elbow. I hear my nails against my skin and wonder if I'm scratching loudly, or if the room is very quiet. I swallow, and I hear that too.

I think about the sounds around your bed, while we were waiting. We could hear everything going on. Cars up on the highway, the birds, a blowfly against the glass. Something must flicker across my face because Jenna's changes.

She shimmies herself to the edge of the bed and lowers onto the carpet, using the side of her bed as a backrest. She rests her chin in her hands and keeps looking at me. There's about a yard between us. Her eyes are bright blue, and boring into mine. They're piercing but gentle. It takes a lot not to look away. Eventually I do.

'Frank.'

I trace my fingertips across the carpet and watch the way they leave lines like I'm drawing in the sand.

'Hey,' Jenna speaks again.

'Mmmm?' I keep looking down. I feel like a spider stuck in my own web. I shouldn't have come. Jenna can see everything, it's so bright in here compared to the shed.

'Look at me.'

Very slowly I raise my head.

She reaches both her hands out, across the space.

'It's okay,' she says. 'I'm here.'

It gets dark. Eventually Jenna pulls me up, still holding my hands, and we lie on her bed. We aren't talking. I'm barely moving, because I feel like it will only take one inch for the walls built up in me to crumble. It's beating inside me, at my heart and chest and throat, tears and yelling and sobbing that wants to come out. But somehow, Jenna's holding me in balance with her touch and her eyes.

The tips of our heads are touching, and her feet rest on mine. It's completely silent.

when jenna and i have sex i cry and she lights a candle
i don't mean to cry
but the candle lighting is intentional
the flame making the moment holy.
we are both trembly
but sure.
jenna betts kisses my mouth my cheeks my forehead
she loosens the tight places
with her fingertips and her eyes
and when the tears come she kisses them.
they aren't loud or anything but they leak then pour
it feels like coming up for air,
like taking a deep breath after holding holding holding
i let go under a sunflower bedspread
jenna betts kissing my mouth my cheeks my forehead
loosening the tight places
with her fingertips and her eyes
sometimes they widen and i remember
that i am taking and making and being
a moment she will never get back and only gets once
and when the sadness comes again
this thought brings me back
to her
and i use my hands gently
hold her to me
strands of hair getting stuck in tears and sweat
salt and candlelight
i kiss her mouth her cheeks her forehead
her neck
jenna betts
in salt and candlelight.

I wake with a start, Jenna's head tucked under my chin. She's breathing deeply, her hair tickling my nose each time she inhales. Adrenaline pumps through my body. I'm planning an escape route, when Jen reaches for my hand and loosely links her fingers in mine. Her breathing stays heavy and slow—I'm pretty sure she hasn't woken up. I let myself drift beneath the sunflower bedspread, as the light outside the window changes from purple, to pink, then gold.

'Frank.'

I blink. Jenna is leaning over me, halfway through pulling her school shirt on. It's gathered around her neck, the sleeves hanging loosely at her sides. Before I can think too much, I grab the sleeves and draw her in, kissing her. Her lips tilt upwards in a smile before she breaks free and keeps getting dressed.

'You should go.'

'Yep.' The nerves kick in once I'm upright. I shouldn't be here. Imagine Mrs Betts walking in to find me, Frank Tetley, in my underwear with her precious daughter on a Wednesday morning. Jen's looking worried too. She's speedily pulling her hair into a ponytail, cursing as strands stubbornly fall free around her face. She knocks her hairbrush off her dresser, whacks her shoulder on the corner of a drawer as she stoops to get it.

'Um,' she trails off.

'Yeah,' I say, as if I know what she's thinking. Shit, I wish I knew what she was thinking. Was last night a mistake for her?

'Right,' Jen says, agreeing to whatever we are saying.

'I'll just—' I gesture to the window.

'Okay.'

'Bye.'

'See ya.'

I turn back to look at her when I'm halfway through the window, one leg dangling in the air, the other on Jenna's rickety desk chair. She smiles. Her smile says something, something there's no words for. I nod, smile back.

* * *

I get back and slip into the shed just before Rose and Alby walk up the driveway, heading for the school bus. Rose and I lock eyes for a moment, then we both shrug it off, mirroring each other. Even though she infuriates me, I hope she doesn't walk laps of the oval today.

9. Rose

Jenna reckons she has the hots for Frank. For my *brother*. She came round the other day, as if she wanted to hang out. Brought cherries, my favourite, and we sat up on the edge of the dam. We talked about music, about the books we are reading, made up new names for the colours the sunset poured across the sky. Marigold. Plum-fuchsia. Rust-urple.

She was holding my hand when she said it. She blurted it out, right after asking how Frank was.

I was replying, saying not good, when her words landed on top of mine.

'I like him,' she said.

I stared at her. 'Like a brother?'

She looked down at our entangled hands. 'Not really,' she said.

I shouted then. Said a lot of things really fast. I said I hated her. That she couldn't have us both. That she should walk up that driveway, and not walk down it again. Ever.

So she did. She left.

I didn't sleep.

I don't think I'll ever sleep again.

There is no one left to lose, except myself.

I can't look at Frank. Wish he'd go get himself lost again. Jen said he doesn't know she likes him. But I already know he likes her back.

* * *

I'm lost on the weekend without Jenna. End up catching a lift with Shane to Mount Barker. He's spent the day at our place, trying to rally the boys to get ready to shear. Come afternoon, they were sitting together on the edge of one of our dams, drinking beers and blowing smoke. Not talking. Not much talking between my brothers these days. I walked the dogs past them, gave Frank the finger as he bounced a squashed beer can on my back. Shane sighed and got up, slapped each of them on the back and whistled for Clyde. He was jumping in the ute when I decided to take the chance and get out of this shithole for the evening. Jenna and I bum around in Barker sometimes on the weekends, window-shopping and eating lollies from white paper bags in the park. I want to call her place, and for Jen to tell me it's all a bad dream. Or a joke. A bad joke. I want to say sorry, and that I don't hate her. Instead, I decide to go mope around Barker on my own, sort of hoping I'll bump into her.

As we drive, Shane plays a band that sound like AC/DC, nodding his head and chewing gum. I nod my head too, hoping it looks cooler than it feels. Wish he offered me a piece of gum.

'Where should I drop ya?' Shane asks as we roll down the main street.

I scan the shopfronts for Jenna but can't see her golden head anywhere. I regret my decision, until Shane says, 'I'm meeting some mates in a bit, but we could have a beer first, if ya want?' I keep my eyes out the window and count to three so I don't seem too eager.

'Sure,' I say. 'If you want.'

Shane pulls into the bottle-o, jumps out, leaves the car running. 'Two secs.'

He comes back with a sixpack of beer, swings the car across the road and pulls up at the park, by the river. We sit on the grass, bindies prickling our bums. Shane cracks a can, passes it to me.

'Who was that you were playing in the car?' I ask.

'Ooh, that's Rose Tattoo.' Shane leans back on his elbows. 'You like them?'

'Yeah, they're pretty cool.'

'Get this—the lead singer's name is Angry Anderson.'

I laugh. 'Surely that's not his real name?'

'Think it's Gary, or something.'

The beer is a bit warm and the mozzies are coming in thick, but I don't want the moment to end.

'Gotta pee,' Shane says, getting up and heading for the toilet block.

'Me too.'

Shane is leaning against the grubby brick wall smoking a cigarette when I come out. He gestures to a peeling poster next to him.

'Did you hear about this?'

I squint at the paper. *Western Australia 1829–1979* is printed alongside a picture of a black swan. *Celebrate the start of WA's 150th year this New Year's Eve at Perth Esplanade. Live acts: Rolf Harris, Fat Cat and Percy Penguin.*

'Um, nah,' I say. 'I didn't hear about it. Was it good?' I ask, assuming maybe he went.

'A Noongar Elder, Colbung, served all white fellas an eviction notice.' Shane blows smoke out of the corner of his mouth. 'They asked him to play the didgeridoo and he took the opportunity. Clever bloke.'

'Wait, who was he evicting?' I ask. 'And where from?'

'All white fellas,' Shane says. 'From the country.'

I nod. 'Okay.'

Shane stubs his cigarette out against the wall. 'Gotta meet my mates, Rosie. You catching up with Jen?'

'Yeah, she'll be here,' I say.

'Sure?'

'Yep. Thanks for the beer.'

Shane hoons away, and Angry Anderson belts into the street. I start to panic a little once it gets dark. There are some dodgy characters in the park, drinking and smoking and shouting at each other. I get up as if I know where I'm going, head up the main street.

In the window of the Chinese restaurant, I see Jenna. She's sipping a drink and laughing. I follow her gaze. Tess. Urgh.

Head down, quick strides. I turn off the main street and wander past fences and letterboxes. Bloody idiot, should have stayed home.

* * *

'Oi, Rosie, watcha doing, bub?' A woman leaning on her gate, ciggie in her mouth. Orange Spirals, but she's not wearing the skirt today. An old t-shirt and loose shorts, tied with a drawstring. I stop. Turn. On the verandah, Herbert is sitting in a camping chair.

Patsy opens her gate. 'Come on in, love.'

It's not like I have anything better to do.

She gestures to a plastic chair. 'Was just putting the kettle on.'

Herbert has a stubby pencil in his hand and the crossword from the weekend newspaper on his knees. He smiles at me but doesn't say anything.

A white kelpie comes to investigate, sniffing my legs eagerly.

'She'll be able to smell your dogs,' Herbert says, reaching out and scratching her neck.

'What's her name?'

'Meeak.' He lifts his gaze, speaks slowly. 'It means moon in our language.'

Patsy comes back with a blue teapot with a crescent moon crack to its surface. The steam smells like lemon myrtle. She pours a cup and hands it to me.

'Your brother up to no good,' she says, lowering herself into an old rocking chair. 'I seen him, Frank, bumming around the shops with smokes. Tell him come here, be in this place.' She points to her heart. 'Tell him here.'

The worn timber boards creak up and down the porch as she rocks.

Herbert has cobwebs on his socks, and his feet are doing that absent-minded dance while he counts out letters. 'Hard to be in this place,' he says, tapping his chest without looking up, 'when this place hurting.'

'Yes, but he can hurt here.' Patsy gestures at the house, at the verandah. 'He can be in this place with us. Like Rose.' She looks at me. 'Good you come.'

We sip tea, and the light fades around us. Eventually the mozzies force us inside. There's newspaper spread all over the floor in the dining room, and across the kitchen table. An assortment of brushes is propped in glass jars, small tins of coloured paint scattered around.

'Patsy up to her tricks again,' Herbert says, but he's smiling. 'She paints pretty things, that one.'

Patsy squirts yellow paint on the underside of a plastic ice-cream container lid. A splotch of red. Some white. She dips her brush in the yellow paint, mixes in the red. Adds a touch of white to the tip. Quick strokes back and forth. She's painting on cardboard squares. Each stroke is rhythmic. Slower now, almost in time with the rising and falling of her chest.

Painting, breathing, dreaming.

'Yes, that's right,' she mutters to herself, sitting back on her haunches for a moment.

She washes her brush in a jar, pats the floor next to her. 'Here, Rosie bub, come do a painting.'

Patsy passes me a paintbrush, a scrap of cardboard, a tin of red paint. She nods encouragingly, re-dips her own brush in the yellow.

Herbert winks at me, looks back to Patsy. She's consumed in her painting now. Rapid-fire splodges form wattle flowers. A grey green for the leaves.

'Mungart tree,' Patsy says. 'The bark makes a good tea for upset tummies.'

Eyes closed, the smell of paint and turpentine in my nostrils.

'Your mum used to sit on the floor with me, just here, and draw her smartypants flower pictures.'

Mallee bush-pea, moojar tree, jam wattle.

I imagine you. Kneeling on the floor, shirt rolled at the wrists.

Herbert says, 'Nice lady, she was.' He clears his throat, closes his eyes. 'Your mum.'

Patsy is quiet, filling in the spaces on her cardboard with sky blue.

'Shame,' she says suddenly, her voice sharp. 'Shame.'

Meeak startles from where she had curled up beside us. She sniffs the air, as if it might tell her what's wrong with her mistress.

'In the past, Patsy,' Herbert says softly. 'You know?'

'Bugger the past,' Patsy snaps, standing up. She wipes under her left eye with the back of her wrist. 'Meeak, come girl, time for a walk.'

Meeak wags her tail, follows Patsy out the door into the darkness.

Herbert drums his fingers on his legs, smiles awkwardly at me. 'Nice painting,' he says, nodding to the red splotch in the centre of my piece of cardboard.

* * *

Patsy returns with a bunch of camphor myrtle, whistling. Herbert's back at his crossword, sitting at the kitchen table, and I've been mucking around with the paints, wondering how I'm going to get home. Maybe I should call Joe.

'Getting late, Rosie, love,' Patsy says. 'Have a kip here, eh?' She pulls a woollen blanket out of the cupboard, tosses it on the couch. 'Meeak will keep ya company.'

For some reason, I think of how you taught us not to fight against the waves at the beach. *Go with the flow*, you'd say. *You're stronger that way. Let it wash over you.*

So I let Patsy tuck the itchy blanket around me. Meeak puts one paw on the couch, tips her head from me to Patsy.

'Go on then, ya cheeky bitch,' Patsy chuckles, pushing Meeak's backside and helping her up. Her big body is warm against me, as she settles her snout under my chin.

'Night, bub,' Patsy says, turning the light off.

'Cheerio,' Herbert calls down the hallway.

I listen to them brush their teeth, murmuring softly. I fall asleep to the sound of the dripping tap.

* * *

A spoon stirring a cup. The smell of coffee. Soft footsteps, the front door creaking. Meeak jumps off the couch. A pale pink glow creeps in the window, where Herbert is tipping his face to the sky. His hands wrapped round his cup, he just stands there. I roll over, turn my face into the couch. Keep drifting.

* * *

Patsy is much louder when she rises. Heavy footsteps down the hallway out the back, the flyscreen door smacking the frame. I swing my legs over the side of the couch, contemplate my navel. That's a term Joe uses. I don't really know what it means. I lift my old t-shirt up and look at my belly button. Do some people get answers from their belly button? Mine doesn't say much, but my belly does say it would like some toast.

I pad down the hallway and out to the back garden, where the weeds are almost as tall as the Hills hoist. Patsy is in her orange spiral skirt again, sitting under a wattle tree. She leans back on her hands, chin tilted upward.

What is it with these two and the sky?

'First of all, you just look around, you can see the clouds, you can see which way the birds are flying.'

I swear Patsy can read my thoughts.

'You listen to what the wind is telling you, and then you smell the wind. You can smell so much. Not as much as in the bush days, but still.'

'What can you smell, Patsy?'

Patsy lowers her face to look me in the eye. 'That ol' Uncle Herbert is burning the toast, Rosie bub.' She stretches an arm out towards me. 'Come help your Aunty up.'

I take her hand. It's small and thin and has specks of yellow and white paint on it.

'Why d'ya say Aunty?' It falls out of my mouth before I can stop it. I'm not complaining. Patsy would make a ripper aunt. Nothing like Aunt Lisa with her downward mouth and pearls.

'We call our Elders Aunty and Uncle,' Patsy says as we make our way towards the back door. 'Shows respect.'

'But—we're not related.'

'We're all from the earth, bub.' Patsy nods towards the kitchen. 'Come on, before the toast catches fire.'

* * *

Herbert is humming—Uncle Herbert, now, I s'pose—scraping charcoal off his toast. Aunty Patsy tuts at him, gets a few slices of fresh bread. Herb winks behind her back. 'Meeak behave herself last night, love?'

I scratch behind her collar. 'Yep.'

He spreads the strawberry jam thick on his toast. You would tell us off if we did it like that. My mouth waters.

Uncle Herbert takes his toast out the front and the rocking chair sets the floorboards creaking again.

Aunty Patsy carries a plate down the hallway. 'Come on, bub.'

We return to the shade beneath the wattle tree. Aunty beside me, her skirt spread out, those orange spirals bright against the dying grass. We take a piece of toast each, munching and listening to the birds.

'Our eldest was good mates with your dad, he was,' Patsy says. She throws her crust to an eager magpie. 'Worked on a farm, out near Gnowangerup. Me and Herb did some work there over the years. Clearing it, making paddocks out of the bush. Used to camp up with the kids.' Aunty Patsy pauses. Plucks three long strands of grass, starts plaiting them together.

I never see her hands still. Dad has told us part of this story, but I want to hear it from Aunty Patsy.

'Our son stayed on when he was big enough, wanted to earn himself some coin. Me and Herb had enough of breaking our backs over that land. Came 'ere with the littlies and Herb would go off shearing at farms round the place. But Bert, he stayed on, met your dad there.'

Patsy tips her head back, talks to the sky. 'Your dad was a good friend of his.'

'Why don't you see Dad anymore?'

A sudden flash of Patsy lobbing that stone on our roof, screeching louder than the pink-and-greys.

Why?

Patsy looks from the sky back down to the grass, rolls her neck from side to side. 'Things change,' she says. 'Let's get you back home, eh?'

* * *

We leave Uncle Herbert at home. 'To man the fort, with Meeak,' he says, winking. 'Nice to see ya, Rose.'

In the car, Aunty Patsy pushes a Tom T. Hall cassette into the player, sings along to 'Old Dogs, Children and Watermelon Wine'.

Her left hand taps her knee, turns the volume down when we near the general store. But still, she doesn't speak. She frowns slightly, hunched over the wheel. I can't tell if she's enjoying herself, or simply dedicated to getting the words right. We are about to pull into my driveway when she looks sideways at me. Her eyes stay on mine, as she turns the car in a wide arc.

Down Gillam Street, onto Ronaldshaw Road. I used to tear up and down these streets on my Malvern Star a few years back. I have a lot of questions, but somehow, I don't need to ask them. Not just yet.

When we turn onto Salt River Road, Aunty starts talking.

'Your old man was like my son,' she says.

'Who? My dad?'

'That's right. Eddie.' Aunty glances in the rear-view mirror. 'Edward Arthur Tetley.'

'Sometimes I forget his middle name,' I admit.

'Do you? Rose Francesca Patricia Tetley.'

'How do you know that?'

Patsy smiles. 'I was there when your mum named ya.'

'When I was born?'

'That's right.'

'But I was born at home.'

'Yes, that's right.'

'In the bath.'

Aunty nods.

Gravel clatters underneath the car. She drives fast. The Blue Ranges loom in front of us.

'You were like my granddaughter, you were,' she says.

Patsy gazes at the mountains, keeps driving that little bit too fast. 'Delivered you and Frank on the farm. Joe didn't need much help, slid out on his own, when he was ready.' She smiles. 'Calmest baby, that one. Frank was a bloody squawker. Late, too. Herb drove me in. We got your mum in the tub. She knew how to listen to her body. Push and pull, ebb and flow. Go with the tides. We were ready when it was your turn. Hot flannels and herbal tea. A woman's body is magic. Wise. Old magic in woman's body.'

We keep heading for the mountains, but I am lost.

'Steve was the first wadjela baby I delivered. Your ma wanted me there, so we had to stay home. Wouldn't have let me in the hospital. Ah. Elena.' Aunty Patsy seems to tell herself the rest of the story, her lips pressed together, her eyebrows occasionally rising up and down.

* * *

Gravel dust, up the side of the car. Aunty pulls over, stops next to a couch honeypot shrub. Could never remember the botanical name for that one. Patsy still isn't talking, so I ask her.

She pauses. Thinks. 'Bullgalla.'

'That's the botanical name?'

'The Noongar name, bub. The real name. Old name.' She opens her door, climbs out. 'Come on.'

I follow as she walks straight into the bush. We reach a clearing and Patsy snaps a sprig from a branch. She closes her eyes, takes a deep breath. Softly slaps the branch across her chest, her back, lifts her legs and circles the branch around them, then round each of her arms. It's as if she's washing herself with the branch. She's humming, opens her eyes. Beckons me over and I stand in front of her. I want to ask what she's doing, but feel like the silence shouldn't be broken, so I close my eyes as Aunty Patsy gently lifts my arms away from my body and starts tapping my body with the branch. The leaves are cool against my skin, they smell peppery and minty. Patsy turns me around, swishes the branch against my back, around my legs, flicks the branch as if she's ridding it of water. Finally, she encircles my head, the leaves tickling my hair. I open my eyes as she tosses the branch into the shrubs.

'Cleansing,' she says. 'Before going bush.'

I can't see a path, but it's as if Patsy knows one. She steps carefully around the scrawling, prickly plants. Here and there she stops to cup a flower in her hand.

'All the time they would tell us when we were young, *This is your Country, your Boodjar. See that tree there, that's your Boodjar. See these flowers, that's your flower. See those hills over there? Don't you fellas go past those hills, that's not your Country.*' Patsy gestures to the Blue Ranges. I keep quiet, stepping in her footprints.

'I was born in Gnowangerup, in the bush. Where the ngank, the mothers, used to go away and have their babies under the trees. Come back with them all wrapped up. Just like that. Had my boys like that too.'

We've come to a clearing, framed by white gums and grass trees. The grass trees are a bright, almost electric green. Some of the gums have been hollowed out by wildfires. We're almost at the base of the mountains, in the thick of the bush.

Aunty Patsy's storytelling voice reminds me of Grandpa, telling us stories around the campfire. Those precious times he packed us up and retraced his botany trips. We held magnifying glasses to banksia flowers, while doctors tried to keep you alive. I stretch my fingers out, imagine warming them against the flames. Fill my lungs, smelling the musty bush smells. The sun scorches the top of my head and that tight band round my chest relaxes a little. The Blue Ranges are stark against the sky. A willy-wagtail dances across the clearing, stops at our feet. Aunty Patsy smiles.

'Djidi-djidi. Might be your mummy's spirit, girl. Checking on you.'

We watch the bird hop about for a while. I think about you, Elena Tetley, with your boots and sunhat, inside this tiny bird. Is it true?

The djidi-djidi skips off into the trees. Aunty Patsy fans her face, blows through her lips. The back of my neck is sticky with sweat.

'Orright,' says Patsy. 'Off we go.' She neatly snaps a sprig from a peppermint tree, swats flies away with it as she walks. I retrace our footsteps behind her, about twenty minutes back to the car.

'Sometimes, you've just got to go bush, and breathe,' Patsy says.

I nod. The Blue Ranges out my window, blurring into a grey streak. Aunty rewinds the cassette, and 'Watermelon Wine' plays again, skipping as we go over bumps. Back onto Ronaldshaw Road, up Gillam Street. Albany Highway stretching in front of us, Perth far away at the other end. Aunty turns up our driveway.

'Home sweet home, kiddo.'

A sinking feeling. Wouldn't mind going back to Aunty's house.

She doesn't stop. Doesn't even cut the ignition.

'Do you want to come in?'

'Nah, not this time, bub. Be good. See you soon.'

I blink, and she's already turning back onto the highway.

* * *

Later in my room, Steve whistles to announce himself. He's holding a copy of *Rolling Stone* magazine. Gets them sent down from 78 Records on Hay Street. The staff in there are the only people in Perth without a suntan. Because of postage, Steve is always a few months behind the latest edition. He gives me the posters from inside sometimes, the ones he doesn't want.

'Blondie?'

'Uh, sure, if you don't want it?'

He tears the poster carefully from the middle, holds it out. 'All yours.'

'Thanks.'

Steve glances at the Patti Smith poster above my bed. 'Heard her new album?'

'Not yet. Saving for it.'

I'm in awe of Patti Smith. She sticks her middle finger to the rules and her music makes me feel like I can do anything.

He waves the *Rolling Stone* at me. 'One of the songs isn't getting any airplay. Used a racial slur in it. She says she was trying to redefine what it meant, or something. I dunno. It's a good song.'

'Where did you hear it?'

'Shane.'

'What does he think?'

'He loves Patti, but he reckons she shouldn't have used it.'

I look at her, high up on my wall, jacket slung over her shoulder, chin tilted up. I wonder what Aunty Patsy would think.

'Thanks for the poster,' I say. 'Can I read the article?'

'Yeah, when I'm done.' Steve turns down the hallway.

* * *

A cup of tea at the table in silence. The smell of the bush on the tips of my fingers. A djidi-djidi is hopping around outside. Have you followed us back?

A knock at the door. What now?

Mr and Mrs Russell.

She's holding flowers and a cake tin.

He's holding an envelope.

Eight cups of tea. The smell of apple cake. Sitting across from our landlords, I'm noticing cobwebs, a damp smell and a miscellaneous food stain on the bench that I swear wasn't there before they arrived. Mrs Russell talks about the cricket, asks about school. Mr Russell scalds his mouth on his tea. Joe gets him a glass of water. When the cake is gone, we go too. We line the hallway, and I take my place at the knothole.

They are talking quietly, so we have to strain to hear the words. There it is, the one we are looking for.

'Evicted.'

They give us one month, to sort the farm and get the rent together, or we have to go.

Normally, I'd call Jenna straight away. But I still haven't heard from her. I figure this means she's chosen Frank, which hurts too much to even think about. She sits with Tess at school. Since that day at my place, I sit at the back on my own. One time, Jen started crying in class and ran out to the toilets. Tess followed, glaring at me before she went. Another time, on the bus ride home, Alby noticed Jenna sitting up the back with

Tess, and me sitting on my own. He puffed his little chest out and walked down the aisle, tapped Jen on the shoulder.

'Don't be mean to my sister,' he said.

Jenna sucked her breath in. 'Oh, Alby,' she said. 'I'm not.'

'You are,' Alby said. 'You've changed.'

I was both mortified and flattered.

In class, if I block everything out, add the numbers, write the words, read the books, then my papers come back with numbers on them that aren't too bad, and a 'B' circled in red pen. The teachers seem to like me better. Mrs Watkins nodded at me approvingly the other day when I sat down alone. Wandered down the back, stood beside me.

'That's it, Rose,' she said. 'You and Jenna are better kept apart. Less trouble from both of you.'

Right. After all the cigarettes and detentions, I reckon Jenna's mum agrees. Things must be simpler for Jenna having Tess as a best friend. Tess's mum didn't just die, and Tess doesn't want to walk laps of the oval every break without fail. I still do that. The laps around the oval. The other day I picked up one of your books about meditating. Maybe that's what I'm trying to do as I walk round and round, the grass itching my ankles.

Eventually though, I decide it's enough. It's Jenna Betts. She's practically my sister. I walk over to her place, knock on the door. Four raps, one—pause—two, three, four. Surely I don't have to lose her, as well as you.

Mrs Betts opens the door. She calls Jenna with a voice like Jen's done something wrong. Jenna, walking up behind her mum, those denim shorts and that yellow t-shirt. My best friend.

We sit out the back, drink orange juice like always. And my heart shatters because my friend Jenna doesn't have very much to say, and I don't have much to say to her and everything feels wrong. I want to ask if she's been seeing Frank, but I don't think I can face the answer. I suck my juice up my straw, slurping in a way that would make Jen laugh. She does, but I feel the sympathy. I decide to leave after that, so I get up and head for the back gate.

'Thanks for the juice.'

Jenna gets up, squinting into the sun. 'Rose,' she calls as I open the gate.

'Yeah?'

Jenna shakes her head. 'See you at school,' she says, from the other side of the gate.

'Do you? Feels like I'm invisible.'

'Rose,' Jenna sighs my name, like it is heavy on her tongue.

'Yeah,' I say. 'What?'

Jenna hesitates. 'I can love you, and your brother, you know.'

That lie she keeps telling herself.

10. Frank

One Tuesday, when I can't be bothered with any of it anymore, I go out and stand on the highway with my thumb out. My pockets are empty, except for some green. At first, I can't decide which side of the road to stand on.

Do I want to go to Perth or Albany?

I'm standing in the middle of the highway with both my thumbs out in opposite directions, when a shit-brown Land Cruiser roars round the bend and beeps at me.

I stay where I am. They can either pick me up or hit me.

The Landy slows, but at the last minute. It's even more beat up than ours. There are surfboards on the racks and a red dog hangs out the back window.

'What the fuck, mate,' says the driver, frowning. He's got long matted hair the same colour as the dog, and a joint hanging out his mouth. His Landy keeps creeping towards me. I keep my feet planted exactly where I am, until I'm staring into the grille, and he has to stop. There's another guy sitting next to him, and a girl in the back.

'Get off the road, man,' the guy in the passenger seat says. He has messy blond curls and a frown.

The driver takes his hand off the wheel and shapes his fingers into a gun. He points it at me, shoots, then laughs.

'Nah, for real, get off the road,' he says.

'Where ya going?' I lift my chin.

'Albany.'

'Can I get a ride?'

He looks round at the others. 'What do we do with this kid?'

'He's weird,' says blond curls.

The girl hangs out the window and examines me. She's wearing a huge black windcheater rolled up at the wrists and her long hair is everywhere.

'Where are you going?' she calls out over the exhaust and some metal song they're playing. She hooks her finger, beckoning me closer.

'Wherever,' I say, scuffing my feet. 'Can I get in, or what?'

The driver cocks his head. 'Hurry up then.'

I get in next to the red dog, who wags her tail like mad and prods my thigh with her paws. I push her sideways and the driver locks eyes with me in the rear-view mirror.

'That's Nelly, if you ride with us, be cool with her, okay?'

I roll my eyes and look out the window. Feels good to be moving, even if I don't know where to. It's like in footy. Never quite knew what was coming next. But whether I got smashed or booted a winner, anything was better than standing still. The music is wild. Crazy, busy stuff. Sounds like the inside of my head. The others are chatting about some shit, but all I can hear is the guitar riff.

'Who's this?' I say.

They keep talking.

'Hey. Who's this?' I shout.

There's a quick pause.

'Oh. Iron Butterfly,' says the driver. 'They're dope, hey.'

The driver says his name is Sam. Next to him is Ben. The girl is Grace. They're going on a surfing trip. They live in Fremantle. They've ditched uni for a few days.

'What about you?' Grace asks.

I look out the window again.

'Weird,' Ben says. Must be one of the only words he knows.

Sam looks at me in the rear-view again, but I pretend not to notice. He's sucking away on his joint, which is shrinking quickly. It's passed to Ben, then to Grace. She goes to give me the roach. I shake my head.

'Got my own.'

Sam laughs, turns the music up.

In Mount Barker, they stop for sausage rolls. I didn't even bring any money. Didn't think that far ahead. While they're eating, squeezing sauce onto the hot pastry, I wander across the road to the bottle shop. Could kill for a beer. It's the fresh air, I tell myself. Makes a bloke thirsty. I walk up to the fridge, pick up a sixpack and walk out again. Don't hesitate at all. The others are back in the car, so I climb in, nestling the beers on my lap.

'Ohhh, fuck yeah, mate,' says Sam.

'Want one?' My head aches as I notice the bottle shop dude marching across the road. The others don't see, so I don't say anything. Sam's already pulling out anyway. As we drive past, the shopkeeper glares and shouts something, but I can't hear it over the magic Iron Butterfly is playing.

'You pay for these?' asks Sam.

I open mine with my teeth and say nothing.

'Jesus,' breathes Ben.

'Nah, you can call me Frank,' I say.

'Chuck us one, Frank,' says Grace. 'You did pay, didn't you?'

By the time we get to Albany the beers are gone and Iron Butterfly has played through on both sides.

'Where do we drop you, man?' asks Sam.

I say the first place that comes to mind. 'Emu Point?'

'Bit out of the way,' says Sam. 'We're headed to Dingo's, but we can leave you in town.'

I know Dingo's, it's where the fair dinkum surfers like Steve go. I've been smashed up real bad out there. Tore my leg on a reef. Snapped a fin. I remember my blood on the sand and Steve passing me his flask to numb the pain. The scar is pretty cool.

They drop me on York Street. The town hall clock says four. I think it's actually right for once. I walk down the street with my hands in my pockets, then walk back up again. Sit on the park bench, roll a gumnut under my shoe. People are looking, but no one notices me, not really. There's a difference. They're all walking along with their plastic bags of shopping and their prams with kids and their dogs on leads. I wonder if any of them have ever been haunted by the smell of hospitals. Sometimes I'm just standing in the paddock and my nostrils burn with the smell of cabbage and piss and disinfectant.

My head's aching and my stomach growls. Maybe I should hitch straight back home. The idea of having to strike up a conversation to ask for a lift is exhausting. I'd have to get back out to the highway anyway, and I feel so tired. I curl my legs up and rest my head on my hands, closing my eyes for a while.

* * *

Twenty minutes later, a family sets up their picnic in the park. They have sandwiches cut into neat triangles and grapes in a Tupperware container, already pulled off the stalk. A boy in school uniform is eating a lolly snake, his fist clasped around the small paper bag at the end of its tail. A girl in the same uniform kicks her shoes off and sits down next to an old lady who must be her grandma. Their mum has gone back to the car to get something. The grandma gets a paper plate out of the basket and puts some grapes on it. I've never seen anyone be so careful about grapes. I used to suck them straight off the stalk. Liked the green ones best. Once I sucked too hard through fish lips and swallowed the grape whole. Stood there spluttering. You whacked me on the back, laughed, then tried to look serious. 'That's not a nice way to eat,' you said. I blinked at you, and you cracked up again. I loved making you laugh. I was best at it. Worst at lots of other things.

The mum comes back with a thermos and little cups like the ones we used to take camping. 'Do you want tea, or Milo, Mum?' she asks the old lady.

'Tea,' says the grandma, a bit indignantly.

The kids both get Milo, and the girl reopens the tin, and spoons extra on top of hers. I feel like a loser, watching some dumb family have a picnic, so I get up and go lean against the library, by the door. The doors slide open. I shift further away from them. They keep opening and shutting, as if expecting me to enter. A woman in heels clicks past. She sees me out of the corner of her eye. I know she does. But she doesn't look. I don't blame her.

Back in the park—the picnic. The boy is still chewing away at his lolly snake, but the girl is saving hers, on the edge of her paper plate.

'He's watching us,' says the boy, standing on one leg and pointing at me with a wobbling finger.

'Don't point,' says his mum.

'Don't stare,' says his grandma, looking at me.

I freeze. Look down. My Dunlops have seen better days. My feet start moving quickly and I keep looking at them. They march up York Street all the way to the top roundabout. My cheeks are hot. Stupid fucking picnic people. A car slows down as it passes me and some shithead hangs out the passenger seat.

'Hey, loser,' he shouts.

I keep walking. Kick a bin as I walk past.

The car pulls into a carpark and swerves back out, doubling past me again. The driver opens his window and his arm darts out. A can of cool drink comes hurtling at me, smacking into my chest with an explosion of orange liquid.

'Fuck you.' The wind steals my shout. The car hoons away in a mess of exhaust smoke.

In the shopping centre, I go to the toilets and clean the sticky Fanta off my shirt. I pat myself dry with a paper hand towel and try to avoid my gaze in the mirror. The shop lights are sharp and mean and I feel dehydrated and achy. In Woolies I grab a banana and eat it as I walk around. Some dickhead in the cold meat section with a pricing gun says, 'Hey, you have to pay for that,' with a loud, nasal voice.

'I came in with it,' I say, and swagger away.

'Prove it.'

'Prove I didn't.' I pick up an apple. The guy keeps staring at me, so I get a trolley and put things in it. Apples, pineapple, bag of carrots. I walk down the aisles, shoving things in willy-nilly. I get razors and aftershave that comes in a can with a pump lid, Passiona and Cheezels. They're things I actually want, so then I make a game of it and get marshmallows, earbuds, cat food, a *Women's Weekly* magazine, dishwashing liquid and a chapstick. I find a packet of mashed potato—how does that work?—and a can of Spam. I hate Spam. Elastic bands and toothpicks. My hands grab at things, and I hurl them into the trolley. The *Women's Weekly* throws up an image of one on your bedside table, so I push the trolley to the end of aisle four and leave it there.

Outside it's drizzling a bit and humid. I'm still hungry. I put my head down and walk along Middleton Road, past the graveyard and the primary school to the skate park.

They built the Snake Run a few years back, and it's epic. One hundred and forty metres long, it gives you the same buzz as surfing. I wish I had my board. There're two guys about my age knocking about and I crave that soaring feeling.

I sit on the grass at the top of the hill and watch.

A skinny, pimply guy is carving up. He kick-turns over and over again, frowning slightly. The other guy is big and fat and not very good, keeps getting in the way.

After a while, the smaller bloke jumps off his board and zips a can of Sprite out of his backpack. It fizzes open and he sinks it almost in one.

'You skate?' he asks.

'A bit.'

He holds his board out to me with an eyebrow raised.

I take it and stand at the beginning of the track. I tic-tac to get going. My knees automatically bend a little and my stomach knits in tight. I've always been good at shit like this. Don't have the tricks of the city kids, but I'm fearless. I ride the concrete curves, my t-shirt billowing out behind me. The other bloke is like a deadweight on the track. I swerve round him.

'Cool,' says the Sprite guy. I ignore him.

After a few goes of the track, he's swung his backpack on and is ready to claim his board back. 'Chuck her this way, would ya?'

He's smaller than me, maybe not as skinny, but I reckon I could take him. I smile.

'Nah, bro,' I say, and go again.

Sprite guy frowns, shrugging his backpack up and down his shoulders. 'One more then,' he says, uncertain how much authority he wants to put in his voice.

I take three more runs.

Then I stop to catch my breath, and lean on the board, looking at him. I'm buzzing, humming with energy. I feel good, in a really bad way.

'Hey,' says Sprite guy. 'Gimme my board.' He still sounds confused, like he can't decide whether to threaten me, or ask nicely. He's sizing me up and can't tell what I'm capable of. Finally, someone paying me some attention.

'Come and get it.' I drop in and soar down the track.

The fat kid looks up and realises what's happening. He plants himself in the middle of the track, feet rooted to the concrete. I gotta give it to him, the guy's got balls. I'm coming real fast, and he doesn't move. He hasn't said anything at all either, just picked up on what's happening and decided to help his friend.

I miss my friends.

I keep going.

I hit him with a thud that knocks the air out of me. Our bodies go down onto the concrete with a crack, and the skateboard keeps rolling.

'Fuuuuuuck,' shouts Sprite guy, running along the side of the track till he gets to us. The fat kid's still not saying anything, but he's scrunched his eyes closed and rolled himself sideways. I landed on him, so I'm mostly okay, other than winding myself and knocking my arm pretty badly. The concrete has tiny bits of coral and seashells in it, it's worse than sandpaper on your skin. Steve reckons one time he dug a fully intact, tiny conch shell out of his leg after stacking it. My elbow is bleeding and my wrist is growing. To be honest, it feels good.

I start laughing.

Sprite guy marches right up to me and punches me in the face.

'What the hell is your problem,' his voice breaks.

My front teeth graze the inside of my lip and I taste blood. Sprite guy seems to think I won't deck him, cos he turns his back on me and drops to his knees in front of his friend, who is still lying on his side with his eyes closed. It'd be a low move, even for me. I get up and limp away, pausing at the bottom of the hill to retrieve Sprite guy's skateboard. I jump on it, and I'm at Middleton Beach in moments.

I skate past the surf club and up the hill, so I can bomb back down it real fast. The wind stings and cools my face where it's throbbing and oozing.

People on the path move out of my way, some staring at me and others averting their eyes. I carry on, riding the path all the way to Emu Point. Jump off the board and jog to catch it where it lands on the grass. I'm hot, buzzing and feeling a little sick. The sun is starting to set. I kick my shoes off, walk into the water. I really hope that kid is okay. Why didn't he open his eyes? My breath is in my ears. I stop at the sheltered bay, before the main beach. People are starting to leave, getting in their cars to go home and cook dinner, and get eight hours of sleep before work and school the next day. Fuck them. There isn't anyone in the bay, so I strip down to my boxers and leave the board and my clothes on the sand. There's a hefty bruise on my right knee. Maybe fat kid wasn't fat enough.

The water stings the tender places on me. My scars look like herringbones, lining my left thigh and my arms. All the weeks without you. I sink to my knees. Water rushes into my open mouth. Bubbles escape my mouth and nose, rising to the light. Salt burns my eyeballs and the back of my throat. My sore arm pulses in the cool. You always used to say the ocean scrubs us clean. It's a healing burn, and I stay there on my knees for a while, until my lungs are screaming for air.

When I come up, the sun has sunk further towards the horizon and is staining the sky blood orange. I go out deeper and roll onto my back. It's nice being held by the waves. I let myself drift.

i started punching people once you got sick
it normally happened on the football field
i was fast, real fast
and good
but if someone knocked me down this rage
came roaring out of me
i was already down
we'd already been taken out
you were dying, cancer eating your bones
how dare anyone take me further.
i'd never remember what i did in those moments
just coach dragging me off
throbbing knuckles
and the smell of kicked-up grass.
when you were still well enough to be there
you wouldn't talk to me as we drove home.
sometimes you cried and once dad left me there
drove right away with you beside him
while i stood in the carpark,
my footy boots hanging by their laces in my hand.
i sat against the change room wall
thinking about how i didn't want you to hate me
before you died.
a few hours later you pulled up in the carpark and
called my name over and over
i was so embarrassed
a little boy hiding in the toilets from his mum.
just come here, you bastard
i wanted to laugh and cry hearing you call me that
so i did.

you found me on the floor
and you edged yourself along the wall to me
using the clothes hooks as handholds.
you crouched in front of me
like when i was a kid
and pulled my hands away from my face
you were so weak, i didn't have the heart to fight
so there we were, looking at each other.
'i didn't mean to,' i said.
'enough,' you said.
my breath jagged like i'd just finished the game
yours blowing softly on my face.
'no kid of mine behaves like that, frank tetley.'
'i know.'
'never again.'
'okay.'
we kept crouching and staring.
'i hate everything,' i said.
'well, i love you,' you said.
and then you shuffled so you
were sitting next to me,
and we curled in on each other
and we cried.

i punched someone in the next game
and coach suspended me for the rest of the season.
dad left me in the carpark again.
you didn't come get me.

Once the sun disappears, the water gets an extra chill. I lie there as shark bait for a while, then slowly wade back to the fading heat of the sand.

I have nowhere to go.

I skate along the footpath, past a few fishermen in the dusk. When I get to the docks, the board makes a racket on the wooden jetty so I jump off. There's a couple of people trying their luck with handlines and rods. Dad says it's not like the good old days when he and his mate Bert used to come and fish here. The old man reckons fish would throw themselves on the line, just about. I sit at the end of the jetty and swing my legs. It's weird being here without the others. We've spent so many Fridays partying on these boats. Some of the best memories I have.

Then I get an idea. The last fisherman has gone. It's only me. I scan the boats. There's *The Rover* and *Neptune's Son*, we've been on both of them before. I like *The Rover* because it's sleek and feels like it would be fast on the water. *Neptune's Son* is old and the turquoise paint is peeling on its hull. I spot *Gypsy*, tied up next to *Warrior*. Good. That's the one.

I step off the jetty and onto her deck, ducking below the roof. They keep the key for the cabin in a little tin under the seat by the wheel. It clicks in the lock, and I push my shoulder against the door. As soon as I step in, I feel relieved. It's cosy and warm, with a sandalwood and coffee smell. There are some cushions on the floor, a pack of cards on the bench, even a packet of cigarettes next to a box of matches. I feel like if there's a god, she's been looking out for me. You always believed god was a woman. You're probably right, if there is a god at all.

Out of habit, I open the fridge to see if there's anything I can nick. There's only a small bottle of milk, but in the cupboard above I find half a box of stale bread sticks and a tin of mackerel. Behind the mackerel is also a bottle of whisky. Normally, we are careful. Little bits here and there mean we don't get caught.

I am too tired, too sore, too done with it all, to be careful. I can't decide what I want first. Bread stick? Mackerel? Cigarette? Whisky? I light a cigarette, opening the cabin window to blow the smoke out. Can't have their lovely cushions smelling of smoke now, can we? I wonder who owns *Gyspy*. Sometimes, Uncle Nic brings his boat down from Perth and we go out for the day. It's strange seeing the boats we like to hang out on, their real owners behind the wheel. They have no idea we spend entire evenings on their beloved vessels. Beers, bongs and Bob Dylan.

I wonder if that fat kid is okay.

The whisky burns my throat. I peel open the tin of mackerel, dip a bread stick in. It reminds me of eggs and soldiers, except it reeks.

What am I actually going to do?

The thought comes suddenly, and raw. I can't answer it, so I drink more whisky. I'm worried about all of them. Dad, the boys, Rose, Jenna.

Rose.

Jenna.

This whisky is good. It's numbing and thawing and hurting and relieving. I drink and drink. There's so much to drown out. I get up for another cigarette and notice a tea candle, sitting in an enamel dish. Light it, then my cigarette, from the flame. Search for the moon through the cabin window. I just want it all to be over.

* * *

I wake up to smoke. Everywhere. The flames are licking the cabin inside out. I'm sweating and shaking and as my eyes startle open, I take it all in. The flames, hot on my face, reminding me of bonfires on the farm. I have a strange, lucid thought. This is the point your survival instincts kick in. Mine don't.

I face the flames the same way I faced Sam earlier. He'd either hit me, or stop, and I didn't care. The flames are the same. They'll either take me or leave me.

Take me or leave me.

I wish for both in equal measure.

hospital light
worse than supermarket beams
a beep a clipboard a plastic tray with a
white sandwich triangle
where are you?

It's me, not you, between crisp white hospital sheets. Skin on fire. Too tired to put it out. Two human shapes, here with me. Patsy and Herbert, I think. Why?

Patsy is looking out the window with her hands clasped behind her back. Herbert's leaning against the wall. They both move towards the bed when they see my eyes open.

'Here he is,' says Patsy.

'Good,' says Herbert. 'About time.'

'Get him a drink,' says Patsy.

Herbert goes out to stand in the corridor. 'Hey, 'scuse me,' I hear him say. 'Kiddo here's woken up. Can I get him some juice or something?'

'Water,' calls Patsy.

'Water, I mean,' says Herbert.

Patsy is holding my hand. It feels like someone has peeled bits of my skin off, all over my body. My right arm is searing and hot, and so is the right side of my face.

'You stay here with me,' Patsy says. I'm not sure where she thinks I'm going to go, I can't exactly do a runner, can I? I close my eyes again.

'Stay here, Frank.'

Open. Patsy, holding a plastic cup to my lips.

'Straw, we need a straw Herb.'

Herbert back in the corridor again. 'Can I get a straw for the boy?'

My head throbs and there's smoke in my nose and ash in my eyes.

A straw, gently placed between my lips.

'Drink, darling.'

Pain in my chest, my throat.

Cold water, putting the fire out.

I close my eyes again.

* * *

‘Second degree burns,’ says the nurse. ‘He’s lucky.’

Lucky? Me? The nurse doesn’t know shit. Cops will probably come soon. Didn’t think this part through at all. Guess I’ve been practising for a cell, all these weeks in the shed.

‘Cops have been already, bub,’ Patsy says, reading my frown. ‘You were out to the world. Probably the drink as much as the fire. But you’ll have to speak to them again, I’d say.’ She grimaces.

‘How come you came?’

‘Us?’ Patsy points her thumb at her chest. ‘I was just getting Herb in the car when we saw you being pushed past on the trolley. Gave us a scare.’

I notice the hospital band on Herbert’s arm. ‘You okay?’ My voice is raspy.

Herbert’s eyes chase his thoughts around the room. ‘Me? Yeah. Alright. Forgot me insulin.’

Patsy clicks her tongue. ‘Silly bugger.’

A second nurse comes in with a clipboard.

‘Hello there,’ she says to me. ‘These will ease the pain.’

A plastic cup with some tablets in it.

Part of me wants to feel the pain, but I swallow and lean back on the pillows.

‘A doctor will be in shortly,’ she says with a business-lady smile.

‘Does Dad know?’ I ask Patsy.

She looks at Herbert. ‘Yes,’ she says. ‘He’s on his way.’

Herbert looks out into the carpark and seems to notice something. ‘Be right back,’ he says.

Patsy sits on the side of the bed, pats my knee gently.

‘Cops said you burned an old widow’s boat,’ she says. ‘Iris. Her husband died a while back apparently. Heart attack. She and her girl go out on the boat to remember him.’

Ouch. Take that.

Patsy keeps going. She says the cops told her one of the fishermen lost his house keys and went back to check his boat. He saw the smoke on *Gypsy* and broke the door down, carried me out, before things got serious.

I wish they'd been more serious.

Herbert comes back after a while, shaking his head. 'Eddie will be in soon,' he says.

But Steve, Joe, Rose and Alby arrive first. They burst into the room, speaking over each other. There's not enough space for all the bodies and voices. My head throbs. I reach out and grab Rose's hand. Can't look at any of them. Close my eyes.

Patsy fills them in. It hurts too much to listen.

'Fuuck,' exhales Steve.

'Which boat?' Rose asks. 'Which one?'

I can't answer her.

'*Gypsy*.' Her voice begs me to say she's wrong.

'That's the one,' Patsy confirms.

Rose drops my hand.

Herbert leaves again. Comes back holding Dad's arm, gently pushes him towards my bed. Dad's not speaking. There are tears streaming down his face. Piss-weak. I close my eyes again. Pretend to sleep.

'Just an accident, Eddie,' Herbert is saying. 'Not sick, like Elena, just hurt himself. He'll be okay.'

'How?' Dad's voice is gravelly.

'He'll heal,' Herbert reassures him.

'How did it happen?' Dad clarifies.

Patsy beckons Dad into the hallway. I can't hear what they're saying, but then—

'Bloody idiot,' Dad splutters.

Next time I open my eyes he's gone.

* * *

I stay in the hospital overnight. Patsy and Herbert go home. The others leave for a while and come back holding steaming parcels of fish and chips, Alby in tow. They sit on the gleaming white floor, grabbing chips and squirting sauce. One of the nurses doesn't approve, and they're gone by six o'clock, leaving a smell of vinegar in the air.

In the morning, a nurse gives me a packet of Panadol and tells me to see the doctor in a few days to check the dressings. Joe's there to pick me up, his hand on my shoulder, steering me towards his car. I look out the window hoping he won't ask questions. In Albany, Joe pulls into the bakery, leaves the car running. Comes back with a bag of hot cinnamon donuts and two foam cups of coffee.

'Breakfast,' he says.

I gulp coffee while Joe pulls back onto York Street.

'Eat,' he says.

The donuts are sweet and doughy. The sugar spills on my legs and makes my hands sticky. In Mount Barker, Joe pulls into the pub, leaves the keys in the ignition, radio on.

'I'll be two secs.'

Four songs later, Joe comes back with ruffled hair, pink cheeks. I'm too tired to ask. When we get to our driveway, Joe refuses to stop at the shed. He parks right up at the front door, cuts the ignition.

'I'm not going in.'

'Yes, you fucking are.'

It's not like Joe to swear. I sneer. Step gingerly onto the gravel. Everything hurts. Dad's in the lounge room. 'I've got him,' Joe calls out.

There's a mumbled reply.

Joe pushes me down the hallway, presses me onto my old bed. Comes back with a big glass of water. His sympathy makes me want to gag.

That afternoon, the cops phone the house. Joe takes the call. I hear him tell Dad. Shit. Will I have to go to court, or straight to jail? What would you think of me now?

* * *

Whenever anyone checks on me, I pretend to be asleep. They each come at some point. Except Dad. His ugg boots don't shuffle down the hallway. Eventually, Joe and Alby go to bed and we lie there in darkness. I listen to the rhythm of their breathing. The wind in the trees. The muffled sound of the TV. Before the sun rises, I slide out of bed. Everywhere I bend pulls bandages. Elbows, knees, ankles. Throbbing skin.

I go to Alby first. The little bugger is curled on his side with his hands folded under his cheek. Always slept like that, even when he was a baby. I used to pretend I wasn't interested in him, let Rose carry him around. I was angry at how he drained you. But sometimes at night I'd get up and stare at him in his cot. Such innocence in all this hell. Wants to be a pilot, and I know he will be. I can imagine him in uniform, round glasses and beaming smile. He's got what it takes to get far, far away from here. Five years old and he's already a better man than I could ever be.

Joe's lanky body spills over the top bunk, all hanging arms and legs. I climb up two rungs, till I can see his moonlit face. Never known a better-hearted bloke. Solid, his feet firmly planted in the earth. Takes me as I am, no explanation needed. I hope the world can return his kindness.

In the hallway, I hesitate at Rose's door. I can't go in.

That's it. It's time.

the paddocks are filled with mist
sunrays in the haze
my favourite time of day.
it's beautiful
too beautiful
for me.

the shed doors keep the light out
deep breaths in darkness.
it will be better for everyone
without
me.

there you are
sunbeams through a gap in the tin
will you take me?
will you let me
in?

11. Rose

Can't sleep. Funny feeling in my stomach. Keep thinking of Frank covered in gauze. Imagine if the flames took him. If he left too. I get up eventually. Need to be close to him, feel the warmth of his body, know that he's still here. I creak the bedroom door open and step into the boys' room. Frank's bed—empty.

He's not in the kitchen, and Dad's still asleep in the lounge room, the TV showing the test pattern to the silent room. The sun is just rising over the paddocks, it's not even six yet. Feet crunching the gravel as I run up the driveway. Shed door's shut. Doesn't look like Frank's been in there. He normally leaves it open a crack.

Something's wrong.

I wrench the door open, heaving it above my head. See his feet first. His slender feet, like yours, standing on the seat of an old chair. His knobbly ankles, skinny brown legs. Everything in slow motion. The end of a piece of rope in his hands. The top tied to the rafters. His black eyes darting to mine.

I can hear a sound, piercing, hurting my ears.

I'm on the chair in seconds. My arms around him, squeezing his body with all my strength. That noise, still ringing in my ears. The chair tips and we fall, landing hard on the concrete. I'm hitting him, shaking him, bellowing. That sound, that sound is me.

The rope swings above us.

12. Frank

my knees are curled into my chest
there's blood and salt in my mouth
some from the fall
some from rose
she has a good swing on her

her fist strikes fast
one
two
three
then rose holds me
she rocks me
nestles my head to her chest
kisses my temples, my cheeks, my eyes
i open them and look at her
i don't see you i just see
her
my sister
rose.

13. Rose

'i'm sorry, i'm sorry,' my brother says
imsorryimsorryimsorry
i have never loved
or hated him
more.

14. Frank

Next there's just pictures. Alby at the shed door, rubbing his eyes. Then he's screaming. Running his little legs back to the house. Joe-Steve-Dad-Alby all at once. Rose's arms locked around my body, howling when they try to pry her off me. Steve and Dad, their hands under our armpits, lifting us. The blood on the floor—my nose gushing with it. The way the rope won't stop swinging. Dad, and his voice. Somehow, he's using it, and it's loud and strong, like I remember hearing it when I was small.

'I'm here, I'm here,' he says over and over. And he is. He's here. He drives the kombi, fast and calm, one hand on my knee, patting it occasionally. Rose is in the back seat, her left hand reaching forwards to my shoulder. I squeeze her hand and don't let go.

In the hospital, they give up trying to separate us. Put us side by side.

A nurse examines us. Me first, then Rose. Talks softly to Dad.

My ankle is sprained, and so is Rose's thumb. Mine from the fall, hers from landing punches.

She catches my eye when she tells the nurse she fell on it.

I didn't expect to be grateful to be alive.

* * *

Shane's mum, Sandy, is our nurse. She has a voice that's cracked from smoking and warm with kindness. She draws the curtain around my bed, and I wave at Rose before she disappears from view. Feel giggly, my bones so heavy on the bed. Guess it's the adrenaline. And the pain relief. Relief.

Sandy's asking Dad something in a low voice.

'Hmm? Just an accident,' Dad says. There's a pause.

The door clicks shut behind them. Must be taking the conversation to the hallway. Seems to take a while. Then she's back.

I sit myself up, and blood pours from my nose again.

'Back again, so soon,' she says, passing me a tissue. I focus on the icepack on my left foot.

'Lucky you didn't break it. Broken a bone before?'

'Loads.'

She looks directly at me. 'Helps with the pain, doesn't it.'

I think she's talking about the painkillers, but then she shifts her gaze to the herringbone scar on my wrist.

My cheeks feel hot.

She checks some of my burns, nodding to herself as she goes.

'They need you here,' she says, eyes on mine again. 'Don't you forget it.' Then she's gone, stepping round the curtain. 'Your turn, Miss Tetley,' she says.

15. Rose

The others go out in search of fresh air. Sandy runs through her checklist with me, examining bruises and scrapes. When she asks if I'm okay, she asks like she really cares. I don't know what to say. I think I'm okay. I'm okay because Frank's okay, just on the other side of the curtain. I give her an oversized thumbs-up with my swollen thumb.

'Alright then, love, we'll get you off this bed so we can let another poor bugger in.'

She nods her head towards Frank. 'Stay with him though, alright?'

I sit on the end of the bed, beside his bandaged ankle. We don't speak, just look. The curtains wrapped around us. There he is. There he is.

My brother.

16. Frank

Jenna.

She stands by the bed, looking at us. Rose, groggy with sleep. Jenna and Rose, staring at each other. Rose propping herself up on her elbow. Jenna standing perfectly still. I can feel the air between them.

A conversation without words. A battle, a truce, a reunion.

Then Jenna, reaching her arms around both of us, drawing us together. My big, bandaged foot getting in the way, a muffled laugh. The three of us, foreheads touching, hands holding, arms squeezing.

There'll be words to say later, and we'll say them. But right now, it's just the three of us on a white hospital bed, and even with the smell of cabbage and piss and disinfectant, there's nowhere I'd rather be.

17. Rose

A cough at the door. She's not what I imagined the owner of *Gypsy* would look like. She's small and withered, bent forward as if the ocean breeze has had its way with her. She's wearing sensible brown shoes and despite her hunch, she walks with purpose. Dad rises from the edge of Frank's hospital bed first, greets her politely.

'Hi,' she says. 'I'm Iris.'

We fall quiet. I edge closer to Frank, shielding him from whatever is to come.

No one speaks.

'Sorry to hear you've hurt yourself,' she says in a matter-of-fact, school-teacher type of way. When still no one speaks, Iris continues. 'I suppose I should provide some context.' She steps further into the room, so that my body is no longer blocking Frank from her gaze.

'I own *Gypsy*,' she says. 'You burned my boat. Was visiting a friend and saw your name on the door.'

Dad clears his throat. 'I'm so sorry, Iris,' he says sincerely. 'As I've told the police, we will be sure to sort this all out with you—'

Iris lifts her hand, silencing Dad. 'Yes, and I trust that whatever's happened here won't get in the way of that.'

Dad starts to speak again, but Frank interrupts. 'Iris,' he says. 'I … I'm so sorry.'

Iris tuts at him in reply.

I want to tell her how much we loved her boat, that I'll miss the safety of the cabin, the smell of coffee grinds and the slight waft of diesel. But of course, I should never have stepped foot on *Gypsy*.

'Well. I've told the cops we can deal with it between us. But you'd better sort it out,' Iris says, and turns on her heel.

Aunty Patsy comes through the door just as Iris goes to step out. They startle at each other, wide-eyed.

'What you doin—' Patsy starts to say, but Iris wraps her arms around herself and hurries away. Something in Patsy flips. 'Yeah, that's right, unna, you run away, you get out of my sight,' she yells after her.

'Patsy …' Uncle Herbert is close behind.

'What's that woman doing here?' Patsy asks, her eyes darting around the room.

We are slow to respond.

'Hmm? What's that about?' Patsy urges, her face pink.

'It was her boat, Aunty Patsy,' Frank mumbles.

'Speak up,' Patsy barks.

'It was her boat,' Frank and I say it together, louder.

'*That* woman? *Her* boat?'

Our silence is all the confirmation Patsy needs.

'We've got to go,' she says, and swoops out of the room.

* * *

They let us go in the evening and Dad drives us back in the kombi. When we get home, Aunty Patsy and Uncle Herbert are waiting. Herbert's forehead is crinkled with worry, while Patsy paces our verandah, spitting a stream of words. 'Our son, *our* son, her bloody boat, got what she deserved …'

Dad frowns, lets them inside. 'What's going on?' he asks.

Patsy keeps rambling, but I don't follow.

Herbert touches her arm. 'Hush, love.' Then to Dad—'Derek owned the boat your boy here has gone and burnt.'

Dad puts his hands on the table, pushes his spine straight. 'What?

'Yes.'

'Iris is Derek's wife?'

'Well, Derek passed recently, but yes.'

'The prick,' Patsy adds. 'If he had another boat, I'd burn it.'

Frank laughs nervously. 'Who's Derek?'

'He was my boss,' Dad says slowly. He's gone terribly pale. 'Back when I was a fisherman … with …'

'With our son,' Patsy says. 'Bert.'

There's a pause. I'm desperately trying to add the pieces together, when Patsy says: 'Derek killed Bert.'

'No,' Dad says. 'I did.'

* * *

A grey day. Rough on the ocean. Hot. The threat of a summer storm breaking the sky. Post catch triumph, homeward bound. Beers in a bucket of ice. Cigarette smoke. Dirty jokes. Leering fishermen. This is what Dad tells us. What he remembers. Bert, quieter with the day's work done. He was able to shrink into himself on that boat, so much so that the other men didn't see him anymore. Except Derek, the boss. He always saw Bert. Seemed to find him an awful pest, even when he was bringing in the most fish. Bert couldn't do it fast enough, smart enough, good enough. Not for Derek.

And so. This grey day. Booze coming out of their ears. Lightning on the horizon. Then the rain, big heavy droplets. The crew squeezing into the cabin, pulling out a pack of cards. Bert, making to step inside, Derek, raising a single hand.

'No space.'

Dad, already in the cabin, locking eyes with Bert. Raindrops in Bert's curly hair. Dad, breathing in. Shrugging his arms in a pathetic apology. Turning away. Sipping his beer.

A few rounds later, a sick feeling in Dad's stomach. He staggered to the cabin door, threw it open. Slid across the deck, calling for his mate. No

Bert. Dad remembers the wind caught his vomit, threw it back in his face. They never found Bert's body.

* * *

Aunty Patsy and Uncle Herbert are quiet when they leave. Dad's story hangs in the air, over cold cups of tea. The wheels on the gravel are the only sound, as we continue to sit.

'They always thought it was all Derek's fault,' Dad says. 'They never knew Bert was left out on the deck. And he shouldn't have been. I should have done something.'

I feel so sad. For Bert, for Aunty Patsy and Uncle Herbert. For Dad. How could he let that happen?

Dad's words are pouring out now, tumbling, like he can't stop. 'I never told them what I saw. I was too scared I'd lose Patsy and Herb. I needed them.' He slams his open palm on the table. 'I really needed them.'

Alby climbs off his chair, headed for the hallway.

'You're named after him,' Dad blurts out, pointing at him. Alby turns back to the table.

'Who?'

'Bert. We didn't want to use his exact name in case it offended them. So your mum came up with Albert. Alby.'

'Oh.' Alby looks older than five in that moment. He's taking in the story, the mood, the weight of his own name. 'Do they even know?'

Dad laughs, without humour. 'No,' he says, rubbing his face. 'No, they don't.'

Eventually, Frank breaks the silence. 'If Aunty Patsy and Uncle Herbert were so important to you, Dad … then why, why did you stop seeing them?'

Dad screws his face up. Sucks his breath in. Sighs.

'Elena,' he says.

'What?' we all say it at once.

'When she got really sick, her old man put his foot down. Doesn't like the Noongars, your grandfather. He and your mum fought about it, and then he and I fought about it. But god, we were all so tired. It was easier to give in. We stopped seeing them when you were little. I told them … I told them they weren't welcome anymore.'

Ah, there it is. There's the why.

18. Frank

I sleep on the couch. Doesn't feel right to go back into the shed, after everything that's happened. Wake with the sun. Stand at the open window for a moment and watch the sunrays hit the haze. The light catching the grass seeds. Not a view I thought I'd see again. Instant coffee. Two cups. I'm about to take it up to him when he climbs down from the loft.

Side by side, just sipping.

'You're up early.'

'So are you.'

'Couldn't sleep.'

Did Bert jump, or did he fall? I know Dad's been lying awake, pierced by guilt.

'It wasn't your fault. Not entirely, anyway.'

My old man inhales slowly, blows steam from his cup. 'You and I have a bit to do today.' He's not wrong. There's about five hundred sheep to shear. A farm to save. But this comes first.

We stop at the florist in Mount Barker. Stand outside, examining the bunches in buckets.

'Your mum liked natives best,' Dad says, turning away from the sunflowers. Two bunches. Yellow verticordia with a firewood banksia bursting out of the middle, tied with a deep red ribbon. One delicate posy of eucalyptus leaves surrounded by camphor myrtle, and some dried everlasting daisies.

We visit Aunty Patsy and Uncle Herbert first. Dad fumbles with the flowers, wipes his hand through his hair, straightens his collar.

I nod at him encouragingly.

Herbert opens the door, smiles in a sad way.

Patsy is at the other end of the hallway. She freezes, eyes the flowers in Dad's hands.

'Bloody men,' she grumbles as she clomps up to the door. 'Now isn't the time for flowers.' But she takes the bunch, nonetheless. 'It's time for a talk, and a cuppa. Put the kettle on, Herb.'

The flowers sit in a large jar, in the middle of the table. I can see Patsy's face through a sea of tiny, yellow stamens.

Dad hasn't said anything since we've stepped into the house.

'Sorry,' he says now, and touches his fingertips together, almost in prayer. Leans his head towards them. 'I am so, so sorry.'

Aunty Patsy grabs the jar of flowers, plonks them on the kitchen bench and sits back down. I can see her face very clearly now. She's not happy.

Herbert arranges his hands in a similar position to Dad's. I wonder if I should be praying too.

Patsy reaches out and snatches Dad's right hand away from his face. 'Enough,' she says. 'You didn't kill my son. Racism, discrimination … history. Hate. They're the things that took Bert from us.'

'But I should have said something,' Dad insists. 'Anything. I was a coward.'

'Yes,' Patsy says. 'You were. But Derek isn't the only one you needed to stand up to.'

Dad closes his eyes. Nods.

'Elena's father made you turn us away. We didn't just lose Bert, but you too. Two sons.'

Herbert remains quiet. He jiggles his knees, and coins tinkle in his pockets. There's deep pain here. It's in the creases of every face at this table.

'Aunty,' I say, in a voice just above a whisper. I don't know when I started calling her that, but it feels right. 'Aunty.'

Patsy drops Dad's hand, turns to me.

'Is there anything we can do?'

'Yes,' she says. 'There is.'

She gets up, goes to the sink, pours a glass of water. Stands facing out of the kitchen window as she drinks. Sighs, returns to the table.

'Your father-in-law broke our families up. Pushed us wide apart.' Aunty stretches her arms out to express the distance. 'I been thinking about him, and all his botany work. All this eucalyptus this, melaleuca that. That's our land he's talking about. He cut pieces of our culture and history with his little pocketknife, you know, and stuck a magnifying glass up to it, put a big fancy white man name on it. Made big money from that, he did. But did he ask any of us? We've got stories and medicine in those plants,' Patsy's voice is hoarse. 'Didn't ask us anything, did he?'

I look to Dad. Uncle Herbert looks at his hands.

'No, Aunty,' Dad says eventually. 'No, Vince didn't ask.'

'Well, you've had your head in the sand long enough,' says Patsy. 'You can do some setting right, Eddie. You tell him—you say, *When you reprint your books next, how about you acknowledge the* people *of the Great Southern, the caretakers of the flowers?* You tell him to say, *This is Menang and Goreng Noongar Country I've been studying. I pay my respects to the Traditional Owners of that land.*'

'Not owners, Patsy, Custodians,' interjects Uncle Herbert. 'No one owns the land. The land owns us.'

'Traditional Custodians, then,' Patsy says. 'Yes, he can say that. You tell him, Eddie.'

'I will,' Eddie assures Aunty Patsy. 'I will.'

* * *

Iris comes slowly to the door. Frowns at the flowers. I step back, giving her space. Dad's waiting in the car. I nod and he pulls out of the driveway, heads towards town.

'Hi,' I say. 'I came to apologise.'

Iris just stands there.

'I hope you like these,' I say, handing Iris the bouquet.

She doesn't take it. Steps out onto the front porch, closes the front door.

'Flowers don't fix much,' she says, leaning on the railing, squinting into the sun.

I lower the bunch to my side. Nod my head, in what I hope is a respectful way. 'I'd like to fix the boat, though. I could do that.'

'Don't think I want you near my boat again, kid.'

'Okay,' I say.

Silence.

I extend the flowers again. Iris keeps her hands on the railing.

'Grief isn't an excuse, you know.'

I drop the flowers in shock.

Iris laughs. It's a hollow sound.

'Wouldn't have minded setting the boat alight myself over the years.' She prods the brown paper encompassing the stems with her toe.

'Derek was sick a long time. But grief doesn't give you a get-out-of-jail-free card, I'm afraid.'

Guess not. I turn to go.

'Frank,' Iris calls.

I turn.

'Come in.'

Iris doesn't make tea. She pours gin, with a hand that trembles. This is not what I expected from the woman with sensible shoes.

Only one glass. One ice cube. Silver tongs drop it into the glass.

Water for me. I gulp it down.

She sits in a rocking chair by the window, and the sun splits her face with a diagonal beam. The flowers lie wrapped on the table.

'We used to take that boat out with our daughter when she was only young.' Iris has an accent, but I can't work out what. I hadn't noticed it before. Her r's are sharp. Scottish? American?

'Stopped liking it the older she grew. Seasickness, she said. Never was when she was little.'

The ice cube tinkles in the glass as Iris lowers it back to the side table. 'As for Derek, the more nets he dragged, the less love he had for our own boat. Fishing sucked the joy out of that man.'

Is she lonely? Should I speak? Is she taking me to court?

'I, however, loved that boat.'

'I'm sorry,' I say. 'I'll fix it. I can fix it.'

Iris holds her hands up to quieten me but doesn't speak. Sips her gin, looks out the window.

'You know your father worked for Derek.'

I think it's a question. So I think I should answer. 'Yes.'

'Shame about the farm. Wasn't much of a fisherman either.'

What?

'He and that boong friend of his are lucky Derek gave them the work.'

'Don't say boong.' I wince as I realise I said it myself.

Iris sits up. 'What did you say?'

'I said, don't call them that. They're Noongars.'

'I don't like your tone,' Iris says. 'He was just a boong.'

'Is that why your husband drowned him?' I hurl the words at her without thinking.

In seconds Iris is standing. She grips my arm in a vice, pulls me up. 'Get out,' she hisses. 'Now.'

I clatter down the hallway, stumble down the steps on my sore ankle. Pause and look back as Iris picks up the flowers.

* * *

Dad sees me in the shade of a peppermint tree, a few yards up from Iris' place. Pulls in, opens the door from inside.

'How'd it go?'

I grimace and hold the flowers up.

'That well, eh?'

'Yeah. She threw them out the window. They were too nice to leave so I grabbed them.'

'It'll work out, mate,' Dad says. 'Let's go.'

* * *

Instead of heading straight back out to the highway, Dad pulls in at the Earl of Spencer. We sit out in the beer garden, quenching our thirst. It's early for a beer, but I'm not complaining. We've never really spent time like this before. There's a hesitancy hanging between us. It feels like making a new friend.

'How are you going to do it?' I ask.

Dad scratches his head, stretches. 'Not sure. But I owe it to her to find a way.'

Grandpa is a hard old man. Once he sets his moustache in a line about something, there's not much changing his mind. He doesn't like Noongars. Never has. Does he even know why?

'Are you going to phone him?'

'Yeah. Might have to. Be good to sit down with him.'

'One hell of a drive.'

'Might be worth it.'

'Got a farm to save first.'

On that note, we drain our beers.

We get home to Steve, Joe, Rose and Alby clearing out the shearing shed. Rose folds her elbows on the end of her broom, grins at me.

'It's our birthday next week.'

'Yeah?'

'I have a plan.'

19. Rose

I sit in the hallway, the telephone book open on my knees. I call Jenna first. She's in. She'll ask her folks to come too. Shane next. My heart hammers as I dial his number.

'Rosie girl.' A smile in his voice.

I ask him.

'Of course. Brilliant. Bloody brilliant.'

'Bring your mum.'

'You bet.'

I find the numbers of Frank's mates, Max and Will. It takes a while to work out which Taylor family is Max's.

'He's out. Do you want to leave a message?'

I'll ring back.

Will answers when I ring the Edwards household.

'Rose.' He says it like I am the last person on the whole planet he expected to hear from.

'Yes.'

I explain quickly. He's not sure. He'll try. He's got football. Or maybe his aunty's lunch. Might be babysitting. But he'll try.

Mrs Mengler and her boys.

What about Gary at the Mount Barker hotel? What's his last name?

I find him at the third Mitchell address. His mum asks if I'm his girlfriend. Sounds disappointed. Passes him the phone.

He's in. Says he'll ask some of the boys from the pub.

I flick through the pages, thinking.

Aunty Patsy and Uncle Herbert. I need to go and see them in person.

Dad and Frank are out, but I tell the boys my plan.

'We can't ask for help,' Steve says, wrinkling his brow. 'We just can't. Too embarrassing.'

'I've already done it,' I say. 'Plus. It's a birthday invitation. They can't say no.'

Joe laughs. 'Good on ya, Rose.'

'I'll ring some old mates of Dad's,' Steve says hesitantly. 'The shearing type.'

We're out in the shearing shed when Dad and Frank get back. They're both standing straighter than they have been. Even so, Dad looks like he's going to fall over when I tell them my plan.

'Careful, old man,' Frank laughs, taking Dad's arm. Then he leans on the fence himself, taking his weight off his injured ankle. 'So, ah, who did ya ask?'

'Gary?' Joe's voice is loud. 'You asked *Gary*?'

'Yeah,' I say. 'What's the problem? He's your mate?'

Joe shakes his head and jogs down to the house.

The rest of us shrug. I continue with the list. Dad's not sure we can ask Uncle and Aunty. But I know we can't do it without them.

This is Noongar Boodjar.

* * *

Dad lends us the car, and we drive over there in the afternoon. Uncle Herbert is sitting in his rocking chair, while Aunty Patsy has her easel on the front lawn, paintbrush in hand. She huffs as we push through the front gate, letting us know this is still fragile territory.

Herbert creaks to standing, shuffles down the steps. 'Hey, you kids.'

Frank leans on the porch, chatting with him, while I stand behind Aunty's right shoulder.

'Looks good, Aunty.'

She's painting the Blue Ranges, a dark silhouette against a fiery sky. Sunset. Sunrise?

'Sunrise,' Aunty Patsy murmurs. 'Bina.'

The bush is green-grey, specked with gold.

Aunty tuts, frowns at the painting. Rubs at a brush stroke with her sleeve, blurring and smudging.

'Put the kettle on, bub,' she says, without turning around.

The pipes creak as I fill the kettle. I stand by the stove, waiting for it to boil, thinking, pondering, searching for answers.

Uncle Herbert wanders in, opens a cupboard and pulls out a biscuit tin. Mills & Ware's Milk Arrowroots and a few Mint Slices.

'Has Aunty Patsy ever had an art exhibition?' I ask, breaking an Arrowroot in half.

Uncle Herbert shakes his head. 'No. Very private with her work, that one. Not many people get to see.'

I take the tea out the front, into the afternoon sun. Herbert brings two camp chairs onto the grass, and Frank and I sit side by side on a wide tree stump. We pass milk, sugar, the biscuit tin.

'What you want, unna?' Patsy is more on edge than usual. 'Already seen you today, Frank.'

'We want to invite you to our birthday party,' I say. I take the risk. 'And also, Aunty, we were wondering if you'd like to show some of your paintings?' I squeeze Frank's arm, willing him to trust me. 'We are clearing out the sheds for shearing, and we could make one into a gallery, for everyone to come and see your work.'

Aunty Patsy shifts in her chair. Stays silent. Moves her gaze to the street, watches a woman walk past with her dog.

'We're cleaning up at the farm,' Frank explains. 'Shearing, fencing, getting back on track.'

'You don't need us for that,' Aunty Patsy says.

Uncle Herbert passes the biscuit tin. We munch. I change tack.

'Aunty, years ago our dad asked you to leave, to stop visiting. It wasn't right. We want to welcome you back. As our friends. Our Elders. Please come.'

'You kids can't fix things for him,' Aunty Patsy says, putting her teacup in the camp chair's cup holder. 'That's for him. His job, you know?'

'Yes,' I say. 'We know. But we can help.'

Herbert shuffles his chair forwards. 'What is it you're wanting to do, exactly?'

Frank explains. Camp out in one of the sheds, up before dawn to beat the heat. The shearing sheds set to go. The group split in two: some shearing, some gardening and doing general maintenance. Most of the shearing done by lunchtime, all going to plan. A quick barbecue lunch. Lemonade and beer. Any final jobs done by midafternoon, in time for festivities. Cake. A swim in the dam. Aunty Patsy's art exhibition. Pizza for dinner. Sleeping bags on the shed floor. My bed made up fresh for Aunty Patsy and Uncle Herbert.

He makes it sound good.

'We don't want you to work,' I add. 'We just want you to be there.'

'Good luck stopping Herb shear sheep,' Patsy scoffs. 'It's what he was born to do.'

'Happy to help,' Herbert nods. 'I'll call some of the other blokes too.' He looks to Aunty Patsy. 'Be nice to hang your paintings, love.'

'We'll think about it,' Patsy says sharply. 'You go now, that's enough.'

* * *

We listen to Cat Stevens on the way home. Dad's favourite cassette, *Teaser and the Firecat*. Frank taps his fingers on the steering wheel and I sing along. My brother smiles.

‘Thanks, Rose,’ he says, lifting one hand off the wheel and squeezing my shoulder. ‘Thank you.’

I don’t need to ask what for. I’m just glad he’s still here.

* * *

The phone rings. She’s terse, sharp.

‘Rose,’ says Aunty Patsy. ‘Yes, I’ll do it.’

‘Oh, that’s great—’ I start.

‘Come around after school tomorrow and help me get things together.’

She cuts the line.

* * *

At lunchtime, Jenna asks if she can come to Aunty Patsy’s. We’re sitting at the edge of the oval, passing her sandwich back and forth between us. Tess is wagging, probably pashing Harry in the carpark. I lean back on my hands. I feel protective of what I’ve created with Aunty Patsy and Uncle Herbert.

‘Yes,’ I say. ‘But there’s some things you need to know about Elders.’

* * *

Uncle Herbert pulls into the pick-up zone. Meeak is on the front seat of the Valiant. He pushes her into the back, leans across and opens the passenger door.

‘Hi Uncle, this is my best friend, Jenna. Can she come too?’

Uncle Herbert nods. ‘Yes, yes, in you get.’

We ignore the group of kids pointing and whispering as we get into the car. Tom T. Hall is still in the cassette player. Uncle hums along.

‘How was your day, Uncle?’ Jenna asks, addressing him as I told her to.

‘Good thanks, kiddo,’ he says, pulling onto their street. ‘How about you?’

‘It was okay,’ she says. ‘We had maths. Rose and me don’t like maths much.’

Uncle Herbert doesn’t reply. I want to tell Jenna she doesn’t need to ramble.

‘Here we are then,’ says Uncle, parking up.

The wind chimes tinkle as we open the front door. I’m conscious of the haven I’ve created here. Of the way Meeak licks Jenna’s fingers, and that Jen takes her shoes off even though she wasn’t asked to. Jenna’s hands behind her back, polite.

‘Where’s Aunty Patsy?’

‘Here I am,’ comes a grumbled reply from the other end of the hallway. She steps into the kitchen.

‘Who’s this then?’

I smile apologetically to Jenna. ‘My best friend, Jenna. She wanted to meet you. To help.’

Jen extends her hand as if to shake Aunty’s, decides against it, and performs a dramatic curtsy.

Aunty Patsy laughs, not unkindly. Steps around her. ‘Kettle, Herb.’

‘Already on.’

Aunty lowers herself to the dining table, opens a notebook. ‘How many paintings?’

I hadn’t thought this far ahead. I give Meeak a good scratch behind her ears. Her back leg itches the air.

‘Rose.’ Aunty Patsy presses. ‘How many, eh?’

‘As many as you like?’

‘Well, I’m not going to bring every painting I ever done down there, am I?’

‘You could do,’ says Uncle Herbert.

Aunty Patsy glares at him.

‘Can I see some?’ Jenna asks. ‘Please?’

Aunty Patsy keeps looking into her notebook. Writes something.

Crosses it out. Shakes her head.

'Aunty,' I say gently. 'I'd love to see.'

She pushes back from the table. 'Come.'

* * *

There are paintings spread over almost every surface in the bedroom. On cardboard, canvas, scraps of paper and even pieces of pinewood. Flowers explode out of the grey-green bush, close-up studies of seedpods, leaves and petals sketched over the oil paint or in spaces between. And among it all, words.

Santalum acuminatum—Quandong/Native Peach—Wolgol

Eucalyptus capillosa—Mallee Wandoo—Muruk

Banksia grandis—Bull Banksia—Mungite/Poolgarla

I recognise the handwriting and it hits me all at once. My hand over my mouth, I stumble back into the hallway. Trembling hands, wobbly legs. Inhale. Exhale. Meeak wags her way towards me, licks my ankles.

'Take your time, Rosie, bub,' Aunty Patsy calls from inside the bedroom. 'Plenty of time. Settle into it.'

I step back through the doorway. Jenna is on tiptoe, examining a painting of the paperbark trees that hug the riverbank.

Melaleuca, Myrtaceae—Paperbark Tree—Yourl/Yorral Boorna

Aunty Patsy stands in the centre of the room, her back straight.

'Your mum,' she says softly. 'Your mum and me.' She beckons me over, towards the bed. I run my fingertips over the painting nearest to me. The raised strokes of oil paint. The indents scratched into the paper by your pen.

'We were working together. Documenting the bush. Noongar way and science way. Our way. Together.'

'When?' I whisper.

'Long time. For years. Until your grandpa convinced Eddie that our people are no good. Until Eddie told us not to come back.'

'I'm sorry.'

Aunty sighs. 'Not your fault. But this—' she gestures at the room, the botanical paintings around her '—this was special.'

'Did Grandpa know?'

Aunty Patsy shakes her head.

Why? You followed in his footsteps, and he didn't even know. Maybe wouldn't have seen the value in what you and Aunty Patsy were working on. All because of the colour of her skin.

'I started painting again when she died,' Patsy says. 'Time to get back into it. Carry on the culture. Not the same without her though.'

'What are you going to do with it all?' Jenna asks.

'We were going to make a book. Maybe show the pictures to your grandpa,' Aunty Patsy looks to me. 'Not anymore.'

'You have to do something with it. It's amazing.' I trace your cursive writing, wondering why you never talked about this. 'We can show Grandpa at the exhibition.'

'No.' Patsy speaks sharply. 'No.' She gathers the paintings up, shuffling canvas, bits of wood, scraps of paper. 'Herb, where's that tea?' She ushers us back into the kitchen.

'Did you want to work out which paintings you'll hang, Aunty?' I ask, blowing steam from my cup.

Patsy shifts in her seat, picks up her notebook and holds it to her chest. 'No. Not sure I want to do it after all, bub.'

My heart sinks. I get a sudden urge to phone you, to tell you about the paintings we've found.

'Mum would have loved everyone to see them,' I say. 'And they're hers too.'

'She's not here anymore, lovey,' says Aunty Patsy. Her words hurt.

Uncle Herbert puts his hand on my shoulder. 'Some people don't want to know, don't want to see ... our people. Culture. They aren't open, like you.'

'But they should be,' Jenna says. 'I want my parents to see who you are and what you do. It's …' she struggles for words. 'It's important.'

Patsy assesses Jenna. 'Yes,' she says. 'It is.' The notebook is still firmly against her chest.

'She'll think about it,' Uncle Herbert says, winking.

'I'll clear the space for you anyway, Aunty,' I say. 'If you want to bring them on the day, it'll be ready.'

Aunty coughs, frowns, changes the subject. 'What about your bees?' she asks. 'Honey been harvested yet?'

The hive is up near some big old gums. Makes enough honey to get us through the year, and to share some with the Bettses.

'Not yet,' I say. 'Joe takes care of the bees.'

'Well, the moojar trees won't be flowering for much longer,' says Aunty. 'Tell him it's time.'

'What does the tree have to do with it?' Jenna asks.

'Like our calendar, bub,' Aunty Patsy explains. 'We look around and we know the seasons are changing.'

* * *

Dad comes to pick us up. He stiffens as he walks through the doorway.

'Hello,' he calls in a forced cheery voice. He pats Uncle Herbert on the back. 'How are you, Uncle?' Nods to Aunty Patsy. 'And you, Aunty?'

Jenna and I grab our bags. We're saying our goodbyes, about to go when Aunty Patsy clears her throat.

'Don't you forget, Eddie, alright?'

'I won't Aunty. I promise.' Dad reaches across and squeezes her hand. 'I promise.'

I sit with Jenna in the back on the way home. 'What do you have to do, for the Elders, Mr Tetley?' she asks.

A pause.

'I have to set some things right, Jenna,' he says.

* * *

The Russells phone to check that we are on track with the farm. Dad promises them everything will be in working order. Lots of promises to keep. We've got two weeks left before the month is up. If things go to plan this weekend, we are going to be okay.

'Aunty Patsy showed me some paintings today,' I say to Dad after he hangs up the phone. I can still see the curve of your handwriting, the joy in the strokes of Aunty Patsy's paintbrush. I know Grandpa needs to see it too. He needs to be at this exhibition. He needs to see what could have been—and what could still be.

I expect Dad to disengage, but instead he says, 'They're amazing, aren't they?'

'I didn't know Mum did that.'

'There was a lot she did that you didn't get to see.'

I swallow. 'I'm helping Aunty Patsy make an exhibition. Here. In one of the sheds. I think Grandpa needs to be there.'

Dad nods, slowly, processing.

'I'll phone him tonight.'

joe never wears a beekeeper suit he
says it's about talking to the bees
'if you respect them, tell them what you're doing,
they don't mind'
he became the beekeeper
when you became
sick
and every year in the late summer
the kitchen bench fills with
mismatched jars of
honey.

Joe, standing quietly beside the hives. The bees swarm around him, brushing his face and arms. Some land on him, but none sting. Joe smiles. He respects this land, you can see it in his careful movements, his gaze lifting to the gums above him, back to the hive. He takes a smoking pot and blows a little smoke around, encouraging the bees to move away. With nimble fingers he uses a screwdriver to lift a frame from the hive, checking for white caps of wax to tell him the frame is full of honey. Gently, he brushes the bees from the frame. They hum around him. Joe puts the frame in a box on the back of the ute and repeats the process, talking to the bees as they land on him. I watch him, imagining you and Aunty Patsy gathering the honey. I wonder about the conversation that passed between you when there was no one but the bees to hear.

When Joe's done, we roll back to the house, setting up to remove the wax and strain the honey.

'Want to learn how to make a honey cake,' Joe says, lifting the tip of a knife to uncap one of the frames. The smell of honey is sweet and thick. Joe passes me the knife so he can put the frame into the old twenty-gallon drum that has been converted into a spinner. Golden liquid oozes from the frame.

'The bees have been busy.'

'They have.'

'Enough to share with the shearers?'

Joe gets a fresh tray. 'That's a great idea.'

We fill the jars and I tie some ribbon around the lids. Alby comes in when we are nearly done, picks up a piece of discarded wax and moulds it between his fingers.

'Can I have a taste?'

'Yeah, mate, go grab a teaspoon,' says Joe.

The honey tastes like hope.

20. Frank

We are finally getting into gear. I clean the shearing board, tinker around with the wool press, making sure it's clean, lubricated and good to go. On Thursday, Joe and I go to the nursery. We get bags of mulch, a bulk pack of gardening gloves, blades for the brush cutter, new secateurs and some packets of everlasting seeds, punnets of coastal daisies and native wisteria. We're loitering around native ground coverings when one of the gardening staff approaches us.

'You two need a hand?'

'Nah, thanks mate,' says Joe.

He nods. Hovers in the adjacent aisle. I catch him peering through a gap in the terracotta pots, straight at me. He lifts his finger, runs it along the pots, as if he's looking for something.

'You right?' I ask.

The man startles. Clears his throat. 'Beg your pardon,' he says. 'But are you a relative of the late Elena Tetley?'

Joe looks up from where he's squatted, an Albany woolly bush in one hand, snake bush in the other.

'Uh,' I say. 'Yeah, we are.'

The gardener steps around to face us. 'You're her sons?'

'Yes,' Joe says, standing up. 'Joe and Frank.'

The man's face splits into a smile. 'Ah,' he says. 'Joe and Frank. I'm Peter.' He stands quite still, gazing at us, for a long moment.

'Sorry,' he says, coming to. 'I always served your mum here. Her and little Rose. How is Rose?'

'Good,' I say. I forgot Rose would come to the nursery with you. It was your special outing, just for the girls. Rose had bright yellow welly boots for gardening in, and a pair of children's gardening gloves with sunflowers on them.

'They were quite the duo,' reminisces Peter. 'How's the garden looking?'

'Oh, well,' Joe says. 'It's a mess. We're fixing it up.'

'Can I … do you … do you need a hand?' Peter fiddles with the zip on his jacket.

'Sure, mate, if you'd like to come,' Joe says. 'You'd be most welcome if you have time.'

'Plenty of it,' Peter says. 'An old fella like me doesn't have much on the calendar. Let me know where and when. I'll be there.'

* * *

Joe says he's meeting someone for lunch, sends me to the supermarket with a list. Bread. Lemonade. Beer. Chips. Sausages. Balloons. Down York Street, past the sandwich bar. Hands in my pockets, limping a little.

'Hey!'

I turn. It's Sprite Guy, his backpack hunched on his shoulders and his eyes narrowed. Three other blokes pull up beside him on their skateboards.

The set of his shoulders says it all.

He's on me in seconds.

I could take him, but not his three cronies as well, and not with my sprained ankle and still-healing skin. I let his fist knock me to the pavement. Close my eyes as their sneakers kick my ribs, my knees, my chin. I breathe as slow and steady as I can, keeping my body loose and open to the blows. When they're done, and I can hear a few of the cronies already rolling down the street, I lick my cracked lips and speak.

'Hey.' I rummage in my pocket. Squint through swollen eyes. He's standing over me, contemplating another kick. I wait. He steps back, uncertain.

‘I’m sorry about your board.’ I hold out twenty bucks. ‘Get a new one. And tell your mate I’m sorry.’

Sprite Guy snatches the note from my fist and spits on the pavement. Then he’s gone.

I limp to the shops, lean on the trolley as I work my way through the list. I must look pretty ghastly, because everyone stares. One little girl walks right up to me and taps me on the back.

‘What happened to you? Did you get hit by a car?’

‘Yeah,’ I say. ‘You should see the car …’

Her mum frowns at me, pulls her daughter away.

I don’t have quite enough after giving the twenty to Sprite Guy. I tell the check-out chick we can do without the lemonade. Back out front, I sit on the wall, bags piled beside me. Everything hurts. My mouth tastes metallic. One of my knees is swelling. It hurts to breathe. But strangely, I feel at peace. Probably deserved that. At least Sprite Guy can get a new board now.

When I get sick of waiting, I stroll towards the pub. Can’t see Joe’s car anywhere. Where’s he parked, the bastard? Past the university, around the corner and through the park. There’s his car. Parked off to the side of the street, facing a cul-de-sac. The handles on the plastic bags are stretched to breaking point, and my whole body feels like a bruise. I make it to Joe’s car, drop the bags by the bonnet. Nearly jump out of my skin when I realise Joe’s already inside. Gary is sitting in the front passenger seat next to him, laughing.

‘Oi,’ I say, rapping on the window.

Joe jumps and whacks his elbow on the horn.

Gary’s face is wide with shock. He flings the door open. ‘Shit, Frank, what happened to you?’

‘It’s nothing,’ I say.

‘Bloody hell,’ says Joe. ‘Get in.’

I grab the bags and sit in the back. Joe moves the gardening supplies to the boot.

'I leave you for half an hour and you can't not get in a fight,' Joe's going on. 'What is it with you?'

'It wasn't a fight,' I say.

'What was it then?' He snaps.

'Karma.'

Joe frowns.

'I'll get out,' Gary says. 'I'll leave you to it. I'll find my own way.' His words rush out after each other.

'Don't be silly,' Joe says, starting the car. He pulls up outside the chemist. Leaves the car running.

'The other guy is fine, by the way,' I tell Gary.

'Right,' he says.

Joe comes back with Panadol, bandages and Betadine. Throws them on the back seat. His brow is furrowed and there are beads of sweat running down his forehead.

'You didn't need to,' I say. 'But thank you.'

The silence feels awkward for some reason, so I keep talking. 'You two had lunch? Where'd you go?'

Still, nothing. Joe's fingers are wildly tapping the steering wheel.

Oh.

Oh.

When we get to Mount Barker, Joe turns onto Ormond Road, pulls onto Hassell. Stops out the front of a red brick and tile home.

'Speak to you soon,' he says to Gary, keeping his attention on his steering wheel.

'Thanks for the lift,' Gary says. 'See you soon?'

Joe nods.

'Ah, see ya, Frank. Get better.'

'Cheers mate.' I smile at him as he gets out of the car.

Joe pulls back out, weaves his way back to the highway. I'm still in the back seat, and we still aren't talking.

* * *

On the edge of Mount Barker, Joe pulls into a truck bay. When I don't move immediately, he snaps. 'Are you getting in the front or what?'

I scramble into the front and slam the passenger door. Joe pulls out again without looking. A truck slows behind us, and the driver leaves his hand on the horn for a good minute.

'Are you—?'

'Don't,' Joe interrupts.

'Was just going to ask if you're okay.'

'Yes. Are you? What *happened*?'

I shrug. 'Got what I deserved.'

Joe slaps the radio on with his palm. Joni Mitchell fills the car with her shrill voice. Joe turns the volume down.

'Don't tell Dad,' he says as we pull up at home.

'I won't.'

* * *

We're unpacking the gardening supplies into the top shed when Rose and Alby get home from school. I tell her about Peter, and her face falls.

'You went to the nursery without me? *We* did the garden up,' Rose says, gesturing down to your garden bed. 'That was us. that was …' She stops, shuffles the weight of her schoolbag on her shoulders, sighs. 'Sorry,' she says. 'It doesn't matter.'

'Nah, sorry, Rose,' Joe says. 'We didn't think. Just trying to get everything ready for your master plan.'

'We can go back, if you want,' I add. 'Is there anything else you want to plant?'

Rose shrugs. 'I'm glad Peter's coming.'

We're loading up the fridge with supplies when Dad rolls down the driveway. He's been out catching up with some of the old shearing crew.

'G'day you lot,' he says. 'Looks fantastic out there. Good on you.'

'Hey Dad,' says Rose. 'Do you reckon Grandpa will come?'

Dad smiles wanly. 'I'm not sure, love. I hope so.'

21. Rose

That evening I stay up well after the sun has gone down. I scrub the smaller tool shed up near the one Frank used to sleep in. I sweep the dirt floor, gather the sticks and honky nuts. Draw the cobwebs out of corners with a broom handle, wipe dust off the awnings.

After school on Wednesday, Jenna and I went to the hardware store. We found long metal hooks, perfect for hanging Aunty Patsy's paintings. In the op shop we found some old doilies, extra plates and cups, a nice vase and some wooden chairs. I called Steve from the pay phone on Hassell Street. We stacked all the things into his kombi. Steve backs it into the shed now, helps me lift everything out.

'Want a hand setting up?'

'Nah, I'm good, actually. Thanks though.'

I take my time. Cover a milk crate with the biggest doily, place the vase on top. Drag an old wooden bench out of the other shed, wipe it down and line up the cups. On close inspection, they need a good wash, so I restack them to take down to the house. I lay the hooks on the table, ready for Aunty Patsy.

* * *

I get up early before school, walk the perimeter of our property. I pick armfuls of bottlebrush and mallee honey-myrtle. Take it all back to the shed. Exhibition space, I'm calling it now. I arrange some of the flowers in the vase. Tie the rest into small bunches with brown string and hang a few bouquets from the rafters. I hope Aunty Patsy likes it. I hope she comes.

* * *

I call her from the school office at lunchtime. I tell Mrs Shepperton, the office lady, that I need to call my aunty. That it's urgent. Nope, definitely can't wait. She watches me out of the corner of her eye, as I try to remember the number. I step to the right, so the wall blocks me from view.

'Aunty,' I whisper. 'Aunty Patsy, it's Rose.'

'Who's there?' Aunty barks into the phone. 'Speak up.'

'It's me, Rose,' I say a little louder. 'Just wanted to see how you're feeling about the exhibition, Aunty.'

Patsy sighs. 'I don't know, Rose,' she says. 'I'm very busy and all that. I don't know.'

'Whatever is keeping you busy, I can help, Aunty,' I say. 'We'd love to have you at our place tomorrow. The exhibition space is all set up. If you want it. No pressure.'

'I'll see, bub,' Aunty Patsy says as Mrs Shepperton steps around the corner, hand out to take the phone.

'Bye, Aunty,' I say.

'Bye, Rose.'

* * *

Jenna comes straight to our place after school. Dad and Steve are out in the paddocks with a few blokes who have already arrived. Joe and Frank are getting the gear ready in the shed. We're switching our school uniforms for old t-shirts, shorts and boots, when the sound of a gunshot cracks through the air.

Jen frowns at me. 'What was that?'

With a sinking feeling, I know. Some of the sheep were so flyblown, they were never going to make it. I still can't believe we let things get this bad. What a waste of life.

Alby sticks his head around the door. 'Sad,' he says.

I grimace. 'Not very pleasant.'

'Are they *killing* sheep?' Jenna squeaks. 'I thought we came here to *shear*.'

'We're all going to hell,' Alby says earnestly. 'Will the sheeps get a funeral?'

'If you want, buddy,' I say. 'But we have to shear the rest of them first.'

'Some get a haircut, and some get to die,' he ponders.

'That's life, I guess. Let's go.'

* * *

The men have gathered around the top shed, getting everything ready for morning. There's already a mix of swags and sleeping bags laid out on the floor. I recognise some of Dad's old mates, people I remember from barbecues when we were small, before you got sick. The farming community used to catch up once a month, and we'd always join in, taking turns visiting each other's vast, dry properties. These must be the guys Steve called. Some of these men have kids at my school. I didn't think they'd show up, or care about us, the troublesome Tetleys.

'Is that young Rose?' One of the men wanders over, ruffles my hair like I'm an infant. I bristle. 'Thanks for organising this, you superstar.'

Oh. That's nice.

The men sharpen the combs and cutters, getting everything ready for the morning. There's a woman in there too, with biceps like a watermelon.

'Who's that?' I ask Frank, as he comes out of the shed.

He grins. 'Remember James, the shearer from near Cranbrook? His partner. She's tougher than the rest of us put together.'

I like that.

Shane pulls up in his black ute before Jenna's parents arrive with the pizza. We sit out on the grass as the night sky creeps in, passing pizza boxes and drinking beer. Just as we're getting ready for our early night, Frank's mates Max and Will arrive.

Frank's face says he wasn't expecting them. He smiles, hides it, then smiles again, as if deciding there's no need to play cool. Men are so weird.

'Hey,' he says, grabbing each of them a beer out of the ice bucket. 'Thanks for coming.'

They roll out their swags on the grass, shake hands with a few of the blokes they seem to know.

Dad's wandering around, making sure everyone has what they need for the night. He seems equally happy at the turnout as he is stressed.

'Thanks, everyone, for coming,' he shouts, banging on the shed door to announce his speech. 'It means the world. Really. Now no more beers. We're up early tomorrow.' He laughs and catches my eye, and in that moment, all of this is worth it.

* * *

Five in the morning, the alarm goes off. Jenna rolls into me, groans.

'Can't the sheep go without a haircut?' she mumbles into my shoulder.

I gently push her off, stumble out into the kitchen. Line up the cups, boil the kettle, four times. Fill the thermoses. Instant coffee, fresh milk, sugar. Jenna and Alby are still half asleep as they stagger behind me, loading up the car. Frank comes out, struggling to get his arms through his t-shirt sleeves. Jenna laughs and sets him free, kissing him briefly. We drive up to the shed where the crew slept. Dad's already there, banging his wake-up call on the tin.

'Coffee,' I call. That gets them stirring.

Bleary-eyed men, sitting up in sleeping bags.

Steve slides the kombi door open, climbs out. Joe and Alby clamber up the hill. Shane takes his cup of coffee, salutes me like an army officer.

'Thanks, Madame.'

Max rubbing his eyes, Will peeling a banana.

'Gotta eat right away, in the morning.'

'Still dark, mate, relax,' Max mutters.

Before the sun, the air is brisk. There are still stars in the sky. The shearing team are setting up their hand pieces. The sound of the sheep is almost comedic. I wonder if they know what they are in for. When we were little, we picked up the wool in exchange for lollies. That'll be Alby this time. The last few shears I've been at school, but today I'm roustabouting. I'll collect the finished fleece, bundle it up, back legs to front legs, then throw it onto the wool table. We'll take off any dirty or stained wool and sort the good wool into parts—head, belly, legs. I haven't been a rousey before, but I've watched my brothers, year after year.

As the sun rises, Frank loads the pack into the wool press, clipping down the edges and making sure it's even. He closes the sides and back of the press. It's ready.

The most important part: music. It's tradition to start with Slim Dusty's 'Shearing Shed Blues'.

Dad whistles for the dogs. Shane jumps on his dirt bike, and so does Max. Joe walks calmly beside them, and while the others shout and bark and snap, he helps guide the sheep into the big pen outside the shearing shed. Shane leaps off his bike and pushes some of the sheep into the shed and the smaller pen.

Dad, Steve and the other shearers stand ready. They each grab a sheep, and the wool cutters buzz almost as loud as the music. My heart is hammering. The beginning always feels like the start of a performance, when you're nervous if you'll remember your lines. And this time, I've got a new role.

'Rose,' Steve grunts. He's squatted next to his sheep, wool falling around him. I grab the fleece, try tuck back legs to front, but it unravels as I heave it onto the wool table.

'S'orright, love,' Dad calls. 'Plenty of time to practise.'

Frank's expertly bundling his wool. It lands in form on the table. He smacks his gum, winks at me. For a bloke who is covered in bandages, he's making it look easy. Cocky bastard. Janelle, with the watermelon muscles, is shearing twice as fast as the men. I stare as she squats and sweats and grunts and pushes her shorn sheep down the race. Jenna and Alby are sweeping, collecting stray bits of wool, adding it to the press. My muscles ache. Who knew wool was so heavy?

We stop at nine for smoko, and a white Holden rumbles down the driveway. Uncle Herbert is in the front passenger seat, another Noongar man driving and a guy about my age in the back. The other shearers shake Uncle's hand. I notice they're respectful, passing him coffee, a cigarette.

'He's a damn good shearer,' Dad mutters to me. 'And they know it.'

Where's Aunty Patsy? Will she come?

We're about to start at it again when another car pulls up. Gary gets out, lifts a tray off the passenger seat. Slides on the gravel, nearly loses the whole lot.

'I, uh, brought jam donuts,' he stammers, looking around at the sweating shearers. 'Thought you might need them.'

The crew whoop and whistle.

Joe is off talking to the sheep, soothing them with his gentle voice. 'Your mate's here,' I call. 'He brought donuts.'

Joe nods, stays put.

I lick sugar off my hands. Chug water from an old milk bottle, pass it to Jenna.

The music is cranked and we're off again. Every now and then I poke my head out of the shed to see if Aunty Patsy is here, but there's no sign of her.

* * *

At midday, Dad fires up the barbecue, chucks the sausages and onion on. Mrs Mengler and her boys have arrived. They're working their way down the driveway, weeding the edges. Uncle Herbert is standing with a ring of the shearers around him. He's talking, softer than the rest of them, but they're all listening, nodding. I sidle up to him, wait for a break in the conversation.

'What's up, bub?' he asks.

'Do you think Aunty Patsy will come?'

He sighs. 'I reckon so, love. In her time.'

I cross my fingers and go to check again. Even if she does come, there's no sign of Grandpa either. I tell myself there's still tomorrow. This isn't over yet.

* * *

By the afternoon break, I've perfected bundling the wool and throwing it on the press. We've done three hundred and fifty sheep. One hundred and fifty to go. Dad calls me over.

'You've done amazing, love,' he says. 'Why don't you and Jenna take off, let us finish up here. You two go get into the garden.'

Part of me wants to stay and finish what we started, but a lot of me has been aching to set your garden straight again. And I don't want Mrs Mengler and her boys to get to it first. We go via the garden shed, taking mulch and some of the seedlings in the wheelbarrow, ignoring our aching muscles.

There's a man standing at the garden's edge, hands clasped behind his back. For a second I think it's Grandpa, but then I realise.

Peter turns, smiles. 'Oh my goodness, you've grown.'

I don't know what to say. I'm thrown into memory. Us walking around the nursery, dreaming of fields of flowers. Peter, helping lift things into the back of the car. The smell of soil, and blood and bone, the windows down on the way home. Our hands in the earth, brushing each other's fingers as we dig a hole for our newest addition. You, squeezing my gloved hand between yours. Dirt on your cheeks, up my forearms.

'It's Peter, from the nursery,' Peter says, gently bringing me to.

'Oh, I know.' I realise I've been facing him with a blank stare. 'I know.'

'I hope it's okay I've come,' he says. 'I always wanted to see your mum's garden.'

I smile sadly. 'Shame we let it go so much.'

'Oh, I don't know,' he says. 'There's still a lot of beauty under there.'

He spots the Papa Meilland rosebush. 'I remember your mum told me this was dying.'

'It was,' I say. 'At one point.'

'May I?' he gestures to the bush.

'Sure.'

Peter wades through weeds, crouches at the rosebush. Inhales, deeply. 'What a beautiful late bloom.'

Jenna has been quietly pulling weeds.

'This is my best friend, Jenna,' I say now.

Peter bows, 'Lovely to meet you.'

'So, Rose,' Jenna asks. 'What's the vision?'

We're plotting out plants and flowers, when a croaky voice says, 'Bit of Koorin would be nice in there. Starflower, you mob call it.'

Patsy.

'Aunty,' I say, jumping up. 'I'm so glad you came.'

She's standing at the edge of the garden bed, arms folded.

'We getting this exhibition going then, or what?'

I'm too overjoyed to fret at her brisk tone.

'Let's do it,' I say, wiping my hands on my shorts.

'Yeah, well, your little mate will be back soon,' Aunty Patsy says, nodding in turn to Jen and Peter. 'This is a job for Rosie and me.'

* * *

Aunty pants as we walk up the driveway to where she's parked her car. She gestures at the passenger seat. The back of the car is filled with paintings.

'Which shed then, unna?' she asks as we climb in.

I direct her to the exhibition space. She backs up to the shed door. I gaze self-consciously at my set-up, hoping it's okay.

Aunty Patsy lifts a small tin drum out of the car. She places it in the centre of the dirt floor. Strikes a match, tosses it in. Smoke rises and the smell of balga and peppermint fills the shed. It's fire season, and we can't light fires elsewhere on the farm. But I know Aunty has permission that runs deeper than council rules. She takes the end of a small branch out of the fire, blows on the tip to reduce the flame to smoking leaves. She taps her chest, her arms, her legs, lifts each foot, wafting the smoke around her body. Beckons to me, and I remember from last time. I stand in front of Aunty, my arms lifted slightly. She circles the smoking branch around my limbs. Then she walks around the shed, tapping the walls down.

Once the exhibition space has been cleansed, Aunty starts unpacking the car. I take a stack of paintings and lay them carefully on the table.

'No one's going to see them like that,' she says sharply.

'Oh, I know, Aunty, I thought you might like to arrange them yourself.'

'Put them wherever.'

I hang the paintings, wiping dust from them as we go. Aunty switches a few around, but mainly she leaves me to it. I get the feeling it's not because this doesn't matter, but because it matters a lot.

'Who will come and look then, eh?' she asks, once it's all set. 'Everyone seems pretty busy to me.'

'They've just about finished shearing,' I say. 'We only have the garden to do, it won't take long.'

Just as I say it, Alby stumbles in.

'Hello little fella,' Aunty Patsy says.

'What's in here?' He wipes dirt and sweat off his brow, looking so much like his older brothers.

Seeing Aunty take his hand, crouching next to him, brings a lump to my throat.

'Your mum and I,' Aunty is saying. She looks up at me. 'Oh Rose, get it together love. No good carrying on like a pork chop.' But she stands up to give me a firm hug. 'We're done in here, bub,' she says to me. 'You did a good job. A really good job. Go on, I'll be here with your brother.'

Outside, I sit for a moment, leaning my back against the tin shed. I can feel you all around me, humming in the air.

* * *

Down at the garden, Gary is helping Peter and Jenna. They've pruned the rosebush back and pulled the weeds that were climbing high around the other plants. The sunflowers and poppies have self-seeded and grow wild, filling the gaps. I'm glad they've been left this way. The lavender hedge has been trimmed, and Jenna is cutting back the daisy bush. After seeing Aunty Patsy's paintings—the spiky, scrawled, Australian bush—I wonder why we planted things that aren't from here. I've never seen you draw anything but native species, but our own garden could be from an English church.

I suppose it's one of those things I'll never get to ask you.

I'm still getting used to that.

Peter is training the new native wisteria plant onto the trellis by the gate.

'What would you like to do with these newcomers?' he asks, gesturing to the packets of everlasting seeds and some coastal daisy seedlings.

We plant the seeds down the sides of the driveway, in the freshly turned soil. The coastal daisies go in an empty corner of the garden bed. Up on the hill, the pen is filling with shorn sheep. Mrs Mengler's son Andrew is mowing the paddocks surrounding the house, and Max and Will have been working on the ones lining the perimeter. The farm looks different. Alive.

I think you'd like it.

22. Frank

sweaty bodies working in sync
the rhythm of each other's breath
the beat of the doobie brothers
my brother
cranks the music—sweet maxine
five hundred sheep
wool, urine and
shit
dave has no front teeth but he's
a man to be respected
the way he turns those sheep around
almost as fast as uncle herbert
dad is shouting
ten more, boys
countdown like it's
new year's eve
five-four-three-two
one.

23. Rose

dad's in the shed with aunty
one foot in the doorway when i see them
quietly step
        back
they're standing side-by-side and silent.
then:
    'mallee wandoo,' says dad
'muruk,' replies aunty.
        hushed voices
        this matters.
the boys traipsing over from the shearing shed
boots kicking up cut grass
shane pulls out a harmonica
plays a few bars then
puts it away
they are met with the smell of peppermint and balga
the sight of the bush and your
handwriting.

Uncle Herbert stands next to the shed doorway with me, smiling broadly.

'Real good, that is,' he says.

Mrs Mengler and her boys come to the door, peer inside.

'What is it?' Mrs Mengler asks, her forehead creasing.

'An art exhibition,' I say. 'It's amazing, go and look.'

'What language is this?' I hear her ask.

Aunty Patsy doesn't reply straight away. Gives her time to let it all sink in. I stay where I am, watching people experience your work. Aunty Patsy is filling the room. Both with her art, and her power. As people realise what they're looking at, they seek her out, ask her questions.

'Noongar way, white fella way, science way,' she says.

It's just wrapping up when Aunt Lisa's car rolls down the driveway. Alby is blowing a party whistle, and it flies out of his mouth as he gasps.

'Blimey,' Dad says, lowering his beer.

Next to her in the front seat, is Grandpa. Sofia, Amanda and Nonna are in the back. Aunt Lisa drives slowly, eyeballing each of us as she passes. She parks up near the exhibition shed.

'Nice of you to wait for us,' she says. 'We had a long way to come, obviously.'

'Happy birthday, you two,' says Nonna, leaning around Aunt Lisa to clasp my hand in hers. She kisses my cheeks. 'Seventeen, beautiful girl.'

Woah. Seventeen. My first birthday without you.

'Not till Monday,' I say.

Nonna flaps her hands. 'All week is a party.'

Grandpa makes his way towards me, smiling. Wraps his arms around me. 'Hello, birthday girl.' I squeeze him back. There's so much I want to say, but I know he has to see for himself.

Nonna has brought cake, a huge sponge from the Re Store in Leederville. Dad lights the candles and Frank and I face each other, the cake between us. I always hated sharing a birthday with my brother. Now,

I have to stop myself from reaching my hands through the flames to touch him, be sure he's still really there.

'Your hair's gonna catch on fire,' he says.

They sing and we blow, half the cake each. One flame remains, right in the middle.

You.

Frank catches my eye. I wonder if he's thinking the same thing. Then he puffs his cheeks up dramatically and blows it out. Wax is dripping on the cake. We take turns to slice it, and careful not to touch the bottom, make our wish.

Fluffy sponge, the middle filled with jam and cream. Generous slabs, passed around on paper plates. Chunks of ice from the esky cooling warm beer in plastic cups. A sense of achievement. Once the cake's been eaten, some of the blokes set up for a game of footy in the freshly mowed paddocks. Jenna's keen to swim in the dam. Frank goes with her. Uncle Herbert is sitting on a chair, shaded by a peppermint tree. Aunty Patsy is stacking paper plates, wiping cream from the knife. Nonna is collecting cups, moving around Aunty without talking to her. I want to take over, encourage these elderly women to sit in the shade together. Where's Grandpa? I need to get him to see the paintings.

I'm hovering around when Aunt Lisa drags me away to her car. She rummages in the glove box, her pearls tinkling against each other, and gives me a small, neatly wrapped gift. The pink paper is tucked and folded at the corners, sticky tape perfectly straight. I'm overwhelmed by the gesture, but also confused. Smothered, cornered, as if I'm in trouble somehow. My fault that Aunt Lisa didn't arrive earlier.

'Well, open it, Rose,' she says.

'You don't want me to wait till the day?'

'Don't think we'll be down here that long.'

'Of course. Thanks.'

I carefully lift a corner, not wanting to tear the paper. Inside is a worn cardboard box. Strange. Aunt Lisa isn't one for second-hand. Was always insulted and unsettled when we gave her dresses from second-hand stores, or vases and ceramics from car boot sales. 'Nothing wrong with giving something an extended life,' you would say. 'Second-hand and given with love means more than a shiny gift without thought.' But both of you would be a little disappointed when gifts were exchanged on Christmas. You'd have fancy new clothes in all the wrong colours and sizes. Aunt Lisa would have a trinket you'd chosen for reasons she couldn't understand, even when you tried to explain. Sentimentality wasn't her forte.

So. This small, worn box. It's a surprise.

Inside is a thin silver bracelet. It isn't a perfect oval, and it's got small scuff marks in places. It catches the sun and I blink.

'Your mum gave that to me,' Aunt Lisa says. 'For my seventeenth birthday.'

I can't speak.

'Here.' She gently clasps the bracelet around my wrist. 'Happy birthday.'

'Thank you,' I whisper.

'You're welcome.' Aunt Lisa swats a fly away from her face. 'Gawd, it's so darn hot.'

We walk back down the driveway. I stare at the bracelet on my arm. It's the nicest thing I've ever owned.

'Where did Mum get it from?'

'The jewellery shop in Nedlands. We used to walk past it on our way home. I'd always stop there and look in the window. Your mum would be ahead, telling me to hurry up. I didn't think she even knew what I was looking at, but she did. She bought the very one I always wanted.'

'Thank you,' I say again.

Aunt Lisa nods. 'Take care of it.'

I notice just before we stumble upon them. Grandpa and Nonna are about to step into the exhibition space. Aunty Patsy is entering from the other side.

'Come and see what we did to Mum's garden,' I say to Aunt Lisa.

* * *

In the shed: one man, two women. Only one of them from here.

Menang Goreng Noongar Boodjar.

The name for this place.

The tin walls creak and crack in the late summer sun. A storm is brewing.

I hope they see it, in the paper, the canvas, the ink and charcoal smudges. The proof of connection, collaboration, that could have been generations earlier.

I loiter outside, giving space for words that I can't say.

Nonna steps out first, into the sunlight. Aunty Patsy behind her.

Through the doorway, I see Grandpa. Hands clasped behind his back. Taking in something you never got the chance to tell him.

* * *

I'm sitting in the shade with Aunty Patsy and Uncle Herbert when Alby comes and plonks himself in Aunty's lap. He's taken a real liking to her.

'Aunty,' he says, playing with a beaded bracelet on her wrist. 'Tell me about Bert.'

Aunty Patsy blinks. 'Why is that, love?'

'Because I'm named after him,' Alby says matter of factly. 'Did you know? Albert. Bert.'

My heart is in my throat. Aunty Patsy's face can't settle on an emotion. Her wrinkles keep moving until Uncle Herbert takes her hand.

'That's real nice, that is,' he says.

* * *

When night falls, the party really begins. The shearing shed becomes a dance floor, the speakers blaring J.J. Cale. When 'After Midnight' comes on, Jenna grabs my hand and draws me into the throng of bodies, wiggling and twisting, laughing and spilling drinks. Alby is jumping up and down, Cheezels on each of his fingers. We're drunk on warm beer, dragging aching bodies into dance moves. We can't stop, or the exhaustion will catch up. Gary is tearing up the dance floor and Joe is bootscooting next to him. Dad's stepping his farm boots back and forth, dust covering his legs. He's grinning, a cigarette lazily in his hand. I even spot Uncle Herbert in there, and his shuffled dance moves fill me with joy.

* * *

I wake early, throw off my sleeping bag. The shed is full of snoring. Even Jenna, in between me and Frank, is still fast asleep with her mouth wide open. Aunty Patsy is in the exhibition space, Aunt Lisa is beside her. Sofia is there too, pulling at her arm.

'Mummy, I'm hungry,' she whines.

'I'm busy, Sofia,' Aunt Lisa says. 'Be quiet or go outside.'

Sofia scowls.

'There's lots of food down at the house, Sofia,' I say. 'Go down and have a look. I'm sure Alby is up, he can show you.'

Sofia saunters out of the shed.

Aunt Lisa looks at me with wide eyes. 'Your mum ...' She waves her arm at the paintings around us. 'And Patsy ...' her voice is incredulous.

'I know.'

'I'll buy one,' Aunt Lisa says urgently. 'I want to take one home. Can I buy one?'

'They're not for sale,' Aunty Patsy says. 'Sorry.'

'But, but I *want* one. This'—she gestures—'this is my sister.'

Aunty Patsy turns away, readjusts a vase of flowers. Aunt Lisa paces the shed, winding her long pearl necklace around her finger. She must've had it fixed.

'Which one you want, then?' Aunty Patsy asks, not looking at Lisa.

'Any of them,' Aunt Lisa says. 'I'll give you whatever you want for it, too. Five hundred bucks. My pearls, even.' She untangles her finger from the string around her neck.

Aunty Patsy catches my eye. Almost smiles. Winks.

'Yes, alright then. Those pearls will do nicely. Take your pick.'

Aunt Lisa whips the necklace off, hands it to Aunty Patsy. She takes a painting from the wall. *Banksia grandis—Bull Banksia—Mungite/Poolgarla.* Your sketches overlap Aunty Patsy's strong strokes of colour. And Aunt Lisa cries. She holds the painting up to her face, wraps her arms around it like she's holding you.

'Careful,' Patsy says sharply. She pats Aunt Lisa on the back. I notice she's already put the pearls on. She winks at me, and I know this exchange wasn't really about the pearls for Aunty Patsy. I help her load up the car.

'Good your grandpa come and see,' she says, stacking paintings in the boot. 'He feel it, I think. Made him stop and think. He talked politely, you know. Asked about our language.'

I don't ask about the book, or anything else. I think maybe this is enough, just for now.

'Come stay soon,' Aunty Patsy says. 'Do some more painting. Together.'

24. Frank

When the phone rings the next morning, Dad gets me to answer it, thinking it'll be a birthday call. We've just finished eating pancakes for breakfast, a birthday tradition, and Rose and Alby have taken the day off school.

'Is Frank there?' I recognise the voice immediately. Iris.

'Yes, I'm here.'

'Oh. Good. You got time to come meet me today?'

I had been hoping for a surf or a skate with Max and Will, then a quiet joint. But I reckon this might be more important, especially if it keeps me out of jail.

'Yep,' I say. 'Where?'

Dad insists on driving me, but he stays in the car. 'Here if you need me,' he says, winding down the window.

Iris is standing in the garage. *Gypsy* is in there. Everything in the cabin has been reduced to a gaping black hole and a pile of melted mess. Structurally, the boat seems to be okay. Iris smokes a cigarette, blows the smoke in my direction. She doesn't say hello.

'You got much money, kid?'

'Uhh.'

'Didn't think so.' She taps ash onto the concrete. Traces her finger along the dusty hull. 'Court would really screw you over.'

'Yeah.' Where is she going with this?

Iris does another lap of the boat. Lights a second cigarette. 'Here's what we're going to do. You're going to fix it. You're going to learn how. You're going to take your time. I've got plenty of coin. I'll get what we need. You fuck it up, I'll take you to court. So, you'd better do a good job. Keep your head down, outta trouble.' She sucks her dart. Blows smoke in my face. 'What do you say?'

When I get back in the car, I tell Dad. He heads towards town as we speak. I don't ask. I'm enjoying the time with him. Dad pulls into the docks at Emu Point and cuts the engine.

'I'll only be a sec,' he says. He hops out, walks towards the boats.

I sit there watching people get in and out of cars, carrying beach towels. A kid rides a bike with training wheels around the carpark.

Funny how this place is special to each of us.

Then I have an idea. The flowers from the other day are still on the back seat. I grab them and go after Dad.

He's sitting on the jetty, dangling his legs above the water.

'Sorry mate, I just needed to—' Dad can't finish his sentence. He doesn't need to though, I get it.

Dad gets up, looks out at Green Island, and the hills beyond.

'This is the exact spot I—'

'I know.'

The exact spot he met you.

We stand side by side.

the flowers drift
upstream
we are remembering
you walk heel
to
toe
jetty beams slick with salt and fish bits
or were they warm in the sun?
i remember a story
while dad remembers
the moment
but we are both with
you.

camphor myrtle and everlasting flowers
drift towards the docks where
the rover and *wind dancer* face each other as if
in conversation
did they see the flames
when i set fire to *gypsy*
when all i wanted was to set fire to
myself?
warrior is moored facing away from
neptune's son as if they are
keeping secrets from each other.
would they stay if we
lifted their anchors?
or would they leave it all behind?
sails fill with wind
an osprey rides the current

everything moving but
dad stands still beside me
we are two men who
left
when you did
but now we are
returning.

the flowers drift upstream.

25. Rose

aunty patsy and i, the grass itching our legs
we sit between the hills hoist and the wattle tree
the rising sun making aunty's pearls sparkle
she paints before breakfast
a pink pompom-like flower with white spikes
an anemone or pincushion
            we don't know its name in any language.
your notes laid out in front of me
grandpa posted them from perth
and i turn page
            after
                page
mapping a botany trip by the location of flowers you have
scribbled next to sketches and scientific names.
but there's none that look like this one
and i want to ask you if you've seen it before
if you know its name.
'aunty,' i say. 'how do you say mum in noongar?'
'in my family, we say ngank,' she says.
'ngank,' i say
and aunty patsy
smiles.
she takes my hand
pinches my thumb between her fingers
'nganka,' she says.

then she looks skywards, the sun kissing her face.
'ngank,' she says, 'is the word for sun.'
'sun and mum, same word. thumb, similar word.
the sun is the mother of creation
your mother is the mother of your family
and your thumb, that is the mother of your hand.'

'your mum here'—she squeezes my thumb
'here'—she points to the sky
'here'—she gestures to the space in between.

nganka,
ngank,
ngank.

Ngank

A pink-and-grey galah carries the word to you.

'Ngank,' it says. 'Ngank, ngank, nganka.'

You look down, from where you've been drifting above the karris. The Blue Ranges smudge the horizon, misty in the morning light. Down there, two people sit between a wattle tree and a Hills hoist. Your friend who helped deliver your children, who taught you about the country you lived on. Menang Goreng Noongar Boodjar.

Your words in ink beside her strokes of oil paint telling a story of consultation, collaboration. Of wisdom as old as the earth. Your daughter, sitting cross-legged beside her. Paper spread out between them. Your words. Your handwriting. Your scrawl. Your friend wears a skirt with orange spirals on it. Your daughter is holding her thumb to the sky.

'Nganka,' she says. 'Ngank. Ngank.'

Thumb.

Sun.

Mum.

A breeze lifts the curls from Rose's face. You see the painting Aunty Patsy is working on, and the name comes to you. The pages flutter and shuffle, until the right one is on top.

Hakea laurina—Pincushion Hakea.

Aunty Patsy will know the Noongar word. She seemed to be able to access her ancient language through the strokes of her brush. You watch her add tiny yellow flecks to the white spikes of the flower.

Kodjet. That's what it is called.

And you know you can leave them now. That Rose is finishing what you began. You rise up, higher and higher until the Blue Ranges fall away and sink into the songlines of the earth.

Ngank yira. The sun, rising.

Salt River Road playlist

Visit bitly.ws/Bqq9

'Moonglow', Billie Holiday
'Space Oddity', David Bowie
'Born to Run', Bruce Springsteen
'Tangled Up in Blue', Bob Dylan
'Ride On', AC/DC
'Crying Song', Pink Floyd
'Where Do the Children Play?', Cat Stevens
'48 Crash', Suzi Quatro
'Hey, That's No Way to Say Goodbye', Leonard Cohen
'Get Rhythm', Johnny Cash
'Stairway to Heaven', Led Zeppelin
'Get Off of My Cloud', The Rolling Stones
'Three Little Birds', Bob Marley & the Wailers
'All Along the Watchtower', Jimi Hendrix
'Layla', Eric Clapton
'Johnny B. Goode', Lobby Loyde & The Coloured Balls
'Come Together', The Beatles
'House of the Rising Sun', The Animals
'Over the Rainbow', Judy Garland
'Dreams', Fleetwood Mac
'Light My Fire', The Doors
'You're My Best Friend', Queen
'Queens of Noise', The Runaways

'Hotter than Hell', KISS

'Lola', The Kinks

'Dancing Queen', ABBA

'Mellow Yellow', Donovan

'Living in the 70's', Skyhooks

'Pale Blue Eyes', The Velvet Underground

'Dreamer', Supertramp

'Friday On My Mind', The Easybeats

'I Wanna Be Sedated', Ramones

'Bad Boy for Love', Rose Tattoo

'(Old Dogs, Children and) Watermelon Wine', Tom T. Hall

'Gloria', Patti Smith

'Heart of Glass', Blondie

'Look for the Sun', Iron Butterfly

'Chelsea Morning', Joni Mitchell

'Shearing Shed Blues', Slim Dusty

'Sweet Maxine', The Doobie Brothers

'Blowin' in the Wind', Bob Dylan

'After Midnight', J.J. Cale

'Albatross', Fleetwood Mac

Acknowledgements

Dad. My man in the moon. My time with you was short, and yet you gave me so much. A man of so much magic and more love than I have ever known. I feel so lucky to be your kid. You are present in every page of this book, as you are the pages of my own life. You are the heartbeat to the story, and you bring the rock'n'roll. I hope I have done you proud.

Mum. In so many ways, this is our story. But we didn't have the Troublesome Tetleys, we had each other. Thank you. For your incredible, unwavering love and support. For reading to me before I was even born. For sharing your wonder and love of the written word, of stories, the ocean. For being my editor, and knowing the Tetleys just as well, if not better, than I do. You are the definition of strength and your belief in me gives me wings.

Dr Brett D'Arcy. Every writer needs a mentor and guide like you, and I'm so grateful you're mine. I don't know that this book would exist if it weren't for you. You made sure I got this done, even when I didn't believe I could. Thank you, for your countless hours, for your careful eye to detail. I couldn't fact-check the rock'n'roll between these pages with Dad, but I could with you. You two would have had a lot to talk about.

Professor Kim Scott. Thank you, for trusting me with your contacts. For sharing your precious time with me, for warning me about the shelf I continued to hit my head on in your office. It's been an enormous privilege to work with and learn from you. I am so grateful.

Uncle Lester Coyne. For opening your doors and heart not only to my questions but also to my friendship. Every second with you is treasured and I am honoured to know you as my Menang and Goreng Noongar Elder. You have helped me connect to Boodjar and also to myself. Beautiful

Linny, thank you for seeing me and partaking in the journey. You bring such generous beauty to every moment and are the best cook I have ever known.

Aunty Averil Dean. For giving me your very precious time and teaching me what strength and determination look like. You gave me much more than advice for this book. I left every meeting with you feeling more myself, and so inspired. I will forever remember you singing 'Old Dogs, Children and Watermelon Wine'. It is one of my most special memories.

Aunty Carol Pettersen. There are direct phrases of your wisdom between these pages. Thank you for sharing your story, your culture, your time. The world needs more women like you.

Uncle Ezzard Flowers. You know the loss that the Tetleys experience oh so well. Thank you for connecting on many levels with this story, and for sharing incredibly special moments with me on country in the Stirling Ranges. For your wisdom and time.

Uncle Glen Colbung. For sharing your memories, your knowledge of culture and your support. I really appreciated your phone calls, asking me 'how's that book coming along'. Here it is, Uncle Glen. Here it is.

To the huge-hearted team at Fremantle Press for believing in me and helping me release the Tetleys into the big wide world. It was always my dream that *Salt River Road* would be published by you. I am so honoured that you took a chance on me. Especially to Georgia Richter, for your time, wit, attention to detail, expertise and care. Thank you for polishing this story and stepping into the world I created with such passion. And to Claire Miller, for your warmth, your kindness, your support and for sharing your love of books with me from the beginning. Thank you to Chloe Walton, for your kindness and care.

Thank you to Noongar Elder and artist Glenda Williams for your artwork. I knew as soon as I saw your painting that I had found the cover of my book, and what an honour it is to have this story wrapped in your work. Your painting connects perfectly with the style of Aunty Patsy's, and the fact that quandongs grow on Salt River Road was a beautiful synchronicity. I hope you connect with this story, as I have with your art.

I am blessed with friends who leave me without the words to describe my love and gratitude. Sophie Vasiliu, Mary Adams, Jem Goodliffe, Han Gunn, Monty Lloyd, Asha Couch. For seeing me, for loving me, for holding me and sharing this life with me.

To the beautiful friends who put a roof over my head when I was in Albany writing, Ella Vervest and Finn Jekabsons, Chris and Kathy Goodliffe and Jack Shiner. Jack, thank you also for the sharing of music and memories.

To my family, both the Schmidts and the Gardens. To Hamish Wight, who also knows the loss of the Tetleys. Marita, Steve, Mia and Ella Ross for your love and your loyalty.

To Peter Milsom for making me feel comfortable in front of a camera and celebrating my wins.

To Katharine Susannah Prichard Writers' Centre for giving me the space to write, to dream.

To the Barton Family Trust for your generous support of the book, I sincerely thank you.

To the wonderful team at Kurrah Mia for taking me on Country.

To Vivienne Hansen, for sharing your knowledge of Noongar plants in your fabulous books.

To Michael Carcione, for believing.

To all the wonderful Western Australian writers, including Madelaine Dickie, Holden Sheppard and so many more, who have welcomed me into your community and helped show me the ropes.

To Alex and Jess, for sharing the writer's journey with me.

To ABC Perth, for understanding when the book had to come first.

To every reader who sees something of themselves here, and to all who have lost loved ones to cancer.

And last but not least, to my four-legged best friend, Rupi. You don't fit under my desk anymore, but you'll always fit in my heart.

Molly Schmidt is a writer and journalist from the coastal town of Albany (Kinjarling), in the Great Southern region of Western Australia. She grew up roaming paddocks and climbing paperbark trees on Menang Noongar country. While writing *Salt River Road*, she collaborated with Noongar Elders from the Great Southern, with the goal of producing a novel that actively pursues reconciliation between non-Aboriginal and Aboriginal people. *Salt River Road* was winner of the 2022 City of Fremantle Hungerford Award. Molly works as a radio producer and journalist for the ABC, where her passion for storytelling is put to good use.

This novel was written with support from the Shire of Mundaring, the Katharine Susannah Prichard Writers' Centre First Edition Fellowship, and the Four Centres Emerging Writer Program funded by the Western Australian Department of Local Government, Sport and Cultural Industries.

CITY OF FREMANTLE HUNGERFORD WINNERS

When Jay's husband lands a diplomatic job in Warsaw, she jumps at the opportunity to escape her predictable life for a three-year adventure in the heart of central Europe. Jay shelves her corporate wardrobe and throws herself into life as a diplomatic wife. Between glamorous cocktail parties and ambassadorial shenanigans, Jay gets to know quirky, difficult, fascinating Poland, with its impenetrable language and unfathomable customs. It's a challenge even for an intrepid traveller with a willing heart. Not to mention a marriage that increasingly doesn't look as if it will survive its third Polish winter.

'Humorous and graceful … [this memoir] depicts a woman's search for identity with a winning mixture of pain and aplomb.' Foreword Magazine

FREMANTLEPRESS.COM.AU

AVAILABLE FROM FREMANTLE PRESS

Black magic, big waves and mad Aussie expats. In Indonesia, Penny is drifting, partying, hanging out – a thousand miles away from claustrophobic Perth and her career-minded boyfriend. But things take a dangerous turn when she goes to work at Shane's Sumatran Oasis. Caught up in the hostility directed at Shane, and flirting and surfing with the hell-man Matt, Penny soon finds herself swept into a world where two very different cultures must collide.

'Where Troppo is particularly sharp … is in its abstract yet precise evocations of the sensory overload of Indonesia and in its dense, poetic riffs on the almost narcotic pull of chasing waves.' Weekend Australian

AND ALL GOOD BOOKSTORES

ALSO AVAILABLE

Life is tough for the Connell family, growing up in a small town where racist attitudes, discrimination and violence against Aboriginal people are commonplace. Lavinia is lucky: her parents ensure her family stays together while other cousins and friends are removed from the state. But violence and adversity occur over and over, even while young Lavinia also excels at sport and school. This is the yarn Lavinia tells her children and her grandchildren, gathered by the fire on the banks of the river where she grew up – the story of one good woman – one moorditj yorga – that reflects the stories of so many strong, determined women of her time.

'This poignant memoir is a reminder that there are generations of Aboriginal women who, in addition to experiencing trauma and pain at the hands of settlers, also have stories of perseverance and strength.' Books + Publishing

FREMANTLEPRESS.COM.AU

First published 2023 by
FREMANTLE PRESS

Reprinted 2023 (twice).

Fremantle Press Inc. trading as Fremantle Press
PO Box 158, North Fremantle, Western Australia, 6159
fremantlepress.com.au

Cover image © Glenda Williams, 'Quandongs', 2023
Author picture by Peter Milsom
Designed by Nada Backovic, nadabackovic.com
Printed and bound by IPG

A catalogue record for this book is available from the National Library of Australia

ISBN 9781760992620 (paperback)
ISBN 9781760992637 (ebook)

Fremantle Press is supported by the State Government through the Department of Local Government, Sport and Cultural Industries.

Fremantle Press respectfully acknowledges the Whadjuk people of the Noongar nation as the Traditional Owners and Custodians of the land where we work in Walyalup.